Captive

A Detective Jade Monroe Crime Thriller
Book 2

C. M. Sutter

AUTHOR'S NOTE

This book is a work of fiction by C. M. Sutter. Names, characters, places, and incidents are products of the author's imagination or are used solely for entertainment. Any resemblance to actual events or persons, living or dead, is entirely coincidental.

ABOUT THE AUTHOR

C.M. Sutter is a crime fiction writer who resides in the Midwest, although she is originally from California.

She is a member of numerous writers' organizations, including Fiction for All, Fiction Factor, and Writers etc.

In addition to writing, she enjoys spending time with her family and dog. She is an art enthusiast and loves to create handmade objects. Gardening, hiking, bicycling, and traveling are a few of her favorite pastimes. Be the first to be notified of new releases and promotions at: http://cmsutter.com.

C.M. Sutter

http://cmsutter.com/

Captive:

A Detective Jade Monroe Crime Thriller, Book 2

A body, wrapped in plastic, is discovered in a ditch along a secluded country road. Detective Jade Monroe, and her partner, Jack Steele, arrive at the scene in minutes. Suspicious looking evidence gives the impression that this young woman has been held captive.

As days pass, more local women vanish without a trace. Jade and her team of detectives fear the worst.

With precious time slipping away, Jade needs to pull out all stops to find this perpetrator, even if that means putting herself directly in harm's way.

Stay abreast of each new book release by signing up for my VIP e-mail list at:

http://cmsutter.com/newsletter/

Find more books in the Jade Monroe Series here:

http://cmsutter.com/available-books/

Chapter 1

They sat around the fire pit they'd built behind the farmhouse. Ten large fieldstones placed side by side created a perfect ring for the blaze. Fireflies flitted in the distance, causing the field beyond them to come alive and twinkle. A half dozen empty beer cans lay at their feet, some smashed and others saved. The brothers talked quietly and planned their next move. The fire mesmerized them—it was soothing and warm against their skin. Jeremy poked at the logs with a stick, causing sparks to crackle and float up into the night sky, where stars hung like diamonds suspended on invisible strings. In the distance, a frog croaked from the pond at the back of the property. Serenity blanketed the night until a woman's screams for help broke the silence.

Matt's eyes darted across the fire pit, waiting for a reaction. Of the two, Jeremy had the more volatile personality. He was the oldest and had shouldered the responsibility of protecting his brother during their years with an abusive father and then, later, with an absentee mother.

Matt spoke first. "This farm was a good choice—no neighbors for miles."

"I've told her a million times to shut the hell up. I can't stand that screeching anymore—she's got to go." Jeremy stood and shoved back the cheap aluminum and plastic webbed lawn chair. It fell over and folded up. He stormed toward the house. "We haven't had any luck with her anyway."

Matt followed on his brother's heels.

The heavy thud of Jeremy's work boots hitting each step echoed off the cement walls as he descended the wooden staircase from the kitchen to the basement. The steps protested, creaking and groaning with age. He flicked on the light and disappeared around the corner. A wooden dry sink stood against a primitive jelly cupboard. Those antique essentials were likely as old as the farmhouse itself and probably held years of canned goods back in the day. Jeremy sorted through the supplies he retrieved from the upper glass doors of the cupboard. He set what he needed on the dry sink, then he poked the tip of the needle through the rubber stopper and into the vial. He drew back the plunger and filled the barrel. Looking with approval at the quantity of liquid inside, Jeremy put the protective cover back on the needle's tip and dropped the syringe into his front pocket. He turned the corner and headed to her cage. The other three women cowered at the back of their confinements. They pulled their knees up against their chests and made themselves look as small as possible, clearly hoping to go unnoticed.

Jeremy jerked his chin toward Matt. "Hold the syringe."

Matt pushed off the cracked cement wall where he stood and did as told.

Reanne screamed and kicked the sides of the cage, trying to stay out of Jeremy's grasp as he approached. He stopped and quickly glanced around the room, spotting exactly what he needed propped against the wall. He reached for it and grinned. In two strides, he was at her cage and jammed the cattle prod between the chain-link openings. He zapped her twice, hard and long. She squealed, grunted, and fell back—stunned and moaning.

"Open the gate."

Matt pulled the key ring off the nail on the wall and pushed the brass-colored key into the padlock. He gave the key a turn, unlatched the padlock, and pulled the gate open. Jeremy grabbed the nearly unconscious Reanne by her legs and yanked her out.

"Give me the syringe." He turned toward Matt and reached for it.

Jeremy held the syringe's end between his teeth and pulled the protective cover off. He knelt by Reanne's side and sank the needle into her carotid artery. She lay motionless within seconds.

"There, that should do it. Go on upstairs, bro. I got this."

"Are you sure?"

"Yeah, she won't give us any more trouble."

Jeremy waited until he heard the upstairs door close before continuing. He had filled the syringe of Xylazine with far more than he needed to knock Reanne out. Chances were she was already dead. He turned his head and gave a warning glare to the rest of the caged women.

"There, now you can sleep, and I don't want to hear a peep from any of you."

Jeremy grabbed Reanne's lifeless arms and pulled her around the corner to the bathroom. He turned the bathtub's faucet to the hottest setting and waited. When the temperature was perfect—a scalding hot, sending steam to the room's ceiling—he closed the drain, stripped off her clothing, and rolled her into the tub. Her body scorched a brilliant red while he stared at her, watching for movement. When he saw none, he shrugged with satisfaction and walked out. Back around the corner, at the bottom doors of the jelly cupboard, he pulled out everything else he needed. Two bottles of bleach, rubber gloves, a roll of duct tape, and a plastic tarp were jammed under, and in, his arms and hands. He scowled at the other women when he heard someone whimper.

"Don't try my patience."

Jeremy returned to the bathroom and cracked the seal of the first bottle of bleach. He tipped the gallon bottle and emptied it over Reanne while she lay in the hot water. He left her like that for a few minutes—stewing in the scalding bleach water. He folded back the sleeve of his yellow rubber glove and checked the time.

"Another minute should do it."

There was a method to Jeremy's madness, and his routine was always the same. He didn't vary from the process that seemed to work well for him. The women he killed never had evidence left on their bodies; the bleach destroyed all of that. He looked at his watch again.

"Here we go."

He twisted the lid on the second bottle of bleach until the plastic seal cracked open with a turn of his wrist. He lifted the foil tab and threw it in the trash can. Jeremy sat on the edge of the bathtub and poured most of the bleach over her head. He stared at her for a moment then lifted the chain attached to the drain plug. The water ran toward the drain and swirled down the hole like a small, forceful cyclone. He watched Reanne's chest—it didn't rise and fall. To make sure she was dead, he poured the remaining bleach from the second bottle down her throat—no gurgling or sputtering sounds.

"Good to go. That should quiet things down around here."

With each corner of the tarp grasped between his fingers, he gave it a quick flick and draped it across the bathroom floor. His rubber gloves helped hold her firmly as he pulled Reanne's slippery body out of the tub and dropped her onto the tarp. He rolled her tightly in the plastic and secured it with duct tape. With a heave, he tossed Reanne's lifeless body over his shoulder then exited the basement through the cellar doors that led upward and outside to the driveway. He shouldered the double wooden doors open and walked out into the dark night.

The flicker of the porch light caught Jeremy's attention as he dropped Reanne into the back of the van. He slammed the doors closed and looked back in time to see the living room curtains flutter. He knew Matt was watching.

Chapter 2

Here at the sheriff's department, we were still getting over our nightmare with Doug, the medical examiner, which had ended just two months ago. He was a sick man with demons that had plagued him for decades. None of us were aware of it until the end, when he was beyond help. Everyone had tried to make sense of it, but it was impossible. We later realized he had been sick for most of his life. The DNA results had confirmed that the bones we found in his basement, hidden behind a wall, belonged to his mother. He had murdered her years prior, and she was possibly his first victim.

Doug had harmed my sister, Amber, and since her physical wounds had healed, I hoped her emotional ones had too. With that incident as a reminder of the dangerous people in all walks of life, and her determination, Amber would go forward with her goal of becoming an FBI profiler. I was certain she'd get there in record time. She had returned to work at Joey's restaurant part-time for now. With school out for the summer, she wanted to relax, plant flowers, and enjoy our beautiful new condo in Ashbury Woods.

Daily life at the sheriff's department was getting back to normal too, and we were moving forward with renewed optimism. Speeding tickets, domestic disturbances, fender benders, and closing out the solved cases filled the days for our deputies and us detectives in the bull pen. Nobody complained, and I was thankful.

"Did you hear about the interviews for chief ME?" I asked as I pushed back my roller chair and walked to the coffee station. Jack appeared to be deep in paperwork. His desk was cluttered with file folders.

"Huh? Um, hang on. Okay, what did you say?" He closed a folder, looked up, and gave me his attention.

"I said, today two people are going to interview for it. Of course, Jason would love to lead, but he doesn't have enough experience under his belt to be the chief ME yet."

"No, but that's cool. Where are the people from?"

"I guess one is a woman from Indianapolis, and the other is a guy from Newark."

"I hope the guy gets it."

I gave Jack a scowl and filled my coffee cup. I made sure to walk past him without offering to fill his cup as I returned to my desk.

"Are you being a male chauvinistic pig?" I chuckled at my own quick wit.

"That was sort of funny, but no, it's just that Newark is at the bottom of my favorite cities list. I feel for the guy—that's all."

"Well, let's see if either of them gets it. So far, the quiet and the lack of bodies in the morgue have been nice." I got back up and filled Jack's cup anyway. He grinned at me.

Clayton entered the bull pen in a huff at eight thirty. "Heads up, guys, we have to go."

"Why?" I pushed back my chair, stood, and then secured my shoulder holster. I could tell by Clayton's demeanor something bad had taken place.

"There's a DB in a ditch just north of Highway 60 on Wayfair Road. A motorist in a high-rise truck called it in. He said he saw something odd and got out to take a look. He realized it was a body when he got close enough."

I stared at Clayton. "What does that mean? Wouldn't you just know it's a person?"

"I guess it's wrapped in plastic, rather suspicious in nature," Clayton said. He rubbed his brow, and anxiety covered his face.

I could read his mind, and I groaned in agreement. "Sounds like another body dump. Wayfair Road is on the county line. It's ours for sure?"

He nodded. "Apparently. All I know is the guy called it in to 9-1-1, and they forwarded it to us. Guess it's on our side of the road. Jan just got the call."

Lieutenant Clark opened his office door and craned his neck out. "What's going on?"

"DB in a ditch out near the county line—suspicious circumstances, boss. We're on our way."

Clark scratched his chin and heaved a sigh. "I hope there isn't more to follow. I think this county has had its fair share for a while. Get Jason, Kyle, and Dan out there. Tell them to get a move on and keep me posted."

"Will do, Lieutenant," I said.

Jack and I took a final gulp of our coffees and headed out. Clayton said he'd run downstairs and give the location to Jason, Kyle, and Dan. He and Billings would be a few minutes behind us.

I grabbed a set of keys, and we left the building. Outside, I clicked the fob, and the lights flashed on the first unmarked cruiser in the lot. I walked around to the driver's side and slid in. It was my turn to drive. Jack opened the passenger door, got in, and fastened his seat belt.

Wayfair Road and Highway 60 fell right at the county line between Washburn and Wausaukee counties. The road literally divided the counties—Washburn extending west from there and Wausaukee heading east, ending at Lake Michigan. If the body was lying in the ditch on the west side of the road, it was our jurisdiction. The east belonged to Wausaukee County. From the sound of things and the call coming into dispatch, I already knew the case was ours.

The radio in the car squawked. Tim Donnelly, one of our daytime patrol deputies, was at the scene with the motorist that called it in. Dispatch forwarded the call.

"Yeah, Donnelly, what do you have?" Jack asked as I drove.

"DB, for sure, wrapped in a plastic tarp. I can only see the top of the head, probably a female. Looks like long brown hair. I don't want to touch anything, so that's all I really have, Jack. Also, there's dew on the plastic, so I'm assuming she's been out here all night."

Jack glanced at me and raised his eyebrows, clearly impressed. "Good observation, Donnelly. Okay, get a statement from the motorist. We're fifteen minutes out." Jack clicked off the radio. "A body wrapped in plastic and dumped in plain sight—that's odd. There are plenty of secluded spots around here. It doesn't make a lot of sense."

I smirked. "Just when I thought life was getting back to normal."

We reached the intersection where Wayfair Road headed north off the highway. I clicked my left-turn blinker and waited until the approaching line of cars had passed. It seemed that every oncoming car was spaced just right so there wasn't enough time to scoot across between them. I'd have to wait for all of them to go by. After the fifth car, I turned left off Highway 60. According to Donnelly, the body was about three miles up. Wayfair Road was the typical narrow road out in farm country, void of a shoulder save a small strip of gravel. Someone had one of two reasons to be driving on it; either they were lost or they lived back there.

I pulled up behind Donnelly's cruiser and parked, then I grabbed my sunglasses off the dashboard and slipped them on before exiting the car. The sun was bright and harsh, and I wanted to see the body and the motorist up close and personal without squinting.

The man standing with Donnelly next to his cruiser looked like the average farmer that lived in this neck of the woods. I gave him the once-over. He wore a sweat-and-grime-stained baseball cap, carpenter jeans, and a plain green T-shirt. I checked his shoes—dirty work boots. His cheeks had a red, chafed appearance. Too much outdoors, I imagined. His neck was as thick as my thigh. The blue pickup truck parked along the side of the road was definitely lifted, with oversized tires and a raised suspension. Running boards lined each side.

Donnelly made the introductions. "Sergeant Monroe, this is Brad Hendricks. Brad, this is our sergeant and her partner, Detective Jack Steele."

We shook hands with Brad and got a quick recap of the statement he'd already given to Donnelly as we walked toward the body.

"So, you live where, Brad?"

He turned and faced north, then he pointed up the road. "Just beyond the second house on the right, ma'am. We have an eighty-acre dairy farm and forty Holstein milking cows. Our family has lived there since my grandpa bought the place in 1965."

"Okay, and where were you going when you spotted the body?" I shaded my eyes with my hand as I looked up at the six-foot-plus man. The sunglasses obviously weren't doing their intended job.

"I was heading to our south fifty-acre parcel of hay to see if it was ready to cut."

I turned my head to follow the direction where he pointed.

"Sure, I understand. Please wait here on the road."

Jack and I approached the wrapped body lying at the

bottom of the ditch. We watched our footing to make sure nothing important was stepped on. We knelt and peered into the top end of the plastic tarp. We couldn't see much other than her hair color and obvious slim shape. It appeared that she had been rolled several times—making the plastic tarp difficult to see through.

"Let's wait for forensics," I said.

Jack and I climbed the bank back to the road to wait for Kyle, Dan, and Jason. I jerked my head toward Brad and approached him as he stood near his truck.

I pointed at his rig. "May I?"

Brad looked surprised. "You want to get into my truck?"

"If you don't mind. I'd like to see how obvious the body was from the perspective you had when you saw it."

"Yeah, knock yourself out."

I glanced at Jack and smiled.

Brad apologized, "Sorry, ma'am. I guess I'm not used to talking to cops, especially female sergeants."

"No problem." I grabbed the handle above the driver's door and pulled myself up.

Two vans and another cruiser arrived and parked just as I climbed into Brad's truck.

Kyle exited the driver's seat of the forensics van and grinned. With a head jerk my way, he addressed Jack. "What is she up to now?"

Jack looked at the truck and, with a hand wave and a chuckle, explained what I was doing. "She's checking out how things look from a higher point of view. Anyway, the body is over here." Jack led the way, fifteen feet ahead.

Kyle and Dan from forensics and Jason McMillian, the only acting ME we had right now, stepped down into the ditch to take a look. I exited the truck by way of the driver's side running board and a two-foot jump, then I caught up with the guys.

"I'll have to cut this plastic open," Jason said. "Do you want me to go ahead, Sergeant, or take her back to the office wrapped like this?"

"Hang on. Dan, snap a few pictures exactly as she is right now, then we'll proceed."

"Yep, sure thing, Jade."

I nodded for Jack to join me over by Brad. We spoke to him for a few minutes more and handed him our cards. "If you can think of anything else, please contact either one of us. Thank you for calling it in."

We took down his information, shook his hand, and sent him on his way. I asked Donnelly to call a few more deputies to come out and block off the road with their cruisers. We had to search the area thoroughly before we'd open up the road to vehicles again.

"Are we good to go?" I asked as we walked back to the body.

Dan responded, "Yep, I have photos from every angle and the ground in the immediate area."

I nodded for Jason to proceed. He cut the plastic and duct tape, then he exposed the nude woman that lay inside.

"Geez, she's telling me quite a story," Jason said.

Jack and I knelt down next to our victim's exposed body. "Holy cow, she can't be more than twenty or so. Okay, talk to me, Jason," I said.

He studied her closely. "She has obvious abrasions on her elbows and knees, and her muscles look seriously atrophied. She's nearly skin and bones." He leaned in next to her head and looked at each side of her neck. "It appears that she's been hit with a stun gun numerous times and likely a cattle prod too." He pointed at every spot. "See these repetitive eraser-sized marks all over her neck and the burns on her body?"

I looked at the obvious burns. Jack peered over my shoulder. "Yep, I see them. They sure look like stun-gun burns—and those?" I pointed at the others. "They're from a cattle prod?"

"Oh, they definitely are."

I took a deep whiff. "Bleach."

"Yeah, she's been doused. It eliminates trace, but we'll check anyway. She's been scalded too. Her skin is loose, blistered, and red. Hopefully she was dead before she went through all of that. Kyle?"

"I have the bags right here." Kyle stepped down and covered the victim's hands with paper bags to protect any trace evidence she might have under her nails.

"Do you see any defensive wounds?" Jack asked.

Jason shook his head. "Doesn't appear so, but that's understandable. Either she was incapacitated with the stun gun or cattle prod or she was already too weak to resist."

I looked around. "Chances of finding anything out here are slim. No clothes—no ID."

Kyle agreed. "We'll do a thorough search of the area anyway."

"Yeah, we'll pitch in too." I turned back to Jason. "TOD?"

Jason tried to move her joints, but she was stiff. "She's in full rigor. Rough estimate, I'd say probably around midnight. Check in with me later. I'll know more then."

"Cause of death? Does anything stand out?"

Other than the repetitive burns and obvious scalding, we hadn't seen anything yet. Jason rolled her over to check her back.

"Wow, I wasn't expecting that."

"I'll be damned. That ought to help us identify her."

The entire back of our Jane Doe was covered with a large Chinese dragon that went from her right shoulder to her left buttock. The colors were still vibrant, and the work was intricate.

"This tattoo was done by the best of the best and not long ago. We should be able to narrow things down by giving that to the media. Dan, get some pictures. Okay, cause of death?"

"Not sure, Jade. I don't see anything obvious yet. I'll likely have an aha moment after reviewing the tox report."

I nodded. "Okay, she's all yours."

Jason wheeled the gurney to where the edge of the road met the gravel, then he retracted the legs to carry it down to the ditch. He and Kyle lifted our Jane Doe up and placed her on the board, then they secured her with the straps. On the road, Jason dropped the gurney's legs and wheeled it to the back of the van, slid it inside, and left. Kyle and Dan took over searching the immediate area where her body was found, while the rest of us spent the next hour walking the edges of the road and the ditches, checking for anything that might seem out of place.

Chapter 3

Jeremy sat at the kitchen table—waiting. He finally heard the sound of his brother stumbling down the stairs from his bedroom. He watched as Matt entered the kitchen. Matt gave Jeremy a long look as he walked across the room. He ran his fingertips through the messy brown hair he often wore in a ponytail since it hung below his shoulders. He stretched and stuck his head in the refrigerator to see if anything interested him. A carton of orange juice behind the milk and a loaf of raisin bread caught his eye. He reached in and pulled it out.

Jeremy frowned at Matt and smirked. "Sleeping beauty finally woke up, huh? It's ten o'clock for God's sake."

"So, who gives a crap?"

"I do, and I've been doing some thinking. These girls aren't selling fast enough. We signed a six-month lease, and we need to take advantage of our time here. We have to get as many girls as we can, get them into the auction site, and make some serious money."

Matt grinned. "I like that idea, and the new mall just out

of town would be perfect. There's bound to be a lot of women that shop there, plus I read the place has a few outdoor cafés. It's supposed to be pretty upscale. We can watch for the right girls from the parking lot."

"I agree, but that's better done at night. We'd have to be super careful—parking lot cameras, you know. We could park off to the side somewhere and watch as girls go back to their cars, distracted with arms full of shopping bags. We'll pull up alongside them and shove them through the sliding side door, opposite the cameras." He paused to give the idea deeper thought. "We do need to be more particular, though. Nobody wants a woman with a tattoo like Reanne's—they're too easy to trace unless they're sold out of the country. I'd much rather make money than kill women because nobody wants them. Sorry about Reanne, but she had to go. She was driving me nuts."

Matt gave Jeremy a long, questioning stare. "So what did you do with her?"

"I dumped her along a farm road about ten miles from here. Don't worry. I bleached her down in the bathtub first. We don't hang on to anyone more than three months. If they don't sell, they die. That's the rules, bro. You know the dr—"

Matt interrupted, "Yeah, I know the drill."

"They're just a commodity. It's like selling a car, so don't get attached to any of them. Reanne was a pain in the ass anyway, and nobody ever bid on her once they saw that tattoo. You like the big bucks, don't you?"

"Yeah, I like the money." Matt poured a tall glass of juice

and guzzled it. He poured a second one and sat down at the table, opposite Jeremy. "So, where do you want to go when our lease is up?"

Jeremy unfolded the map that was jammed into the napkin holder. He spread it across the table. "I'm thinking Vegas. There's plenty of open space just outside the city. With the amount of hot babes there, we can cherry-pick from the cream of the crop. We'd only need to sell eight high-quality girls, then we'll be set for a year. We'll go to Europe for a while. We're due for a ski trip again."

Matt's eyes lit up. "Yeah, skiing sounds great."

"Anyway, we have three women left. Let's grab as many more as we can and get them sold. When we leave here, we'll hit Vegas with plenty of fun money too." Jeremy poured himself a cup of coffee while a new idea popped into his head. "I think we should check out a beach somewhere. Any tattoo a chick has that fits under a swimsuit should be okay. We have four more months here. I'll even extend my rules by an extra month. Any new chick we can't sell in four months dies, then we leave for Vegas. Beth is on the chopping block, though. We've already had her too long."

Matt nodded then dropped two slices of raisin bread into the toaster. "Okay, so what's on the agenda?"

"We'll give them breakfast first and then clean them up and take new videos and still shots. They'll be for sale on the auction site later. This will be Beth's last chance."

Matt ate his toast while Jeremy made the preparations for the girls' breakfast.

Jeremy reached into the upper cabinet door and pulled

out a box of breakfast bars. A bottle of Alprazolam sat on the counter. He dropped six tablets into a mortar then closed the bottle lid. With a pestle, he ground the pills into a fine powder and divided it into thirds. He scooped each amount into a bottle of water and handed them to Matt.

"Here, shake these good."

Jeremy pulled out two chewy bars for each woman and headed to the basement. Matt shoved the rest of his toast into his mouth and followed Jeremy with the water.

Ten cages lined the basement wall, but only three were occupied. The whimpering began.

"Shut the hell up," Matt said.

He set the water bottles on a table and waited as Jeremy tossed two breakfast bars into each cage. They watched the women eat.

Matt spoke up. "Back up so I can put the bottles inside. Don't do anything stupid, either. Drink all of it. Each of you will take a shower and put on clean clothes. It's auction day."

Matt turned the keys and opened the padlocks. He set a bottle in each cage and stood there to make sure the women drank the water.

Jeremy went to the bathroom and returned with three towels.

"Strip off those clothes and put these towels around you. We'll be back in ten minutes. After your showers, you'll get clean outfits to put on."

Matt clicked the padlocks closed, and the brothers disappeared around the corner. The door to the next room creaked when Matt opened it, and they walked in.

"Damn mice," he said when he heard something scurry by.

Jeremy hit the light switch. The room was full of camera and video equipment. The computer sat on the desk next to a closet-sized area used as a photo booth. A bright light hung above the space. The women couldn't be given too much room in case they tried to run.

Chapter 4

The hour-long search through the brush in the ditches and along the roadside produced nothing. Our killer was careful and thorough, even down to bleaching and scalding the body to remove trace evidence. We returned to the station to brief the lieutenant on what we had, which wasn't much.

I went downstairs and passed Kyle in the hallway. He told me he had just fingerprinted our Jane Doe. He would enter her prints into the IAFIS database, and he'd know soon enough if she was in the system. Without a match, we'd have no idea who this young lady was. We'd have to depend on the tattoo to give us answers.

"Let me know as soon as you find something out."

"I will," Kyle said.

I entered the cold autopsy room to check on Jason's progress. Our victim lay on the stainless-steel table, her head resting on a block. A cart containing scissors, forceps, a bone saw, chisels, bowls, and a scale sat alongside the body. I tried not to give their use too much thought.

Jason pulled a sheet up to Jane Doe's neck and paused

his preparations when I entered. "Jade."

"Hey, Jason. How's it going?"

"Just getting under way."

I walked over to the table our victim was lying on and gave her a long, thoughtful stare. I wondered who she was and how she ended up in this terrible predicament. She had family somewhere. Weren't they looking for her?

"So, what more can you tell me?" I asked.

Jason pointed at the table in the corner. "Let's have a seat. I have a few hours of work to do, but I have an interesting theory. It might actually hold some weight."

"Okay, I have an open mind." I sat at the table and rested my hands in my lap. "Go ahead."

"I'll get to the obvious first. I'd say she's in her early twenties, no defensive wounds, has been deceased for about fifteen hours, and other than the tattoo, she has no identifiable markings such as birthmarks, scars, or piercings. She has plenty of stun-gun burns, yet I don't see what would be the COD. She wasn't stabbed, shot, or strangled. She hasn't expelled any water, so even though she was scalded, she didn't drown. I'm thinking the submersion in water and the bleaching was done postmortem. I noticed evidence of bleach in her mouth too. I'm certain something will pop on the tox report. Now, on to my theory."

I took a deep breath and pulled out my notepad to jot down what Jason was about to tell me.

"I think this young woman was caged, as in held prisoner."

I dug my fingertips into my temples and groaned.

"Okay, why did you come to that conclusion?" I began writing as he talked.

"Her elbows and knees were scuffed raw, as if she was confined in a tight space. I did a scraping of the scuffed areas and took a look under the microscope. There are very minute traces of metal dust, likely from bars or a chain-link cage, embedded in the tissue. Also, she wasn't getting any exercise, hence the atrophied muscles."

"Couldn't that come from lack of food?"

"Sure, in conjunction with no exercise. Her skin is unusually pale for summertime, like she never went outside."

"Maybe bedridden?"

"I don't think so. That wouldn't explain the scuffed elbows and knees. Have you ever heard of incidents like this?"

I sighed and let my breath out slowly. "Sure, I've heard of it but never witnessed anything remotely similar. I wouldn't even know of a particular case to cite. So you think it could be black-market human trafficking?"

"It's possible, but if that's the case, there are likely more women out there. I've seen TV documentaries where women are sold via darknet auction houses. The search engines go from surface web to deep web and then dark web, which ensures anonymity. The dark web conducts the searches and the darknet is the networking platform. The location where these women are held captive isn't important. These auctions are online and can take place in the most remote areas or right next door. You never know who is running them. Anyone, anywhere, with an account and the knowledge of how to access these sites can buy a woman from the darknet. I'm just throwing it out there, Jade. Let's see what the tox report tells us. No matter what, I doubt if the bleach killed her, but I do think she was overdosed with something."

I closed my notepad and slid it into my pants pocket. "Is there any way to put a rush on the tox results?"

"I'll see what I can do."

"Okay, I'm going to see if Kyle got a hit on the prints yet. Thanks, Jason."

He nodded and walked back over to our victim, where he continued his prep work.

The forensics lab was the first room on the right nearest the staircase to the upper levels. I went down the hall and entered through the glass double doors. Kyle was sitting at his computer, and Dan was checking the duct tape under the microscope.

I walked over and stood at Kyle's back. "Please tell me you got a hit."

"Sorry, Jade, nothing yet. Want some coffee?"

"I'd love some, thanks." I walked over to Dan. "Find any fingerprints on the tape?"

"Sorry, but no. It's been rolled over itself deliberately."

I smirked. "Our guy is pretty smart. He wants to hide potential fingerprints. How about freezing it?"

Dan grinned. "That's just what I was about to do. I'll get that started and move on to the tarp."

I nodded a thank-you to Kyle when he poured several

cups of coffee and handed me one. I sat down at the table with the guys to brainstorm for a minute.

"So, unless her prints come up, we have nothing other than looking through the missing persons database. We don't know if she's local or not. If she isn't in the system, we'll move forward locally with the tattoo first, then the nationwide missing persons database. We'll get the media involved and release a sketch of her face too if necessary. How much longer, Kyle?"

"I'd say an hour at the most. I'll call your desk phone when I'm done."

"Thanks. Dan, will you print out ten pictures of her tattoo for me?"

"Sure thing. I'll bring them upstairs when they're ready."

I headed back to the bull pen with my Styrofoam cup of coffee to tell the guys Jason's theory. I pulled out the notepad and sat at my desk. Lieutenant Clark came out of his office and joined us.

He grabbed an empty chair and sat down. "What's the word on our vic?" he asked.

"Kyle is still scanning IAFIS for her prints. If she isn't in the system, we'll go back to the old-school method. A lot of phone calls and letting the media help us out. I'd like to go through the missing persons database too and see if any descriptions pop for someone with a large dragon tattoo on their back. She could be from anywhere, boss, but we'll check within the state first. Nobody has been reported missing in Washburn County as of"—I looked up at the clock—"thirty minutes ago."

"Is there more? It looks like something is weighing heavily on your mind."

"It's a theory that Jason presented." I tapped on the desk with my pen.

"Uh-oh, her nervous energy is kicking in," Jack said.

I smiled—Jack knew me well. "Jason thinks our Jane Doe might have been caged."

The lieutenant wrung his hands. "What the hell? That's something we haven't had to deal with yet. Get busy, guys, and come up with a plan of action. I'm going downstairs to talk to Jason."

"All right, everyone, you heard the lieutenant. Let's start going through the DOJ database. Start with Wisconsin and type in her approximate age, height, weight, hair color, and the keywords 'dragon tattoo.'" I turned in my chair. "Jack, call North Bend PD first and see if anyone local has been reported missing in the last forty-eight hours. Maybe the system hasn't been updated."

"Got it."

I went to the whiteboard and wrote down our Jane Doe's vital statistics, according to Jason, so everyone had the information in front of them.

"Clayton, will you make a fresh pot of coffee, please?"

"Sure, Jade." He got up and went to the coffee station.

Two hours and two pots of coffee later, and with no luck searching the Wisconsin database, we had moved on to the nationwide database. I stretched and rolled my neck. My shoulders were stiff from leaning forward over the desk, staring at my computer.

"Anybody find anything remotely promising?" I looked from face to face.

They groaned their response. Nobody matched Jane's description with a large dragon tattoo so far, and Kyle had come upstairs an hour ago and informed us that her prints weren't in the system.

"This is too time consuming. Even if there is a photo in the database, she might have gone missing as a child, and the description won't match. We have to go with the media."

I called downstairs to Jason. "Hey, Jason, can you take a picture of our Jane Doe? Something that is suitable to put on the air?"

"Doubt it. Her color is off, and her eyes are closed. People aren't as easily recognized when their eyes are closed. I think a drawing and description would be better. I'll call Marie and see if she can stop in. If she comes in now, we'll have it ready for you in a few hours. The photo of the tattoo should help too."

"Thanks, I appreciate it. We haven't had to use a sketch artist for so long I almost forgot we had access to her. How about a break, guys? My eyeballs are beginning to blur."

We sat in the lunchroom and discussed Jason's theory.

"What do any of you know about human trafficking?"

Billings huffed as he fed a handful of change into the vending machine and pushed button A2. A second later, a bag of potato chips fell to the hinged door below. "I don't know a damn thing, Jade. This town is too small for something like that to be going on right under our noses."

"Yeah, I thought the same thing, but a lot of new faces have popped up in the last year. North Bend is a desirable community—maybe for criminals too. I've certainly never dealt with anything like this, that is, if she actually was caged." I looked at Jack. "I wonder if Lindstrom or Colgate ever has."

"We can sure ask if we have to. Milwaukee is a big city, and Chicago is only ninety minutes further. It isn't impossible."

I agreed. "It's something we can chew on. Let's get the description, drawing, and the photo of the tattoo ready for the media first. Jason pushed the tox report. He said he'd have it back tomorrow. I'm sure that's going to tell us more."

Chapter 5

"Melanie and Liz are getting bids, but it's moving pretty slow," Jeremy said. "It doesn't look like anyone wants Beth. Shit. I can't lower her age now—everyone already saw what I wrote, and this is the third time I've listed her for sale. If she doesn't sell this time, she's going to disappear too. Guess nobody wants a woman over twenty-four." Jeremy looked at the clock on the computer. "There's only two hours left, and the numbers aren't even close to the reserve." He pounded his fist on the desk. "That jerk from Miami is still the top bidder for Mel and Liz. There's no way in hell we're giving him a package deal for both of them."

The brothers sat at the computer and refreshed the bids every few minutes. In a few hours, the clock would stop counting down, the bidding would end, and the fees would still be owed, sale or no sale.

"The bidding has to move five thousand bucks for Mel and Liz before the reserve is hit. We're going to owe money on Beth." Jeremy jotted down notes to himself. *No large tats and nobody over twenty-four.* He was getting agitated. "Get them back out here. I need them to look excited. Better yet, they have to look hot."

Matt chuckled. "Got it." He left the video and computer room and headed to the dimly lit area where the girls were held captive. "Get up." He rattled their chain-link cages with the cattle prod. "Let's go, or I'll zap you. We need a do-over, and it better be good. Look seductive and hot. If you don't get sold, it'll be your fault, and you'll pay the price." He opened the first cage and pushed Melanie out with the prod. He held the stun gun in his other hand. "Get out there and act sexy," he barked. "Your life depends on it—now move."

Melanie stood in the small picture booth Matt had made, wearing the same blouse and skirt she had on earlier. "Keep those top two buttons open," Matt instructed. He tied a red scarf around her neck to hide the stun-gun burns and brushed her hair. "That's better," he said with a look of approval. She shook with fear, and tears streaked her cheeks.

"Hold on," Jeremy said just before Matt began taking pictures. He walked out and grabbed a wet washcloth from the bathroom. He returned and threw it at Melanie. "Fix your damn face and look happy. Now start over and smile seductively."

Matt began clicking the camera, and Melanie forced a sexy smile. She knew what was in store for her if she didn't.

Jeremy nodded. "Yeah, that's much better. Okay, put Mel back in her box. Don't bother with Beth—she's a waste of time. Get Liz in here. It's her turn." Jeremy uploaded Mel's new pictures to the auction site then went back to hitting the refresh button.

By three o'clock, both women had new photos on the site, were back in their cages, and the auction had ended. At least the reserve had been met on Melanie. She would be gone by Friday, and the confirmation had just come through for eight thousand dollars via wire transfer. A man from Morocco bought her and was sending a representative out of New York to pick her up at an agreed-upon location.

Jeremy shut down the computer and walked into the darkened room. He rattled her cage. "It's your lucky day, Mel. You'll have a new owner as of Friday, and you'll be living in Morocco—how cool is that?" Jeremy laughed at the thought of eight thousand dollars. The instant transfer had already confirmed the money was in their joint account under fictitious names.

Melanie's fear of the unknown came through in small sobs. She knew better than to cry out loud. Reanne's screams had gotten her killed. Mel tried squeezing her hand through the chain links to reach for Liz in the next cage.

"Get your hand back in the cage before I break it."

She hadn't realized that Jeremy was still standing in the doorway, watching her. She quickly pulled her hand back, scraping the skin off her wrist in the process. She lay down in the cage and kept quiet.

Jeremy shut off the lights and went upstairs. His fingers wrapped around the handle of the refrigerator, and he yanked it open. A cold beer would be good. He pulled out two cans and followed the sound of the TV playing in the living room. Matt sat on a chair with his feet propped on the ottoman and watched a crime thriller. Their dog, Cage, lay at the end of the couch. Jeremy handed his brother a beer then plopped down with a heave on the opposite end of the sofa. The dog lifted his head, looked at him, and moaned. With a curled fist, Jeremy punched the cushions and grabbed a few pillows, trying to create a comfortable spot to watch TV. The same routine occurred every time they turned on that crime thriller series. Jeremy watched the program, then he paused the TV during commercials and jotted down notes for future reference. As usual, a ring of condensation formed below Jeremy's beer can. He'd watch the water run down the sides of the can for a few seconds then turn his focus back to the TV when the commercial was over. This time, he watched the program for five minutes, then he paused the TV before the commercial, breaking their routine.

Matt sat up straight. "Hey, what are you doing, man? It isn't a commercial yet, and it was just getting to the good part."

"Plan on the beach tomorrow. We need two new girls. We'll do the model-photographer ruse, and this time we need to know their age before we grab them. I don't want anyone over twenty-four. No noticeable tats either. The business cards, camera, and Xylazine have to be ready to go."

"Yeah, no problem. I'll get everything ready. Two syringes, then?"

"Bring extra—just in case. I don't want anything to go wrong. We have to come up with a plan for how to grab them too. We can only do two at a time."

Chapter 6

"I think this sketch will do the trick, Marie—appreciate it." I held the drawing next to the face of our unidentified female victim, and the likeness was spot on. With the photo of the tattoo on her back and the sketch of her face, if this Jane Doe was local to our TV viewing area, somebody would recognize her.

I rapped on the lieutenant's office door. He looked up from his paperwork and waved me through. Jack joined me.

"Jade, Jack, anything new?"

"No, boss, but I want to get this composite and photograph on TV before the evening news. Just wanted you to take a look and give us the okay."

Lieutenant Clark closed the folder he had lying on his desk and slipped on his reading glasses. He extended his hand, and I gave him the two pictures. We waited for his opinion.

"The sketch looks remarkably like her. You have her vital statistics to add to the broadcast?"

Jack spoke up, "We sure do, boss. Her height, weight,

hair and eye color, approximate age, and the general location where she was found will be added to the newscast. I can notify the local stations right away so it gets on the six o'clock news. We just need your go-ahead."

Clark scratched his forearm. "There aren't any missing women with her description in Wausaukee or Washburn Counties?"

I responded, "No, sir. Even if we looked over every photo in the statewide database, she may look entirely different than when she went missing. We don't know how long that's been. Also, as Jason pointed out, her muscles are atrophied. She may have lost significant weight since she was last seen. I think putting the sketch and dragon-tattoo photo on TV will give us something more definitive."

"Okay, get it out there. I want to see it on the news in"— he looked at his watch—"less than an hour."

"Thanks, boss. We'll get right on it."

Jack closed the lieutenant's office door at his back and returned to his desk. I headed to the coffee station and felt the side of the stainless-steel coffee pot—cold. I started a fresh pot.

"I'll call the local NBC and CBS stations, and you call ABC and FOX."

Jack looked up and acknowledged me. "You got it, partner. The sooner the news stations can squeeze our segment in, the better."

We sat down and called the station managers for each TV channel that broadcast in southeast Wisconsin. We explained as much of the situation as we could and faxed over the sketch, the description of our Jane Doe, and the photograph of the dragon tattoo to every news channel.

I hung up, sighed, and waited for the brewing coffee to beep. I needed to be revived. "Okay, let's take a break. We'll see if anything shakes out after the news bulletin. I have a feeling we're going to be pulling late hours if the calls actually start coming in. We should think about dinner while we still have time."

Billings stood and offered to go out and pick up the food. "I need a dose of fresh air anyway," he said. "I'm going to Jimmy's, so here's the menu. Write down what you want. I'll call it in and pick it up. They're pretty fast."

Billings started at my desk and handed me the menu. I browsed the three pages and decided on a large Caesar salad with strips of broiled chicken. I didn't eat as healthy as I should when I worked late, and salad seemed like the best choice for a guilt-free meal. I wrote down my order and tossed the menu across my desk to Jack's.

"Have at it, partner. You're up. Thanks for the offer, Billings. I appreciate it." I leaned back in my chair with my eyes closed. "Somebody tell me when ten minutes has passed. I need a power nap, then I have to call Amber."

"Jade… Jade. Hey, partner, wake up."

I opened my eyes and squinted at him. I gave Jack a scowl. "What the hell are you doing?"

He laughed. "I'm kicking your desk. You didn't wake up when I called your name."

Clayton added, "Yeah and you were sawing some serious logs too."

"I was not." I stretched and yawned. "I'm going to make a quick call to Amber. Thanks for waking me up, guys."

I walked into the lunchroom to clear my head and get my bearings. I needed blood flow to my extremities too. I tapped Amber's name on my contact list and waited. She answered on the second ring.

"Hi, Jade. When are you coming home?"

"I'm not sure, Sis. I wanted to let you know that I may be late. We have a missing person's bulletin going out on the six o'clock news on all the channels. With any luck, the phones will start ringing. As much as I don't want to stay too long, we have to see if any viable leads come in." I yawned again.

"You sound really tired."

"Yeah, I am, but I think I'll hang around for a few more hours. It's nothing that a pot of strong coffee can't fix. Jamison and Horbeck can take the calls after that. Anyway, we're ordering takeout, so go ahead and have dinner, honey. Don't wait for me."

"Okay. I'll feed the kids and lock the doors."

"Thanks, Sis. See you in a few hours."

I hung up and heard Billing's voice coming from the bull pen. He was back with dinner, and in thirty minutes the news would start. I returned to my desk and saw a steaming cup of coffee waiting for me. My salad sat next to it. "There is a coffee and food fairy after all." I plopped down in my chair and dug in.

Chapter 7

"Check it out, man. Hurry, get up here!"

"What's going on?" Jeremy ran up the stairs and followed Matt into the living room.

"Watch the news. They showed a picture of Reanne. The segment is coming up right after the commercial."

Jeremy rubbed his forehead. "Shit! I have to think about this. This is just the local news, right?"

"Yeah, only the Milwaukee stations."

"Okay, we should be good, then. Nobody from North Dakota is going to see this. Man, they're quick around here. I figured a small Podunk town like this wouldn't put anything on the news, let alone on the same day. The last girl I dumped never got her fifteen minutes of fame at all."

The third commercial ended, and the news was back on. The anchorman showed the sketch of Reanne's face and the photo of the dragon tattoo.

"Woo-hoo, there she is! That drawing is pretty damn good. Looks just like her."

"Matt, shut the hell up. I'm trying to think. I wasn't expecting this."

"What's the problem? We aren't in North Dakota anymore."

"Yeah, I know, but that was just stupid on my part. How could I be so careless? From now on, they're getting buried."

Jeremy was angry with himself and went back downstairs to finish passing out dinner. He glared at the women.

"One peep from any of you and you'll all be buried in the woods."

With the twist of a key, he released each padlock and opened their gates.

"Get to the back of your cages," he ordered.

The women complied. Jeremy put a plastic plate with two hard-boiled eggs and two pieces of bread in each cage. A bottle of water was tossed in too. He checked the time.

"You'll get a bathroom break in an hour. I'll be back then."

Jeremy turned off the light at the top of the stairs and slammed the basement door. The chair cushion in the living room caved in when he sat and reached for his laptop. He did a Google search while Matt watched a sitcom.

"Okay, shut that thing off. I want your full attention."

Matt reluctantly turned off the TV and tossed the remote back on the coffee table. It skidded across the surface and fell to the floor on the other side. He huffed, "Yeah, now what?"

"The sooner we get these chicks sold, the better. I'll

admit, we've been lazy. I've checked this out. Tomorrow, we're going to hit Bradenton Beach. According to the information online, that seems to be the most popular beach in the Milwaukee area. Google Images show a lot of babes out there. It's our best bet."

"So where is it?"

"It's right on Lake Michigan near downtown Milwaukee. It's a popular place for sunbathing. We're taking Cage along. He knows how to charm the ladies."

Chapter 8

We watched the segment about our victim on the TV in the lunchroom. The news stations did a good job of broadcasting the information and pictures just as we asked them to. The phone number at the bottom of the screen came directly into the bull pen. Each news station was given a different phone number that rang at one of our desks since we didn't want to miss any calls.

Fifteen minutes later, the phones began to ring. For the next hour, we were taking calls from every mother, father, sibling, and neighbor of this girl, and none of the calls seemed legitimate. We wrote down the information and recorded the calls anyway.

Horbeck and Jamison came in at seven o'clock and took up some of the slack.

I pressed my temples as I looked over what I had written down from the callers. From tips about our Jane Doe being somebody's pastor's wife, to the neighbor's babysitter, then on to someone's son's fourth-grade science teacher, I didn't know if any of the calls would pan out.

Jack's desk phone rang, and he picked it up. I watched the expression that crept across his face. He seemed interested in whatever this caller was saying. He scribbled information in his notepad, thanked the caller, and hung up.

"This may be legit," he said. "The caller is from Pleasant Prairie, near Kenosha. She said the sketch looks just like her niece from Grand Forks, North Dakota, who went missing three months ago. She doesn't know anything about a dragon tattoo, but she was going to call her sister and ask. The niece's name is Reanne Orth, and she's twenty-one years old."

I perked up. "Is she going to call us back?"

"Yeah, she said in five minutes."

"Okay, Jamison, log on to the missing persons database for North Dakota and check if anyone named Reanne Orth is listed. If you find her, see if the dragon tattoo is also listed with her description."

"I'm on it, Jade." Jamison went to work, and within a few minutes he had something. "I found her, but the picture doesn't look like the same girl." He hit the print button on the computer screen, and the printer in the bull pen sprang to life.

We gathered around the monitor and leaned in.

"I'm printing out ten copies," he said.

I nodded. "Thanks, Jamison. Let's see what the description says. They have her listed as one hundred thirty-two pounds with blond hair. No wonder we didn't notice her in the database earlier. This poor girl barely weighs one hundred pounds, according to Jason, and her hair color is different. I wonder how the aunt even recognized her."

"She told me she wasn't absolutely sure, that's why she hesitated to call. Her husband finally convinced her it was Reanne," Jack said.

Horbeck maximized the screen. "That's our girl, but it's weird that the tattoo wasn't even mentioned. No wonder that keyword didn't help us locate her in the system."

I poured coffee for everyone. "We might be on our way to North Dakota in the morning."

Jack's phone rang again. He picked up before it had a chance to ring twice. "Hello, Detective Jack Steele speaking." He seemed to be listening intently. "Yes, okay"—he nodded and gave us the thumbs-up—"I completely understand, and we'll tread lightly. We'll need the parents' names. … Uh-huh, thank you. Phone number and address? Okay, Mrs. White, I think that should do it for now. … Yes, I have all of your information as well. Washburn County Sheriff's Department thanks you, and our condolences go out to your family. … Yes, good night."

"What did she say?" I turned my chair to face Jack as I sipped my coffee.

"Well, I have the parents' info. I guess the mom has been a basket case ever since Reanne went missing. Apparently she's anti-law enforcement since the local cops didn't pursue the case. They said she was over eighteen and could do as she pleased. Reanne had a few minor run-ins with the law in Grand Forks, so they chalked her up as a runaway."

"Was that the 'tread lightly' part?" I asked.

Jack nodded.

"They have a point, though. Maybe Reanne did leave town on her own volition and got into trouble with a stranger she met along the way. She could have been picked up hitchhiking or even left and assaulted by someone she knew. Either way, somebody still killed her, and they tortured her before she died. Jack, make the call to her folks. I'll call the lieutenant and update him. We'll likely be flying out tomorrow. Get a feel from the mom and see what she says."

"Yep, I'm on it."

I tapped the buttons on my desk phone to call Lieutenant Clark's home number. I had it programmed. I glanced at the clock—eight thirty. At least I wouldn't be waking him up.

"Jade, what have you got? I saw the news. They did a great job on our Jane Doe segment."

"I agree. We found her, boss. Her name is Reanne Orth, and she's from North Dakota."

"I'll be damned. Who called it in?"

"Her aunt lives in Pleasant Prairie and thankfully recognized the sketch of her face. I had Jamison track Reanne down in the North Dakota missing persons database, and he found the listing. It's her, boss, minus thirty pounds and with a different hair color."

"No wonder we missed her in the database—and the tattoo?"

"Funny thing—it wasn't mentioned in the description. One would think that the tattoo would be an important key element to put in a missing person's description, unless—"

"Unless what?"

"Unless she got it in the last three months, but a tat that size takes time. Maybe she had it all along and her folks never knew about it."

"Either way, you and Jack are on the first flight to what city tomorrow?"

"She lived with her parents in Grand Forks."

"All right, book it for both of you. Keep me posted. Jade?"

"Yes, Lieutenant?"

"Tell everyone 'good job' for me."

"Will do, boss. Good night." I clicked off and went back to work on my computer. As I waited for Jack to end his phone call, I checked the flights going in to Grand Forks. He hung up after ten minutes.

"Well?"

"I told the mom, Charlene, we found Reanne and had her here at the ME's office. I wasn't going to give her details, but she did ask how she died. I only said it looked like foul play. She had a hard time talking. Apparently, Mrs. Orth is a homemaker, and her husband is a parts driver for car dealerships. She said she'll be expecting us tomorrow. She broke down, and the husband, Jeff, had to finish the conversation."

"I can only imagine how heart wrenching that call had to be for both of them."

Jack agreed. "So, what did the boss say?"

"He said to take the earliest flight out. I'm checking on

availability now. It looks like there's a nine forty-five flight with six seats left. What do you think?"

"Sounds fine with me. We'll grab breakfast on the go."

"Okay, I'm booking it now."

With the tickets purchased, boarding passes printed, and the rental car reserved, I called downstairs and left a message for Jason.

"Hey, Jason, it's Jade. Jack and I are flying to Grand Forks, North Dakota, in the morning. We found out our girl's identity. Billings and Clayton can give you the details when you come in tomorrow. Anyway, I'd like a call as soon as you get that tox report back. Thanks." I looked at everyone in the bull pen and gave them a thumbs-up. "Clark said good job. I'm out of here. Tomorrow is going to be a busy day." I put away the clutter on my desk, grabbed everything I needed, and headed out. "Night, guys."

The guys waved, and I left. As I pulled out of the parking lot, I wrapped my Bluetooth ear piece around my left ear and called Amber. I glanced at the time; it was still early enough to sit down, relax with my sister on our deck, and have a glass of wine. First, I'd give Polly and Porky a little bit of love—Spaz too.

I arrived at the condo I recently began to call home. Every time I pulled into the driveway, I smiled. Amber already had two glasses of wine waiting on the deck out back. The low-watt floodlights illuminated the woods beyond the deck just a little. Now and then we'd see a raccoon skitter by, and on occasion, if we were lucky, we'd see a deer. After relaxing with the wine and a decent amount of girl talk, I went to bed and hoped for at least five hours of sleep.

Chapter 9

"Got everything we need?" Jeremy asked as they loaded the van.

"Yeah, it looks like it." Matt opened the passenger side door and reached in. He popped the glove box and made sure the ice pick was still in there. He yelled to Jeremy at the back of the van, "The tire-puncturing device is on board, sir."

"Real funny. Just don't forget your role today. I'm the schmoozer, and you're the photographer. We have to locate the best two girls arriving at the beach together. Knowing which car is theirs is the third most important thing."

"What's one and two?"

"Damn it, Matt. You're supposed to know these things."

"Dude, calm down, I'm just kidding. No visible tats and nobody over twenty-four. I got it, trust me."

Jeremy puffed out a sigh. "Sorry, I'm a little edgy. As soon as we get two new girls, I'm getting rid of Beth. Nobody wants her anyway, and she's costing us money."

"Is she going in the woods?" Matt's eyes lit up with intrigue.

"Definitely." Jeremy looked left and right, then he exited the long gravel driveway and turned left onto the blacktop road. Soon, he'd be merging with the freeway traffic and heading south to Milwaukee. "I'm not taking any more stupid chances. Sorry, brother, that was my bad. Hope it blows over. Let's go over the plan one more time."

Matt slapped his hands together. "Okay, I'm ready."

"We sit in the van and do surveillance until we find the right girls. They're the ones we'll focus on. You're in charge of the camera and the cooler. I'll have my shirt off and my shades on. Cage and I will start playing on the beach. When I throw the ball, it will accidentally on purpose land on the ladies' blanket. That's how we segue into the introductions."

They both laughed.

"Pretty good idea, huh? Cage will love the attention." A wide grin spread across Jeremy's face.

"Yeah, Cage always makes it work like a charm."

"A dopey puppy and an alleged model and photographer—we're golden, man. Anything model-related draws women in. You know how they love being photographed. If we can't connect with the two we pick out, we'll find someone else. We might have to find a few sleeping beauties on the beach and give them a jab when they're least expecting it," Jeremy said.

A plastic grocery bag filled with breakfast bars and apples, along with a thermos of hot coffee, would be enough to hold them over during their surveillance. It could be hours of sitting and watching, but it was a price they were willing to pay.

Getting there early gave them plenty of parking options, and once they arrived, Jeremy found the best parking spot along the curb on the main road. The beach and Lake Michigan were only fifty yards to their right. They drank coffee and waited as Bradenton Beach began to fill with sunbathers.

Chapter 10

I pulled into Jack's driveway and honked three short beeps. We had two hours and fifty minutes to get to the airport, take the shuttle to our terminal, get through security, and find our gate. General Mitchell International Airport was just over an hour south of North Bend. We'd be fine as long as we didn't hit morning-rush-hour traffic. That was where my driving expertise came in. My pop taught me years ago how to be an aggressive driver when necessary. I figured it might be necessary if Jack didn't get his butt out here. I honked again then finally saw the front door open. I laughed at the sight of him. I'd swear on a stack of Bibles that he had just woken up ten minutes earlier. He opened the door of my Mustang and threw a backpack over the seat then climbed in.

"Why do people get up this early?" he grumbled.

"My best guess would be to get somewhere on time." I glanced at my watch. "You're lucky you're predictable. We wouldn't have had time to stop and get coffee from Pit-Stop, so I already did."

He perked up. "You got coffee?"

"Um, yeah, it's right next to you in the cup holder."

"Bless you, woman. Did you remember the boarding passes?"

"Seriously? Women never forget anything, Jack. Remember that. It might serve you well someday."

"Thanks for the coffee, partner."

I glanced both ways as I backed out of the driveway. I gave him an eye roll and shifted through the gears as I headed south.

"Have you ever been to North Dakota?" I asked.

"Nope, have you?" Jack sipped his hot coffee cautiously.

"Not that I can remember. I've always imagined folksy people living there."

"How did you arrive at that conclusion?"

"Not sure—probably because Fargo is nearby."

"Yeah, I always thought of that wood-chipper scene in the movie *Fargo* as pretty folksy."

I laughed. "Smart-ass… guess you got me on that one. Traffic is light, so that's a good thing."

"Yeah, because normal people are still in bed."

"Get a grip, Jack. It's almost seven o'clock. You're usually up by now anyway. You can take a nap on the plane; you'll have a few hours to relax."

"Just giving you a hard time, partner."

"I know. So what are you expecting from Reanne's family? Get any vibes from them?"

"Only that they're really upset with the local cops. I'm glad we're intervening. I don't think they would have let the city boys talk to them now after the fact. If anything, they're probably angrier than before."

We reached the airport, and I pulled into the park-and-ride and found an open slot. The shuttle stopped behind my car. Jack took my briefcase and his backpack and handed them to the driver. We boarded the van and were taken to the curb at departures.

"What concourse are we leaving from?" Jack asked.

"This way." I pointed to my left. "We're flying out of Concourse C."

Getting through security was a breeze—no hiccups, thankfully. We found our gate and had forty-five minutes before our flight. I pulled out the boarding passes and handed Jack his. Boarding would begin in fifteen minutes. Several sections of the daily newspaper had been left behind on the seat next to me. Jack asked for the sports page. I took the cooking section and browsed through it for a recipe that might interest me. Someday, I'd be as good a cook as Amber, or maybe not. I'd probably just let her have that role permanently. I tore out a recipe for Swedish meatballs and gravy anyway and put it in my purse.

We got in line to board the aircraft, and twenty minutes later we were taxiing down to the runway. Jack was sound asleep by the time he fastened his seat belt. The engines revved, and the airplane thrust forward. That was my favorite part of flying. I loved feeling that force and watching the ground disappear beneath us. I reclined my seat and closed my eyes too.

The voice over the intercom woke me. We were making

our descent into Grand Forks and would be on the ground in twenty-five minutes. My neck ached, likely from sleeping in an awkward position. I reached back and rubbed it.

Jack was still sound asleep. I leaned against his shoulder and whispered, "Jack, wake up. We're about ready to land."

"Huh, what?" He ground his fists into his eyes and yawned.

"We're going to land soon. Wake up."

"Yep—I'm awake. Any coffee?"

"It's too late. The flight attendants are already picking up the trash. We'll get some as soon as we're inside the terminal. We'll have plenty of time while we wait for the rental car."

"Yeah, okay, sounds good."

We landed uneventfully, which I was thankful for. As much as I loved takeoffs, the landings unnerved me most of the time.

Inside the airport at Grand Forks, we hit the nearest coffee kiosk then took the escalator to the lower level where the rental car agencies were. I had placed the order for a subcompact last night after I purchased the airplane tickets. We wouldn't be going far, and the price was reasonable.

"Jack, do you have the Orth's address programmed in your navigation?"

"Yeah, it looks like their house is about ten miles away. I'll drive."

I smiled. "Sure, no problem."

We found our small white rental car in row five and took off. The Orth home was on the edge of the city nearest the airport. We headed east toward the University of North Dakota. According to the navigation system on Jack's phone, their home should be just a few blocks south of the college.

Finding the house was easy. Jack pulled up to a modest white single-story bungalow, grouped on a street of similar looking houses. With the large trees in the neighborhood, I assumed these houses were from the 1950s. Jack parked in the driveway, and we followed the sidewalk to the front door and knocked. A slender middle-aged woman with blond hair opened the door. She seemed like a nice lady at first glance. She was dressed casually in jeans and a floral top, and her hair was pulled back with several barrettes.

"Mrs. Orth?"

"Yes."

"We're from the sheriff's department in North Bend, Wisconsin." We pulled out our badges.

"Of course. Please come in."

We stepped inside and made our introductions, then we shook her hand. She was alone and said her husband couldn't get off work. We nodded.

Mrs. Orth pointed at the couch. "Please, have a seat. I made coffee. Would you like some?"

"That would be great," Jack said. "Black for both of us."

Jack and I had an agreement that whenever we conducted interviews at someone's home, we'd drink our coffee black. We never wanted to inconvenience anyone. Once Mrs. Orth sat down, we began the interview.

Jack pulled out his notepad, flipped to a blank page, and

wrote as I asked the questions.

"Ma'am, did you get a chance to review the email I sent you last night?" I asked.

"Yes, and that was helpful. Trying to think of all Reanne's friends' names and contact numbers would have taken time."

She handed me the sheet of paper where she had written the information.

"Thank you." I continued on, "Did Reanne have a job?"

"She worked at Black Label Tattoos downtown. I've already spoken to them. Heck, I've spoken to everyone she ever knew or had contact with. The local cops weren't any help at all. My husband and I did everything on our own."

"Did Reanne hang out with anyone that seemed shady, maybe people it might not have been in her best interest to associate with?"

"Hang out with? I'm not sure. She had her usual group of friends, but in a tattoo parlor, you'll likely find some undesirables."

"What was Reanne's role there?" Jack asked.

"She took the phone calls, set up appointments, and showed albums to people that weren't quite sure what they wanted. I guess you'd call her the secretary or receptionist."

I opened my briefcase and took out the dragon tattoo picture. "Ma'am, did you know Reanne had this on her back?"

Mrs. Orth broke down in tears. She reached for a tissue from the dispenser on the coffee table and wiped her eyes. "I found out, and we argued about it. I wondered where her paycheck was going. She always seemed short of money. I lost it when she showed me the tattoo and said that was the reason why. Apparently, the guys at the parlor had been working on it for months during their free time. It cost her over a thousand dollars. I'll admit, I was furious. She stormed out of the house and drove off. That was the last time I ever saw her."

"She left in a car?"

"Yes, her own, but we got it back the next day. It was found abandoned with a flat back passenger tire about five miles from here at a swimming lake all the kids go to. We assumed she didn't have the money to repair or replace the tire. We figured a friend picked her up and she just needed a day or two to blow off steam. She never came home and never answered her phone after that day."

"So the car was never checked over by law enforcement?"

"No—we didn't know a crime had been committed." Mrs. Orth stole a glance at Jack, then she stared at the floor. "I'm sorry—if only we had known. Maybe there was evidence in the car. We took the car in and had all the tires replaced. They were due anyway. The man at the garage said the flat tire looked like a nail puncture, but nothing was in the tire."

I patted the back of her hand. "It's okay, really. Mrs. Orth, had Reanne seemed different, depressed, agitated, or worried about anything?"

"Not that I noticed, but she's twenty-one. Kids do weird things." Mrs. Orth continued looking at the floor. "I meant to say she *was* twenty-one. How did she end up in Wisconsin, officers?"

"Well, ma'am, that's what we're trying to find out. Have you contacted a funeral home yet?" I asked.

"Not yet. We're grieving and still trying to process this."

"We understand, ma'am. I have a forensic artist's sketch of Reanne. We'll need you to confirm it's her." I took the sketch out of my briefcase and turned it toward Mrs. Orth.

"It's her. My sister and brother-in-law were certain of it when they saw that local news broadcast last night. I trust their opinion."

"Ma'am, is there anything else you want us to know about her?"

"She was a good kid. Everyone that age fights with their parents, you know?"

We nodded.

"But all in all, she was sweet and didn't give us any trouble. She wasn't into the drug scene and didn't smoke. She went out on Friday nights with her friends, usually to Boomers Bar on Fifth Avenue, the typical thing young adults do."

"Thank you, Mrs. Orth." We handed her our cards. "We'll be in Grand Forks for most of the day checking out some of these places and names. Please call if there's anything else you'd like to discuss." We shook her hand. "We're sorry for your loss. We'll be in touch to let you know how soon we can release Reanne's body."

She escorted us to the door, and we left. We heard the door close at our backs.

Jack climbed in behind the steering wheel and looked over at me. "Who do you want to check out first?"

"Let's go with the tattoo parlor, then Boomers."

My cell rang, and I looked at the screen—Jason was calling. "Hey, Jason, what have you got?"

"The tox report came in, and I'll admit, I wasn't expecting this."

"And that's what?"

"Xylazine overdose, enough to put down a large animal."

"Holy crap—horse tranquilizers?"

"Yep, she must have gotten injected right in a major artery. It likely killed her within seconds. I didn't notice needle marks on the initial exam, but now that I know what I'm looking for, I'll check the carotid and femoral arteries under a magnifying glass."

"How does one get Xylazine?"

"It's available online to pharmacies and veterinarians. Whoever did this either has a fake license or they broke in somewhere and stole the drug. That would be nearly impossible to track across all of the pharmacies or vet clinics throughout the country. The drug could just as easily come from Canada or Mexico too."

"So we know what killed her, but we can't track the killer from the drug?" I asked.

"Yeah, it's unlikely."

"Damn it. Okay, anything else?"

"Yeah, put me on speakerphone."

I pressed the speaker icon on my cell. "Okay, go ahead."

"We have a new chief medical examiner."

I heard Jason chuckle. I turned my head toward Jack and grinned.

"Who is it?" Jack asked.

"It's the woman from Indianapolis. I met her earlier, and she's pretty cool. She'll start next week."

I laughed and gave a fist pump. Jack groaned.

"Okay, Jason. Thanks for the update."

"There's one more thing, Jade."

"Yeah, go ahead."

"Dan said he lifted fingerprints from the duct tape, but they aren't in the system. He checked nationwide."

"Damn it. Okay, thanks. See you later." I hung up.

Chapter 11

"Grab the binos. Those two might have potential," Jeremy said as he leaned forward and pointed through the windshield.

Matt slapped at the floor behind him, grabbed both pairs by the straps, and pulled them over the seat. He handed one set to Jeremy.

"Yeah, they look good."

"Never mind, the blonde has a sleeve tat. Whatever happened to the girls without ink? They're getting harder and harder to find."

"That should make them more valuable." Matt shook the thermos. There was still coffee sloshing around inside. "Want some more?"

"Yeah, sure. Another hour and this beach will be packed. There's no way we're going home empty handed," Jeremy said.

Matt poured the last two cups from the thermos, screwed the lid back on, and set it on the floor. He leaned back in his seat with the cup in his hand. The coffee was tepid at best. "When are you going to get rid of Beth?"

"If we snag a couple of girls to take home with us, Beth will definitely meet her maker in the next few days. Maybe we'll do it when Melanie leaves. Liz will be the only one left since we began this road trip and grabbed Reanne in Grand Forks. I'll admit, Matt, your suggestion of getting them as we go was brilliant. It's easier, and there isn't a bread-crumb trail. None of the girls are from the same town. These next two will be the exception, but the cops will look for them in Milwaukee, not out in Podunk farm country."

Matt sat up straight in his seat and put his cup on the dash. "Hey, check those two babes three cars up. I don't see tats on either of them." He adjusted the focus on the binos. Jeremy did too.

They watched as two young women exited a green car and opened the trunk. They pulled out a cooler and a large blanket then headed for the beach.

"Yeah, I'm liking the looks of it so far. I like the fact that they parked under that big tree too. It darkens the area a bit so they won't notice the flat tire right away."

"Plus the curb helps. I think they're perfect."

A sly smile crept across Jeremy's face. "I agree, bro. Let's wait until they're settled on the beach. We have to make sure no boyfriends show up."

Jeremy checked the time—twelve fifteen. "If nobody else shows up in an hour, we'll get started. You walk out with the camera strap around your neck and the blanket on the cooler. Spread the blanket out and start taking pictures right away. Take shots of the lake and harbor first so you don't seem invasive. Get a couple of beach shots after that, then I'll show up with the pooch and a ball. Make sure you lay the blanket right next to the women so we can strike up a conversation."

Matt grinned. He was ready to get the sham started. "How much time are we going to give ourselves?"

"A few hours. If it doesn't seem like they're ready to leave by four o'clock, we'll hit them with the needle. They'll just seem like they had too much to drink, and we'll walk them to the van. Remember, anything we touch goes in our cooler. Don't leave any bottles or cans behind."

"Wish me luck." Matt grabbed the door handle and stepped down onto the curb. The gear he needed was pulled from the back of the van, then he took the sandy path to the beach.

With the binos pressed against his eyes, Jeremy watched Matt get closer to the women they chose. He saw Matt spread out the blanket and place the cooler on it, then he exchanged a greeting with the ladies.

Good job, bro. Work it.

Jeremy continued watching as Matt lifted the camera hanging from the leather strap around his neck and started shooting toward the water. Still watching through the binos, Jeremy saw Matt turn and talk to the women some more. They were already intrigued.

"No sense in prolonging this—it's time. Come on, Cage, we have work to do."

Jeremy clipped the leash on the dog collar and put a bottle of water in one pocket of his cargo shorts and the ball in another. He slipped off his shirt, put on his shades, and locked the van. The man and dog headed down the path.

Cage relieved himself in the bushes and sniffed a few tree trunks, then they continued on. The dog trotted alongside Jeremy, secured with the leash, as Jeremy walked across the warm sand, shirtless and looking as good as any male model. Both brothers were easy on the eyes—they were lucky that way. Jeremy had ice-blue eyes and wavy black hair that just skimmed his shoulders. Women fawned over him—and Matt too, with his wild-child long hair. Their good looks always worked to their advantage. Jeremy felt the stares of approval as he headed toward his brother.

Their eyes made contact, and Jeremy gave Matt a subtle nod as he and the pup approached. Matt knelt and called out to Cage. With the camera on his subject, Matt snapped shots of the dog as it ran toward him. This ruse had been used often in the past and worked to perfection. A camera and a dog were all that were necessary.

"Aww… look at the cute pup. What kind of dog is that?"

The ladies were hooked already. Jeremy noticed how the women gave him an approving smile when he reached their blanket.

"Ladies. So you like my dog, huh?"

"He's adorable. What is he?"

"Cage is a rambunctious mountain cur. He's only six months old with an overabundance of energy." Jeremy extended his hand. "I'm Jeremy, and it looks like you've already met my photographer brother, Matt."

"We're Carley and Gina. Are you really a photographer?"

Carley shielded her eyes with her hand as she looked up at Matt.

"Yeah, I sure am. Actually I photograph models, and my brother is one of my main clients."

"You're a model?" Gina asked as she grinned at Jeremy.

"Yeah, I have been for almost two years. We're out here to do some magazine cover shots and let Cage have a few hours of exercise. Nice talking to you, ladies, but I have to stick close to Matt. He says when and where to set up. Come on, Cage."

Matt waved Jeremy over. "Right here, bro. The sun glistening off the sand is perfect."

The photo-shoot ruse had begun. Matt photographed Jeremy in the sand, against the water, and playing with the dog.

"Jeremy, throw the ball for Cage so I can get a few shots of both of you."

Jeremy wound up and threw the ball toward the ladies' blanket. Cage ran for it. The plan was flawless.

"Sorry," Jeremy yelled, his hands cupped around his mouth.

Sand skidded over the blanket when Cage bounded across it, coating the ladies.

"Oh my God," Carley said, "your dog is too much fun." She instinctively wiped the sand off her arms and legs.

Jeremy sat down, with Matt right behind him. "Cage, come on, boy. Take a break. I'm really sorry about that."

"No problem," Gina said. "He's so cute. Cage is an odd name. I hope he isn't always caged." Gina laughed at her own dim wit. She was already flirting as she flashed a grin Jeremy's way.

He gave her the once-over. She had long dark hair, nice teeth, pretty hazel eyes, and a good figure.

She'll go for top dollar, he thought. "Of course not—Cage is far too important to us to be confined like that. He has free reign of the house."

Jeremy sized up Carley too while he sat on the blanket next to them. She had smooth shoulder-length brown hair and brown eyes. Deep dimples popped on her cheeks when she smiled. Her skin was flawless.

"Do you brothers live together?" Carley asked.

"Yeah, sure do, in a high-rise over there." Matt pointed toward a group of tall condos a few blocks in from Lakeshore Drive.

"Wow, that's so cool."

Matt inched closer to Carley. "Where do you ladies live?"

"We live in Riverwest. We're best friends and roommates."

"How about a beer?" Jeremy asked. He opened the cooler and pulled out four of them before Carley and Gina had time to respond. "Where are your boyfriends? Ladies as beautiful as you two must have guys lining up to take you out."

They laughed. "School is more important right now. There's plenty of time for a serious relationship later," Gina said.

"So, what are you both—eighteen?" Matt asked to

confirm their ages. "Maybe we should have asked before offering you a beer."

Hmm… that was smooth, bro, Jeremy thought as he gave Matt a subtle wink.

Carley laughed. "I'm twenty, and Gina is twenty-one."

"Nice age. Perfect in fact." Jeremy glanced at Matt again and raised his right brow.

Chapter 12

I looked at the time on our rental car's dashboard. Three o'clock came and went, and our flight back to Milwaukee was at six. We'd struck out with the tattoo parlor where Reanne worked and at Boomers Bar. Mrs. Orth had been pretty thorough when she and her husband interviewed people at all of the places Reanne frequented. Everyone told us the same thing they had told the couple—Reanne disappeared without a trace. She never mentioned to anyone, including the friends we spoke with, that she had plans to leave town. The last communication she had was with her best friend, Lacy Meeker, then Reanne vanished. We interviewed Lacy after visiting the tattoo parlor and Boomers. She showed us the last text she'd ever received from Reanne, which said that she was going to the lake to chill out and asked Lacy to meet her there. The text showed the message came in at four thirty that day.

"That's where her car was found with the flat tire the next day," Lacy said. "She wanted me to meet her, but I had to work. Nobody ever saw her after that."

I wrote the information down. Lacy said she couldn't think of anyone that had a problem with Reanne—she had no enemies.

I asked her if any of their friends were missing other than Reanne. Maybe somebody she was acquainted with abducted her. As far as Lacy knew, everyone Reanne ever hung out with was still in Grand Forks.

Jack and I thanked her and left our cards. We got in the rental car and drove away.

"Are you hungry?" Jack asked. "My stomach is doing some serious growling."

"Yeah, I guess. Take your pick. There are plenty of restaurants around here."

Jack turned in at a twenty-four-hour diner, parked, and we walked in. The place was crowded for midafternoon. That told me the food was probably good, even though I usually thought of food as nothing more than sustenance—something that kept me alive. I never craved anything in particular, except maybe a chocolate bar slathered in goo and nuts.

The hostess seated us at a dark red vinyl-covered booth. The seats were cracked with wear, but the decor was pleasant. I opened the oversized menu and chose a turkey club. Jack took his time and browsed every page. He finally decided on the steak sandwich on sourdough bread with a side of waffle fries. The waitress brought our waters and filled our coffee cups. She took our order and left.

"So, it's pretty obvious that Reanne was snatched right in Grand Forks. Her car was left behind, and she disappeared in broad daylight. You'd think somebody at the park would have seen or heard something." I pressed my temples, hoping that would flip a switch—it didn't.

"Sounds like the flat tire could have been a deliberate act to keep her from leaving. Mrs. Orth said the car was parked in the last open spot, and the flat tire was on the passenger side. Reanne wouldn't have noticed it. Somebody could have punctured the tire then lay in wait and watched for her to return to her car. The friendly, concerned stranger could have pointed it out as a distraction," Jack said.

"That certainly makes sense, but he must have seen her arrive to choose her as his victim. I mean, he wouldn't have picked a car with a family in it." I shrugged and took a gulp of coffee. "The guy saw her early on then waited for her to return to her car. That's when he pointed out the flat tire. She probably looked down at the tire, and he clubbed her from behind. No—that would be too noticeable, but he had to do something to disorient her enough to get her in his vehicle without attracting attention. Shit!" I looked around, hoping nobody other than Jack had heard my exuberance.

"What?" Jack leaned across the booth, his eyebrows raised so high they almost touched his hairline.

I whispered, "I know how he did it—the Xylazine. The guy pointed out the flat tire, Reanne walked around the car to check it out, and he jabbed her in the neck. All he needed to use was enough to throw her for a loop. She'd be too messed up to yell for help. Chances are, he parked right next to her. Grab and go—he'd be out of there in seconds."

I jerked my head toward the approaching waitress. Our

conversation would be silenced until she came and went.

"Here you go, folks. Can I get you more coffee?"

"No, thanks, we still have plenty in the carafe," I said.

"Okay, well, enjoy your meal. Just give me a holler if you need anything else."

Jack smiled. "Will do."

I whispered again, "I'm calling Jason back to ask him if he's noticed a needle puncture in her neck or anywhere else yet. So, a small amount of Xylazine was likely used to incapacitate her, then he used it again when he killed her. If it went down the way I think, the flat-tire scenario is the ruse, then she got nailed in the carotid artery. My question is, if she was picked up in Grand Forks and dumped in Washburn County, did our killer pick up more women on the way? And why come to our area at all?"

"Valid questions, Jade. Knowing the method isn't going to give us the killer, but it might be a way to figure out what locations are easy grab-and-go spots where plenty of women hang out. The killer obviously took Reanne from a park. Popular swimming areas and parks would be a good place to start. Mall parking lots would be primo, but there are cameras. He'd have to be more careful there." Jack leaned across the table. "Wouldn't you think there's a nationwide database of pharmacies and veterinarians that have had dangerous drugs stolen?"

"I'm not sure, but call Billy and Todd. If anyone knows, they will. Jason thought it would be hard to track, but see what they say. I'll give Jason a call."

We ate, paid the bill, and left. We had to start making

our way to the airport to return the rental car. I called Jason as Jack drove and told him to be extra thorough when checking for needle marks. Chances were, she could have evidence of more.

Chapter 13

"What do you think, Gina? Should we head out?" Carley checked the time on her cell phone.

"Yeah, I suppose. This has been fun, guys, but if we don't get going, we'll be too drunk to drive." Gina laughed. "I think we've both had too much beer already, and I'm the only one that's legal to drink. I guess I'm driving."

"How far do you live from here? We could give you a ride home, and you could pick up your car tomorrow," Jeremy said, trying to encourage the women to agree.

"Nah, we're good—too much of a hassle. We'd have to get a ride back tomorrow, plus it isn't far," Carley said. A hiccup popped out of her mouth as she spoke. She chuckled.

"Hang on. Don't leave yet. I'm going to put Cage in the van, then we'll help you ladies carry your things to your car," Matt said.

Jeremy gave him the go-ahead look and nodded.

"What a gentleman," Gina said. "I guess chivalry isn't dead after all."

Jeremy grinned. *But you might be if you don't sell quickly.*

He watched as his brother left with Cage. Jeremy took in the surroundings. The number of people on the beach had thinned. Matt shouldn't have any trouble puncturing the tire without being noticed. He had become quick and efficient at it.

Matt returned in less than ten minutes. Jeremy watched his brother's face for a sign. Matt tipped his head. All was good.

He whispered to Jeremy as the girls gathered their belongings. "There was an empty parking spot in front of their car. I pulled the van in there. It's going to make loading them much easier."

"Perfect. This should be a piece of cake."

Matt handed Jeremy one of the syringes he had pulled out of the glove box when he returned Cage to the van. Jeremy dropped it into the front pocket of his cargo shorts.

"Let us give you a hand," Jeremy said. He reached for the ladies' cooler and picked it up with their own.

Matt helped Carley shake the sand out of the blankets and fold them. He wedged them under his arm, and the four took the path back to the road.

"We're right up here," Carley said as she pointed at a green Toyota. She clicked the key fob and popped the trunk.

Jeremy sat his cooler down on the curb and put the ladies' cooler in their trunk. Matt dropped his blanket next to the cooler. The flat tire would be hidden from view with those items until it was time for the women to see it.

Jeremy scanned the street and the beach to make sure nobody was in their immediate area. The limbs of the large tree Carley had parked under kept the car somewhat hidden. Jeremy nodded at Matt. The coast was clear.

Gina leaned back against the trunk and twirled the key ring around her index finger. "This was really fun." She openly flirted with Jeremy as she talked. "Maybe we can do it again sometime."

"Maybe. That's weird. The car is leaning toward the curb."

"What?" Gina turned her head to where Jeremy had pointed.

"Looks like a problem with that back tire," he said.

Jeremy had already popped the protective cover off the syringe in his pocket. Matt nodded, indicating that he had too.

Gina walked around the car. "Damn it, Carley. Your back tire is flat."

Carley came around the car to take a look. The ladies knelt cautiously at the back tire, apparently to avoid scraping their bare knees on the curb. With his head on a swivel, Jeremy did a final check in every direction. A second was all they needed. The brothers crowded behind the girls and sank the needles into each of their necks.

Short yelps of pain—mixed with surprise—came from Gina and Carley. That was the typical response. They slapped at their necks and wobbled. The Xylazine took effect quickly and rendered them unresponsive. They were dumbstruck, gurgling, and nearing unconsciousness.

"Hurry, open the back of the van," Jeremy instructed, jerking his head toward the vehicle.

Matt ran ahead, opened the back doors, and put Cage in the front seat. He came back around the car and lifted Carley. She was deadweight and limp. He threw her arm around his shoulder and nearly dragged her to the van. He did the same with Gina, shoving them both in and slamming the van doors behind them.

Jeremy was already wiping down everything he touched at the car. With their coolers and blankets tossed in the backseat of the van, and after a final check of the surroundings, he nodded. "Let's go. Get in the back and tie them up." Jeremy climbed in behind the wheel, and they took off.

The quarter dose of Xylazine the ladies got was enough to knock them out for a few hours. There would be plenty of time to get back to the farm and introduce both of them to their new home. A dark, musty basement and a three-foot-by-four-foot chain-link dog cage would be their new digs until they were sold. At least they'd have roommates.

An hour later, Jeremy pulled into the secluded driveway. Gravel crunched under the tires as he backed the van against the outer cellar doors. That entrance came in handy and was the easiest route in and out of the basement of the old farmhouse. A few moans sounded from the girls as they were pulled out of the van. Their arms were tied behind their backs, and their ankles were tied together. Duct tape covered their mouths, almost to their ears.

"Get the cages ready," Jeremy said as he flung Gina over his shoulder.

Matt unlocked the cellar door, flipped the wall switch to light the steps, and ran down before Jeremy to ready two vacant cages. "Go ahead," he said as he came back up the steps to grab Carley.

Both brothers were strong and capable. Matt flung Carley over his shoulder and followed Jeremy downstairs. The three caged women cried out when they saw two more women being carried to the empty enclosures.

"Shut the hell up over there," Matt said with a threatening glare. "You should be happy to have new roommates. There's so much to talk about, and you better do it while you can, Mel. You're out of here tomorrow."

The brothers smirked as they shoved Gina and Carley into their individual cages and secured the padlocks. They took the cellar steps out and slammed the heavy double doors behind them.

Jeremy headed toward the barn.

"Where are you going?"

"We have work to do, and there's only a few hours of daylight left. Come on. Give me a hand."

The faded, warped barn doors weren't opened often, but Jeremy knew what he needed would be inside. He grabbed the old iron handles and pulled. The doors resisted but spread open with a creak.

"What are we looking for?"

"I know there are a couple of shovels in here. I saw them when old man Miller's son showed us the place. Push those doors open wider so we can see."

Matt entered the barn and turned to face the doors.

With a strong kick from his work boot, he got them to spread farther apart. "How's that?"

"Better. Here we go. There's plenty of tools back here." Jeremy walked halfway through the barn and found the rakes, sledgehammers, and hoes propped against a sidewall. Several shovels were mixed in with the rest of the tools. "Here, take one and come with me."

Matt never wandered around the property as Jeremy did. He wasn't one for the country life and wide-open spaces. He'd thought Jeremy was crazy when he said he wanted to rent the farm. Old man Miller owned a hundred acres that were part of the farmstead the brothers rented from him several months back. The house had stood empty for nearly a year until Jeremy saw an ad in the newspaper and called. The description of the secluded location was too good to pass up—it was perfect for their needs. Crops thrived on the farmland years ago, but these days, only broken remnants of dried-out cornstalks stood in the fields. A rickety house in need of updating and a barn that had seen better days were all that remained of the hundred-acre spread. For six hundred dollars a month, it was a steal, and Matt reluctantly went along with it.

Each brother carried a shovel, and Jeremy led the way. They stepped over the fieldstone rock wall behind the barn and entered the woods, where they continued on for five minutes more. Jeremy stopped, jammed the end of the shovel into the ground, and took in his surroundings.

"This should do it. Start digging."

"Is this for Beth?"

"Yes, it's for Beth."

Chapter 14

We sat at our gate and waited. Boarding to Milwaukee would begin shortly. Jason called me back, saying he did see several nearly faded puncture wounds on Reanne's neck and one other that looked more recent. Once he had confirmed that, and with his theory that Reanne had been caged, we knew there might be a dangerous individual roaming freely and possibly looking for more women in our area.

The flight to Milwaukee wouldn't land until after nine o'clock, and then we'd have another forty-five-minute drive to North Bend.

I glanced at Jack, sitting to my right. He looked tired. "Let's call it a night when we get back and start fresh in the morning," I suggested.

He agreed. "Sounds like a good idea to me."

It didn't take long to settle in once we boarded the airplane. We taxied out to the tarmac and waited our turn. The pilot announced we were third in line. Once the engines revved and the plane thrust forward, it was a little over a two-hour flight back to Milwaukee. The first hour was spent with coffee as we went over everything we had learned from Reanne's family, workplace, and friends. We rewrote the day's events in an orderly fashion, listing the most important notes from the interviews we conducted. That information had been scribbled in our notepads. Tomorrow, we'd sit in the bull pen and have a powwow with our team. I put the legal pad back in my briefcase and slid it under my seat.

I looked at my watch—seven fifteen. The flight attendant collected the Styrofoam cups and pretzel wrappers from the complimentary beverage and snack service. Jack and I folded up the tray tables, reclined our seats, turned off the overhead lights, and closed our eyes for the duration of the flight.

The aircraft wheels were lowered, and the sound woke me. The flight attendants were already walking the aisle, picking up last-minute garbage. We were reminded to stow anything we had taken out of the overhead compartments, raise our seat backs, and close our tray tables. Everyone should remain seated with their seat belts fastened for the rest of the flight. I chuckled and thought how easily I could have been a flight attendant. I had their spiel memorized verbatim.

I gave Jack's shoulder a nudge. "Hey, wake up. We're in Milwaukee."

Two slits opened slightly, and a frown furrowed his forehead. "Man, I can't open my eyes. It's like they're superglued together." He fisted his hands and ground them into his eyeballs.

I smiled. "Better?"

"No."

"Poor baby. Good thing I'm driving."

"Yeah, no kidding. I'm beat."

The plane hit the runway, and the wheels screeched. We taxied to the gate, then the lights came on. I looked at the other passengers, who groaned and had puffy, tired red eyes.

"What's with everyone anyway?" I asked, whispering to Jack.

"What?"

"Well, it isn't like we just flew twenty hours from Tasmania. It was a two-and-a-half-hour flight, for Pete's sake. Come on. Let's go."

We stood and waited our turn to exit, Jack hunched over so he wouldn't crack his head on the storage compartment above him. The process always reminded me of the way people took turns to go to the front of our church for communion when I was a kid. One row would empty before the next could step out. On airplanes, I always insisted on an aisle seat so I could charge to the front before anyone had a chance to stand up. After years of dirty looks from other passengers, I'd mellowed slightly and learned to wait my turn.

We walked through the near-empty terminal, down the escalator, and out the door to the park-and-ride shuttle stand. The green-and-black van approached, and we stepped aboard. I dug the green row reminder card out of my purse and handed it to the driver. Jack pulled a few dollars out of his wallet and gave them to the driver when he dropped us off at row A, slot 17, right where my car was parked.

"Are you hungry? I can find a quick drive-through, and we can eat on our way home. To be honest, I could use another cup of coffee," I said.

"Yeah, sure. It's on me, though—you choose. I'm cool with anywhere that's convenient for you," Jack said.

"How's this?" I asked as we came up on a fast-food restaurant a block from the freeway entrance.

"It works for me."

We ate in silence as I drove. We each chose a chicken wrap—easy to manage and not too messy. The coffee was hot and strong—just the way I liked it. It perked me up a little too.

"Jack?"

"Yep."

"We have no idea if the perp just passed through and dumped Reanne along the road or if he's made himself at home in our area."

"I'm leaning toward the latter."

"Okay, I'm listening."

"I could see a dump as he's passing through if Reanne was found just off Highway 60, but she was three miles up a narrow farm road. He'd have to get off the interstate, go to Highway 60, and then find a backwoods secluded farm road somewhere. It seems like too much work if he was just passing through."

"That's true, but the tarp and tape? Isn't that telling us he stopped and shopped somewhere, unless he just carries those supplies in his vehicle? Maybe he's an opportunist and doesn't plan who his victims are, or when he's going to grab them. That would tell us he *does* carry those supplies with him." I turned to check Jack's temperature on my theory. "What if he's a cross-country killer and the marks on Reanne's elbows and knees are from cages inside his vehicle? Maybe it's just what the women are transported in once he snatches them."

Jack nodded. "Good point, but what about the bleach and the scald marks on the body? Wouldn't he need a private place like a house with a bathtub to do that? He certainly couldn't take a risk like that in a hotel room."

"Yeah, those are all valid concerns to run past everyone in the morning. I think I'll let it go until then. The gerbil on the wheel needs a rest."

"We're almost home, partner. So when are you and Amber going to invite me to dinner? You do have a party-sized deck, you know. I sort of recall helping you carry your lawn furniture out there."

"You're right. How about after this case is solved? I'll have Amber give me her work schedule, and we'll make a definite plan. Now that I think of it, I did just buy a new grill. You guys can break it in with brats and burgers while I supervise and set the table. When we plan a date, have your folks come too, and I'll invite Mom and Bruce. I'll get my first party out of the way, hopefully sooner rather than later."

Jack agreed. "Okay, you've got a deal. I'll be the grill master, and all you have to do is make sure there's plenty of beer."

I grinned.

"See you in the morning," Jack said as I pulled into his driveway.

I watched him walk up the sidewalk with his backpack slung over his shoulder. He turned back and waved when he reached the front door. I waved back then drove home.

The overhead garage door lifted and creaked as I waited in the driveway to pull in. The condo was dark. Amber was closing Joey's tonight. Spaz lay on the couch and lifted his head when I walked in. He wasn't quite interested enough to get up and greet me properly, but I gave him a head scratch anyway. He purred.

Polly and Porky were sleeping soundly on their perch, so I left them alone. I didn't need to hear birds chirping anyway when I was dead tired and going to bed.

We'd start the brainstorming, hopefully rested and refreshed, first thing in the morning.

Chapter 15

Jeremy got an early start. He'd have to take Melanie to the designated location later where the buyer's representative would pick her up. He wrote down the address and programmed it into his GPS. Neither of the brothers was familiar with the area. From what Jeremy had been told, the rep would be flying into O'Hare on a private plane and would meet him near the state line. Jeremy calculated the distance was about ninety miles from the farm.

The sun had been up for only an hour, but he was already hard at work. His body glistened with sweat, even in the shade cast by the overhead tree limbs. Jeremy had to finish digging the hole for Beth. He left a note on the table for Matt to feed the girls and to make sure Melanie showered. She needed to look nice for her new owner. If the buyer was pleased with her, the chances of future sales would be good.

He had two more feet to go. Jeremy wiped his brow with his forearm and rubbed his watch against his cargo shorts. The crystal was coated with dirt. Eight o'clock—there was still plenty of time. He speared the ground with the shovel head and cracked open the water bottle that was in his oversized side pocket. He sat down against a tree and took a deep swallow. A mosquito buzzed on the back of his hand. He watched as it filled its belly with his blood. He smashed it with his other hand then smeared the blood across his shorts. He took another swallow of water, got up, and began digging again.

An hour later, the hole was finally deep enough for a body. Jeremy headed inside to see if Matt had gotten up yet. Matt's sleeping habits annoyed him. His younger brother needed to be a bit more ambitious. Jeremy didn't like carrying the brunt of the responsibility all the time.

The kitchen screen door slammed behind him when he entered but not before a few pesky flies managed to get through. He slapped at them as he walked toward the living room. Jeremy peeked around the doorway—nobody there. He heard voices coming from the basement—at least Matt was up.

He opened the door and descended the creaking stairs. What sounded like distant voices from upstairs were now clearly panicked cries for help. Jeremy rounded the corner at the bottom of the stairs and entered the large room with the caged women.

"What the hell is with all the noise?"

He saw Matt sitting on a chair five feet from the cages. Lying next to him on the floor were the stun gun and cattle prod. Five bottles of water and ten breakfast bars sat on a small table to his right.

"Did you just come down?" Jeremy asked.

"Yeah, sorry, bro, I got up late. Their food is ready, but these two? Apparently they don't know the drill yet. They can sure yell."

Jeremy approached the cages that held Gina and Carley and crouched down in front of Carley's gate. "Haven't your roommates gone over the rules with you yet?" He stared at both newcomers. "I bet you weren't expecting this yesterday, were you?" He grinned at his brother. "Your throats must be parched from all the yelling you're doing. Water would taste good right now, wouldn't it?"

Carley spat through her pen, just missing Jeremy's face.

Jeremy turned to Matt and laughed. "That was close. I guess Carley needs to be taught some manners."

He stood and winced at the pop that came from his knee. Memories of his own childhood abuse entered his mind for a second. He dismissed them and walked toward his brother, his hand outstretched. Matt picked up the stun gun and cattle prod and handed them to Jeremy, then he sat back in his chair and rubbed his hands together with anticipation.

"Pay attention, ladies, and watch how this is done. You see these bottles of water? I want to give each of you water to drink, but you have to do as you're told. Watch Beth over here. She'll be the guinea pig for this demonstration."

Jeremy approached Beth's cage. She cowered toward the back and whimpered.

"Okay, I'm going to open her pen and place the water bottle inside. If she makes a move toward the gate, she's going to get zapped. Let's show them how this works, Beth."

Jeremy motioned for Matt to bring the keys over. Matt unlocked the padlock and opened the gate. He stood back and watched—excitement was written across his face.

"Okay, come on, Beth. Come forward like you want to escape. Pay close attention, girls. You seriously don't want this happening to you. It really hurts, right, Beth?"

In a flash, Jeremy reached in and hit Beth with the cattle prod. She grunted, fell back, and twitched for a few seconds.

He jerked his head to the sound of Gina screaming. She wrapped her fingers through the wire links and shook the cage. Jeremy slammed Beth's gate and walked over to Gina's pen.

"Let us out of here! I want to go home," she screamed.

"That's a big no-no, Gina. I thought I *just* made it clear to you what the consequences were for misbehaving. Besides, you're never going home. Now everyone is going to be punished for your behavior." Jeremy pulled the stun gun out of his back pocket.

"You're going first, Carley. Brace yourself, it's going to hurt."

Jeremy grabbed Carley's hair through the wires and pulled her head back. He zapped her neck with the gun and gave it a few extra seconds. She screamed, grunted, and jerked as her body hit the floor of the pen.

"Who's next?"

Jeremy approached the cage with Liz inside and zapped her, then he nodded for Matt to help out. "Hit Gina with the cattle prod. You want to keep your distance from her. She looks like a fighter. I'll let you slide, Mel, only because you're leaving us. I'm sure your new owner doesn't want to see burns on your body when he gets you. Consider yourself lucky. Your roommates got your share instead. Now eat your damn breakfast. None of you are getting water, so you can thank Gina for that. We'll be back in an hour, and I don't want to hear a peep from any of you before then."

Jeremy dropped two breakfast bars through the wires of each cage. He and Matt turned the corner, clicked up the volume on the baby monitor, and left. They slammed the door behind them at the top of the stairs.

"Let's see if these new girls have any bright ideas," Jeremy said as they entered the kitchen.

"Does it matter? Mel and Beth will both be gone."

"Nah—it doesn't matter, but it is amusing." Jeremy turned the volume up to high on the baby monitor that sat on the kitchen table, poured two coffees, and waited. The monitor came to life with conversations from downstairs. Laughter filled the kitchen as the brothers leaned in closer to listen.

"I have to get out of here. I'm going to make a run for it when they let me out to shower. It's the only chance I'll have before I'm gone for good."

"Mel, you can't leave me. I'm afraid."

Matt said, "That sounds like Liz."

"I'm leaving no matter what. They've already sold me."

The sound of a cage shaking made the brothers laugh.

Jeremy grinned at Matt. "That has to be Gina. The others know better."

"Stop doing that, Gina. There's no way out. You're just going to get us zapped again. You're better off complying. Don't give them a reason to get mad at you. You won't win."

Matt took a gulp of coffee and said to Jeremy, "Good advice."

The voices continued.

"There has to be a way out."

"There isn't, and I want to live. They killed one of us a few nights ago. She screamed a lot too, and now she's gone."

"That sounds like Beth and Gina talking," Jeremy said with a smirk. "Sorry, Beth, you may want to live, but that just isn't in the cards anymore. We didn't dig that hole for nothing."

Chapter 16

We had already been brainstorming for over two hours. Three pots of coffee into it, we'd concluded that Reanne was snatched randomly from a popular swimming lake in Grand Forks. Now, she was found dead over six hundred miles away in our county. According to Jason, she hadn't been sexually assaulted, only zapped numerous times with a stun gun and cattle prod. We all agreed that Reanne had been caged. We just had to figure out if it was during her transport or if the killer had a place where he was staying.

The motive could come from one of two directions. We were dealing with somebody who was moving across the country and snatching women as the opportunity came up. This method would be difficult to track since he could be a serial killer who would capture women in one location, then torture and kill them somewhere else. The other scenario would be that he actually was collecting women as he traveled. Once he had enough, he'd have to hunker down somewhere, keep them caged in a stationary location, and then sell them on the darknet.

Lieutenant Clark leaned back, causing his chair to squeak. "Okay, if our guy is selling women, why kill one? Isn't that like getting rid of the goose that laid the golden egg?"

I nodded. "But maybe she did something that enraged him. Killing her might not have been his original intention. We need to find out if any other dead women have been discovered between Grand Forks and here with burns from a stun gun and cattle prod. At least that would tell us if he was killing them for fun or if Reanne's death was the exception to his sick intentions. We'll have to come up with the most likely route between the two areas and see if anything pops."

"That's easy," Jack said. "The most direct route is Interstate 94. I think we should check less obvious alternate routes too. If he just kills and dumps them, he may not want to be on such a public stretch of highway."

The lieutenant agreed. "Okay, Clayton and Billings, you guys get started on that. If he is stationary, we'll need to establish a perimeter to stay within, meaning our own county. We'll focus initially on the eastern section of the county. Wausaukee County could also be a possibility. I'll talk to the sheriff's department over there and give them a heads-up. If he's transporting women, we're likely looking at somebody with a van or something larger."

"Boss?"

"Yes, Jade."

"We could check into moving-truck rentals that came from Grand Forks, but we have no idea if that was his starting location."

"True, but Reanne went missing several months ago. Would anybody keep a moving van for that long? He still needed a means to dump her body. I'm thinking this guy has his own vehicle. Okay, let's narrow down what we do know."

Jack began. "He may be familiar with the area just because of the dump spot. To me that means he's found a place to stay even if it's temporary. He's likely driving his own vehicle, so it has to be at least the size of a van, and he somehow has access to Xylazine."

"Did we get anything on that?" the lieutenant asked, looking between Todd and Billy.

Todd spoke up. "There was a report two years back about a break-in at a veterinarian's office in LA. Nobody was ever caught on that one. Also, a pharmacy in Miami reported Xylazine and a few other drugs stolen last August, but the thief has already been apprehended. The database goes back three years in the US, and those were the only two reports where Xylazine was mentioned."

Clark groaned. "What ever happened to good old-fashioned murders committed by jealous husbands in their homes? At least we'd have a location and a name."

I poured more coffee for everyone. "This isn't going to be an easy case, especially if we have no idea if the perp dumped Reanne and continued on or not. He could be in Ohio by now for all we know. What we do know is she's dead, and somebody has to be held accountable for her murder."

Lieutenant Clark's phone rang on his desk. He turned

and headed for his office. "Clayton and Billings, get started on those routes. Todd and Billy, thanks for the help tracking down the Xylazine." He looked at Jack and me. "Excuse me for a minute, guys. I'll be right back."

We watched through the glass wall as he sat at his desk and talked on his phone.

"This can't be good," I said.

The expression the lieutenant wore told us something bad had happened. He hung up and came back out to the bull pen.

"That was Lieutenant Colgate calling to give us a heads-up. After seeing the news broadcast from the other night about Reanne, he thought we ought to know that two young women vanished without a trace from Bradenton Beach yesterday. Their car was left behind with a punctured back passenger tire."

I hit the desk with my open hand. "Son of a bitch, it's the same MO as Reanne's. What about tracking their cell phones?"

"Not happening—they were left inside the trunk along with their purses. It looks like one of them had anti-seizure medication in her purse."

I groaned. "Shit—she's probably epileptic."

Clark squeezed his temples. "Jade, check the fax machine, please. Colgate sent over the photos and vitals on the missing girls. Our guy is obviously still in the area. Get Todd and Billy back up here. I want them sitting in on this."

"You got it, boss."

I grabbed the sheets on the girls from the fax machine then ran down to the lower level of the building. The tech department was down the hall. I stuck my nose in the door and saw maps on the computer screens.

"What are you guys doing?" I asked.

Clayton walked in. "They're giving me a hand with the routes. We're looking for a few secondary roads leading from Grand Forks to our area. The interstate doesn't make sense. I was going to print them out and bring them up to the bull pen."

"Well, Clark wants everyone upstairs again. I think he has some questions for you guys."

Billy pushed back his chair. "Sure, let's go."

"Have a seat, guys," Clark said when Todd and Billy entered the bull pen. Clayton and Billings came in behind them. I handed the lieutenant the photos of the two girls that went missing yesterday in Milwaukee.

"Normally, this wouldn't be an issue for us, but because Jack and Jade went to Grand Forks and found out more, I'm thinking it's related. Apparently, Reanne's car was found with the back passenger tire punctured." Clark pointed at the photos he had pinned to the corkboard beside him. "These two ladies went missing at Bradenton Beach yesterday, according to the Milwaukee PD. The car was left behind, and the back passenger tire was punctured. Lieutenant Colgate told me that the car was probably wiped down. There weren't any fingerprints on the vehicle other than the owner's"—he looked at the sheet with the girl's information on it—"Carley Donovan, twenty years old, and her friend, Gina Sansone, twenty-one. The fourth district PD has already interviewed the families and friends. So far they have nothing. Billy, Todd, how do we access the darknet without our IP address coming up as the location of the Washburn County Sheriff's Department? If our guy is actually selling girls, wouldn't he post photos of them?"

"Yeah, he sure would," Billy said.

"Well, we know what these latest missing girls look like. We also know that Reanne had scrapes on her elbows and knees that had traces of metal in them. Right, Jason?"

"That's correct, Lieutenant."

"Okay, for now, we're going with that theory. We need to get to the darknet so we can gain access to these auction sites. Is that possible?"

"We can definitely hide our IP address, Lieutenant, but finding their site, if it's actually out there, is tricky. Something as vile as human trafficking is likely found in the dark web which we'd have to access first. The darknet auction sites move around a lot to avoid detection. You have to be one of them to get in and bid on women."

"Is there a way to see what's going on without being detected or without logging in?"

Todd looked at Billy and scratched his head. "Maybe, but it depends on if they show teasers on their home pages. The administrator can add photos to it, but the viewer can't go beyond that page, meaning we couldn't get in, but we could see whatever is posted on the home page. That also depends on if they actually update that page with real photos of girls they have held captive and who're for sale or if they're just posting random pictures from the Internet. If these people are smart, they'd never show real photos to anyone other than registered bidders."

"Can you guys at least try? Would their IP address be blocked?"

"Yeah, they'd hide their IP address, but we can give it a shot."

Chapter 17

Jeremy checked the clock above the stove. Beth had to be dealt with first. He'd get that out of the way and still have plenty of time to shower and clean up. Mel had to get ready too. A freshly washed outfit draped across a hanger was for her to put on later, after her shower.

"It's time." Jeremy pushed back the kitchen chair and opened the basement door. "I'll get her. You fill the syringe with a double dose."

"Yep, got it," Matt said.

The brothers took the stairs to the basement. Matt hung back and pulled a syringe and the Xylazine out of the jelly cupboard. He spun the roller chair toward him and sat while he poked the needle tip through the rubber stopper. He pulled back the plunger and drew a double dose into the syringe. He checked the amount through the clear plastic barrel then covered the needle with the protective cap. Matt looked around the corner and nodded to Jeremy that he was ready.

"Let's go, Beth. You're looking awfully pale. I think you need some sunshine."

"What? Why? I don't want to go outside. Please, I'm good. I like my cage." Tears rolled down her cheeks as she scooted to the farthest corner of her enclosure.

"That's nice. Let's go."

Matt spoke up, "Either come outside on your own or get the prod, it's your choice. Either way, we're going outside, and you're coming along."

Matt unlocked the cage, and Jeremy grabbed Beth by the legs and pulled. She kicked, grabbed the sides of the cage, and held on while she screamed for help.

"Zap her," Jeremy yelled. "That skank just kicked me in the face."

With the cattle prod between the links, Matt zapped Beth in the chest. Her hands twitched and fell to her sides as her grip on the cage loosened. Jeremy yanked her out and heaved her over his shoulder. With a nod toward the cellar door, Jeremy motioned to Matt to open it and the outer wooden ones at the top too.

"If she wakes up, nail her again. I don't want to look scratched and bruised up later when we dump off Melanie."

Matt followed Jeremy into the woods, with the cattle prod centered at the base of Beth's neck. She moaned and began to squirm.

"Hit the bitch again before I drop her," Jeremy yelled.

Matt zapped Beth in the neck. Her body arched unnaturally then slumped back over Jeremy's shoulder. The grave lay straight ahead where the mound of dirt and shovels interrupted the flat forest floor. Jeremy dropped Beth to the ground.

He straightened his shoulders and cracked his neck. "Got the needle ready?"

Matt nodded. "Yeah."

"Okay, do it."

As he knelt on one knee, Matt turned Beth's head to expose her carotid artery. He sank the needle into her neck and pushed the plunger in until all of the Xylazine was gone. Each brother found a tree trunk to sit against while they waited.

Jeremy looked at his watch. "We'll give it another few minutes. She's probably dead already, but it's better to be safe than sorry. Let's strip off her clothes. Somebody else can wear them."

"When are we going to take pictures of Gina and Carley?" Matt asked as he pulled the T-shirt over Beth's head.

"Probably tomorrow. We have a long drive ahead of us, and I might want to go out and celebrate later. That's eight thousand bucks we just got for Mel. Gina and Carley should bring that much too. Liz, I'm not sure. Maybe six thousand if that guy from Miami is still interested."

Matt put his fingers against Beth's neck and tried to find a pulse. There wasn't any. He nodded at Jeremy. "She's gone."

"Good, let's finish this up. Give me a hand."

With a heave, they lifted Beth and threw her in the hole. A thud sounded when her head cracked against a rock. Without missing a beat, they each grabbed a shovel and threw dirt over her face.

The deed was done within a half hour. Jeremy patted the grave with the shovel head to flatten it out. He returned the shovels to the barn and set them inside.

He wiped his brow and turned to Matt. "I'll take a quick shower, then you can. After that, we'll get Mel ready. She might need to get dosed for the drive. I'm not about to listen to her wailing for two hours. Get a syringe prepared to go."

"Sounds good. I'll give them something to eat while you clean up." Matt headed to the house with Jeremy right behind him.

Chapter 18

"Woo-hoo, don't you look pretty?" Jeremy's face lit up as he looked her over. Melanie came out of the bathroom and wore a clean dress. Her hair was glossy and smooth. Jeremy sniffed the air. "Man, you even smell good. Let me take a look at your forehead." He brushed her hair aside as she stood frozen in place. "Yeah, it's just a little bump. Your hair will cover that. See what happens when you try to run? It didn't work out very well for you, did it? Hey, bro, come and take a look at the new and improved Melanie."

Matt came around the corner and smiled. He had just filled a syringe for the drive to the state line. "Wow, you should have gone for at least ten grand the way you look now. Maybe we should keep you for ourselves." He licked his lips slowly and deliberately.

"Too late, brother, we've already been paid."

Melanie trembled as she stood in front of Jeremy and Matt and looked over at the three women still caged. She had known Carley and Gina for only a day, but Liz had been with her for two months.

"Just think, Mel, you're going all the way to Morocco. Man, who knows what that dude is going to act like with a hot, blond babe like you? He's going to be out of his mind with ideas." Jeremy laughed. "Okay, it's time to go. We don't want to keep your new owner's representative waiting. Say your goodbyes and make it quick."

Melanie wiped her eyes with the back of her hand. "Where's Beth? I want to say goodbye to her too."

"Yeah, Beth is gone. She asked us to say goodbye on her behalf."

"Where did she go?" Mel coughed between sniffles.

"Where is Beth, Matt?" Jeremy looked at his brother with a questioning smile on his face.

"Hmm… oh yeah, the last time I saw her, she was in the woods."

"That's right, she's in the woods. Now say goodbye to your friends. It's time to go."

Melanie began sobbing as she ran to Liz's cage and held her hands through the wires. "You'll be okay, Liz." She leaned in and whispered, "The cops will find you, all of you. You'll get out of this, just don't make these two mad, and do what they say. Tell the cops where they sent me when you're rescued."

"Okay, that's enough blabbering." Matt pulled Mel backward by the hair. "Get upstairs." He pushed her toward the cellar doors with the prod.

Jeremy opened the back of the van and set a cage inside. Mel and Matt stepped out into the late afternoon sun. The brightness made her squint.

"Get in. You have a choice, Mel, and I'm only going to explain it once. You can sit in the cage quietly and accept your fate, you can get zapped every time you make a fuss, or you can get hit with the needle. Which do you want?"

"I'll be quiet."

"Good choice. Here's a bottle of water for the ride. Remember, one peep and you get the needle or the prod."

She climbed up on the bumper and crawled into the cage. Jeremy handed her the water, closed the gate, and padlocked it. He slammed the back of the van shut and got into the driver's seat. Matt set two bottled waters in the cup holders and got in. Jeremy exited the long driveway and turned left onto Division Road. He headed south for ten minutes on different country roads, passing an occasional tractor before reaching a main highway. Jeremy turned east and drove for another fifteen minutes, then he merged onto the interstate. They would be at the Wisconsin and Illinois border in an hour. The rep they were meeting was supposed to be at an abandoned ski hill just west of Union Grove. He would be in a black SUV. The syringe of Xylazine would be given to him in case he needed it.

Just before dusk, Jeremy turned off the frontage road and into the entrance of the long-forgotten ski hill. A broken ski lift and a chalet with most of the windows shattered stood ahead to their left. The thick chain that had been stretched across the weedy driveway and holding a yellow "No Trespassing" sign had been taken down and was lying to the side. A lone black SUV sat idling with its fog lamps on. The gravel crunched under the van's tires as

Jeremy pulled up side by side with the other vehicle. A large man in a dark suit exited the SUV. Jeremy killed the engine, and he and Matt exited the van. Whimpering sounded from the back. Jeremy heard it just before he closed the door.

"Shut the hell up," he said in a snarled whisper.

The three men met at the rear of the van, shook hands, and introduced themselves. They talked for a few minutes before Matt opened the back doors.

"One moment," the rep said. He excused himself, returned to the SUV, and tapped on the driver's side window. The window came down. The rep spoke to the driver for a few seconds before the SUV started, and the driver turned the vehicle around in the driveway. The headlights illuminated the back of the van. Mel squinted and covered her eyes with her hands.

"Much better," the rep said.

"Put your hands down so he can see your face," Matt instructed.

She reluctantly complied.

The rep lifted his cell phone and began taking pictures. "These are for the buyer. He wants to make sure she looks the way she did in the auction photos. I'm sure you understand his concern."

Jeremy nodded. "Pull her out, Matt, so Mr. Lawrence can get a better look."

Matt unlocked the cage and grabbed Mel's arm. "Get out."

She crawled out of the cage and slid off the bumper. She stood and smoothed out her dress while more pictures were taken.

"Wipe your face. Your makeup is running," Matt said with an air of disgust. He turned her in different directions while Mr. Lawrence snapped a few more shots.

"It will be just a few minutes. I'm sending these photos to the buyer."

"Sure, no problem—how about a bottle of water?" Jeremy asked.

"No, thank you. Ah—there we go. The photos went through. It should only be a few minutes more, gentlemen."

They waited in silence.

"Yes, very good—our buyer is pleased. Let's go." He took Melanie by the arm.

Matt handed Mr. Lawrence the syringe of Xylazine and showed him the amount in the barrel. "Half of this will knock her out for a good three hours. Don't give her all of it at once. It'll kill her."

"I understand. Thank you, gentlemen, it's been a pleasure. I'm sure we'll be in touch."

"See ya, Mel. Have a nice life." Jeremy turned and got into the driver's seat of the van.

Matt walked around to the passenger's side and climbed in. They heard Mel's wailing as they drove away.

"How about grabbing a couple of beers on our way back?" Matt said.

"Yeah, I like that idea. We have eight thousand reasons to celebrate." Jeremy turned to his brother and high-fived him.

Jeremy's cell phone, lying in the cup holder between the seats, rang as he drove. He lifted it to see who was calling.

Not many people had that number since it was a burner phone. The screen illuminated, showing the caller was Mr. Lawrence.

"Crap, this can't be good." He grimaced as he answered. "Hello, Mr. Lawrence."

"Jeremy, I just wanted to tell you what a spitfire you sold us. My client will be amused."

Jeremy smiled. "That's good to know. What did Melanie do?"

"She obviously had her own agenda. As you drove away and before she was loaded in the SUV, she twisted out of my grip and ran toward the woods. My driver and I chased her down, of course, and quickly caught her but not before we each got a few scratches and bites in the process. She's resting comfortably now." He laughed into the phone. "She'll be sleeping for hours, and by the time she wakes up, we'll be over the Atlantic. I doubt if she'll try to make another break for it at thirty thousand feet."

Jeremy breathed a sigh of relief. "Sorry about that. I did hear her threaten to make a run for it, but she tried that earlier—hence the knot on her forehead. What is it they say? If at first you don't succeed, try, try again? Good night, Mr. Lawrence. We appreciate your business."

"Good night, Jeremy."

The brothers drove the ninety miles back to the outskirts of North Bend while drumming their fingers to the music playing on the radio.

"Hey, check out that bar," Jeremy said as he pointed and slowed down. "Want to stop and have a few?"

"Yeah, definitely. This looks like a pretty happening place." Matt scanned the parking lot when Jeremy turned in.

Jeremy shut off the van and got out. "Let's see what makes this place so popular. It's got to be the women. That might even give me some ideas."

They walked toward the front door, checking the roofline as they got closer.

"I don't see any cameras," Matt said.

"Sucks for them. Let's see what's inside."

They entered the jam-packed bar area. There was barely room to pass by another person and definitely no place to sit at the bar. Two guys stood, and Matt grabbed their bar table just before a couple got to it.

"Sorry, folks. You snooze, you lose," Matt said as he claimed both chairs. He saved one for Jeremy, who was squeezed between other patrons at the bar, ordering their beers.

"Pretty crazy place you've got here," Jeremy shouted to the bartender through the noise.

She smiled and nodded while she filled the pints he ordered.

"They come here for her." A voice sounded to Jeremy's left.

He turned his head and grinned. "Are you talking to me?" He noticed the woman's good looks and gave her the once-over.

"Yeah, I said she's what brings in the business."

"Knock it off, Jade. You're embarrassing me."

"Jade? Nice name—it matches your eyes."

"Thanks, that was smooth. Back to her, though—it's true, just look at that face."

"I certainly can't disagree. I'm Jeremy and new in town. May I buy you two a beer?"

"Sure, and by the way, you better be nice to your bartender. Amber is my little sister."

Jeremy looked back and forth from one beauty to the other. They were both gorgeous. The dollar signs rolled in his head. The playful spark in Jade's eyes made her look very appealing. "Oh, I intend to be nice to her. Amber, huh? So when do you get off work, Amber? I'm having a 'get to know your neighbors' party at my house." He looked at Jade and gave her a dimpled grin. "I'd love it if you were both my guests of honor." *Jade looks to be my age, older than most of our girls but very hot. I bet she'd still go for a good price.*

Amber leaned forward over the bar. "I work until closing. Sorry, dude, but you don't need to worry about being nice to me. It's Jade you have to watch out for."

"Really, why's that?" He gave Jade another look of approval.

"She's a sergeant at the sheriff's department, and she has a wicked gun."

Jeremy's excitement quickly diminished, but he couldn't let on. He laughed instead. "Yeah, you look like someone who could easily handle herself."

Amber passed the pints across the bar. Jeremy handed her thirty dollars and told her to keep the change. "Nice meeting you ladies."

"You too, Jeremy, and thanks for the beer," Amber yelled out.

Jeremy carried a pint of ale in each hand and placed them on the table. "Can you see that chick bartending from here?"

Matt craned his neck, trying to look around the sea of people. "Nah—can't see shit."

"Yeah, she's pretty damn hot, and young. She barely looks old enough to be a bartender. There's another hot-looking babe sitting at the bar—long black hair, huge green eyes. She gave me a smile and started talking, so I bought her and the bartender a beer. Turns out they're sisters, and the one sitting on the barstool is a cop. Damn it, they would have gone for top dollar. I think we should steer clear of this place. Drink up, brother—we need to go."

Chapter 19

It seemed that whenever we solved a case, I'd finally have a weekend off. Lately, that wasn't happening very often. Other than the week I took off while Amber and I moved, and she recuperated, we'd all been putting in extra hours.

"Clayton, you're catching on," I said, joking with him when I walked into the bull pen. "It's about time somebody other than yours truly brought doughnuts in on a Saturday."

He chuckled. "Yeah, I figured it was time I paid my dues."

I walked over to the open box on the table at the back of the bull pen and peered in. "Oh, yum—French crullers, my favorite." I grabbed two and a napkin then sat at my desk. For a split second, I thought about that hot guy standing next to me at Joey's last night. I was flattered when he bought Amber and me a beer. I guess I still had something going on, and Amber? She would be gorgeous forever. I smiled then forced my focus back on work. "How's it going with the roads between here and Grand Forks?"

"We've picked two alternates, but we're still checking out the interstate too. We'll split up the areas into counties and cities. It might take all of us working together, but we can make contact with the larger cities' PD and sheriff's departments and see if anyone has been reported missing or if any bodies have been found with the same MO as Reanne's," Clayton said while he chewed on his sugary treat. "If anything pops, it will likely be handed off to the FBI. We can't get them involved unless we know there have been other crimes like this committed."

I nodded as I tore off a piece of the doughnut and popped it into my mouth. "Yeah, murders crossing multiple state lines, that's definitely the FBI's job, not ours."

Jack walked in and headed directly for the doughnuts.

"You're amazing," I said.

"I am?" He turned and grinned at me, almost blushing and most likely expecting a compliment.

"I swear, you're like a dog. You probably smelled those doughnuts before you even got out of your car."

His smile quickly evaporated, and he was fast with a comeback. "Yep, you're right, Miss Piggy. How many have you had already?"

I frowned. "Just two, and I'm done, thank you very much." I wiped my hands on the paper napkin, balled it up, and threw it ten feet to the garbage can. "Swish—nothing but net and another three-pointer for me."

Jack laughed. "So what's on the agenda?"

Billings and Clark walked in, and they both headed directly to the doughnut box.

I shook my head. "We're going to divide up the cities and counties along the routes between here and Grand Forks. We should be able to complete that in a few hours if we all pitch in. We'll make phone calls and see if anyone has been reported missing or, worse, has come up dead in those areas with obvious stun-gun and cattle-prod burns on their bodies."

Clayton added, "We're focusing on the towns around Interstate 94 and State Highways 10 and 75. Keep in mind, just because there may not be reports of missing or dead women between there and here doesn't mean there aren't any. Driving from Grand Forks only takes a day. Our perp could have been staying somewhere in North Dakota or Minnesota for the last two months and recently headed our way."

"I think after we make these calls and either confirm or rule out other women between the two locations, we should begin knocking on doors in our own county," Jack said.

We all agreed.

"We can start that next week." I got up and made a fresh pot of coffee. We'd be at our desks and making calls for a while.

We divided up the police departments and sheriff's departments in cities with a population over fifteen thousand and dug in.

Chapter 20

"We need to get Carley and Gina up on the site today. Weekends are always busy."

"What about Liz?" Matt asked as he headed into the kitchen.

"Maybe later. Two new girls are going to get more attention right out of the gate." Jeremy laughed at his own comment. "Hey, that was funny, man. Right out of the gate—like literally."

Matt chuckled and grasped the chrome refrigerator door handle, giving it a tug. "Want breakfast before we start?" He pulled eggs and bread and butter off the shelves.

"Sure, why not? It's the weekend. We have a few hours before the site really gets rocking."

The heavy cast-iron skillet clanked as Matt set it on the stove and turned the burner on. He sliced a pat of butter off the stick and whacked the knife against the skillet. The pat fell and sizzled across the heated pan. Matt twirled the skillet, coating the bottom with the butter, then cracked four eggs into it. He popped two slices of bread into the toaster.

Jeremy busied himself making a pot of coffee while Matt cooked. He topped off two glasses with chilled, pulp-free orange juice, and Jeremy placed them on the table.

"So when do you think we can check out the new mall?" Matt asked as he flipped the eggs.

"Tonight sounds good to me. I bet that place will really be busy. The outdoor cafés too. It should be a warm night. Seeing tats isn't going to be easy, but we'll grab anyone that looks young and hot. They can go for a cheaper price, or we'll sell them overseas if we have to. We need to ramp things up. We can't forget our binoculars either."

They sat at the table and ate in silence.

Jeremy cleared the plates and set them in the sink. He closed the drain with the stopper and turned on the faucet. "These dishes can soak for a bit. Why don't you pick out a couple of sexy outfits for Gina and Carley? I'll go wake them up."

Matt went to the closet down the hall and opened it.

The basement door creaked. Jeremy flipped on the light and headed downstairs. With only one half-sized window in the room, located at the top of the opposite wall and with a window well around it, the girls were still able to see a small amount of daylight peeking in every day. At least they knew if it was day or night.

"Time to rise and shine." Jeremy pushed a banana through the cage wires for each girl. "How about that? Something different, right? It's Saturday—that means a busy auction day." He pointed at Carley and Gina. "You and you are going to get your biweekly shower. Matt is going to give you clean clothes to put on. Cool, huh? You're going first, Gina. No funny moves or you're really going to be hurting—understand?"

She mumbled something under her breath.

"I didn't hear you. What did you say?"

"I said I hope you rot in hell."

Jeremy laughed and picked up the cattle prod. "I probably will, eventually, but this is going to hurt like hell right now."

He was at her cage in two strides. The prod, jammed against her side, made her flail and screech as he zapped her with it. She fell back, stunned and groaning.

"Are you ready to cooperate now?"

She nodded.

"Good. I'm going to open the gate. You have ten minutes to shower and clean up. Got it?"

"Yes."

"Matt is bringing an outfit downstairs for you to wear for your photo shoot. You'll dress, comb your hair, and come out. Do as you're told and you won't get zapped again. Now move."

Jeremy unlocked the gate and opened it. Gina crawled out. He pressed the cattle prod against her back and pushed her into the bathroom. Matt came downstairs with the outfit and threw it at her. He closed the bathroom door and locked it from the outside.

After she showered and dressed, Gina knocked on the door. Jeremy unlocked it and pulled it open. She stepped out where they were waiting.

"Now *that's* what I'm talking about." Jeremy whistled. "If you do what you're told and act hot for the video camera, you might get an extra snack." He grinned at Matt. "She's going to hit ten grand, I can feel it. Let's get started." He pointed at the door going into the video room. "Over there."

Inside, Jeremy had the video equipment ready to go and was logged on to his account on the darknet auction site. He'd upload Gina's still shots and video as soon as Matt was finished working with her. He tapped several buttons and set her reserve at eight thousand dollars. He was hoping that once the reserve was hit, a bidding war would begin. They could only be so lucky. Gina's auction would last until four p.m. It took Matt thirty minutes to get the perfect shots of her. Several threats of agonizing pain convinced her to put her best foot forward and look sexy for the camera. When Matt finished, Gina was put back in her cage, and he began the same process with Carley. Her reserve was set at eight thousand dollars too. Her auction would end at five o'clock.

"I don't know, dude. I'm thinking Gina will go for a higher price. It's that Italian look, you know what I mean?"

Matt nodded. "Yeah, she's pretty damn hot."

Chapter 21

"Any luck so far?" Billings asked as he stretched and coughed into his fist.

I pulled off my reading glasses and looked from face to face. "Apparently not. Nobody between here and Grand Forks has come up missing in the last few months?"

Jack answered, "The sheriff's department in Fargo said they had two runaways last month, but they both returned home three weeks ago. They were siblings. Other than that, nothing stood out on their end."

"Anyone else? Clayton?" I pushed back my chair and walked to the watercooler. I filled my Styrofoam cup.

"Sorry, Jade. I've got three missing-dog reports in Alexandria, Minnesota, and a wife that voluntarily left her husband in Rochester."

"Who would even report that?"

"Apparently the husband did, but they found the wife staying with her sister in La Crosse."

I groaned. "Are we at least halfway done?"

Jack tore open the cellophane and popped a chocolate

chip cookie into his mouth. "Yep, I think we're close."

"Having lunch? And I was going to suggest we all take a break and go out for a burger somewhere."

Jack stood and folded the cellophane cookie bag in half. He set it on his desk, the opened side down. "I'm ready. Let's go."

I rapped on Clark's half-open door. "Boss, we're taking a lunch break. Want to join us?"

"Nah—the wife says I need to lose a few pounds, but thanks. I'll stick to my celery and carrot sticks." He rubbed his expanding stomach for emphasis.

"You sure?"

He rolled his eyes. "Don't tempt me—maybe next time."

I looked at the clock above the bull pen door. "Okay, we'll be back by one o'clock."

He nodded and went back to reading the report on his desk.

We all walked to one unmarked cruiser. I had the keys. The guys chuckled.

"What—is there a problem?"

"No, ma'am," Clayton kidded.

"I didn't think so. Now get in." I smirked at the guys.

"I have shotgun." Jack climbed in the passenger side and looked over his shoulder at Billings and Clayton. "Buckle up," he said when they got into the backseat. "She's nuts behind the wheel."

"Hush. That's only when there's an emergency. I don't abuse the lights and sirens, even though I've been tempted many times. So, where do you guys want to eat?"

"Let's go to Toucan Grill," Billings suggested.

"That sounds good to me." I pulled out of the parking space and gunned the cruiser through the lot.

Toucan Grill was a funky little ice cream-and-hamburger stand along Main Street. The service was fast, and the food was good. We sat at a picnic table facing the street and waited for our orders.

"You know, we may have to let this case go after a week or two. We have absolutely nothing to go on. Clark said the Milwaukee PD didn't have any leads with the two missing girls from Bradenton Beach either. I think we should establish a perimeter around the area where Reanne was found and start knocking on doors beginning on Monday. Somebody might have seen something that could be relative to the case and they don't even realize it," I said.

The waitress appeared with a large tray full of red plastic baskets, each lined with waxed paper and filled to the top with food. We all ordered the same—a double cheeseburger, fries, and a large soda. I gave Jack my pickle.

I took a gulp of soda to wash down my burger. My cell phone was vibrating in my pocket. I pulled it out and slid it across the table. "Jack, answer my phone. It's Clark." My mouth was still too full to talk.

"Hey, boss. Jade's mouth is full."

I kicked him under the table. He winced.

"Yes, right away. Uh-huh, we're almost done." Jack hit the red icon to hang up and passed the phone back to me. "Let's go. Milwaukee PD finally got a lead on Gina and

Carley. We're having a conference call in twenty minutes with a Lieutenant Gibson from the fourth district police department."

I threw Jack the car keys. "I'll get the bill. Pick me up at the curb."

We headed back to the sheriff's department, and I hoped this potential lead could help us apprehend Reanne's killer. The four of us entered the bull pen with ten minutes to spare. Clark rose from his desk when we arrived.

He looked at his watch. "We're gathering in the conference room in seven minutes. I've already started the coffee."

"Thanks, boss." I pulled a thermal carafe and a half dozen Styrofoam cups out of the cabinet above the coffee station. I jerked my head toward Jack. "Come here and give me a hand. Grab a tray and take these cups and the sugar and creamer to the conference room. I'll be in with the coffee as soon as it beeps. Should only be a minute or so."

"Okay. We won't start without you."

I walked down the hall to the third door on the left. I entered the room, the gold thermal coffee carafe in hand. Everyone was already seated and waiting. Our conference room was bright and airy with a bank of windows facing the south side of the building. The early-afternoon sun still glowed through the last few windows. An hour from now, it would disappear from our sight and shine on the west side of the building. Our conference room wasn't used often. The chairs were still comfortable and new looking, and the long walnut-veneered tabletop remained clean and unscratched. I placed the carafe next to the tray Jack had carried in and took my seat.

Clark made the introductions once we were live on the conference call. I went over the visit Jack and I had paid to Reanne Orth's family in Grand Forks, North Dakota. I explained to Lieutenant Gibson why I thought the cases were related.

"Sir, the way the perpetrator disables our victim's cars was too similar to be a coincidence. The girls were abducted from parks—swimming areas, to be exact. Both cars had the back passenger tire punctured. The method was identical. Anyone could have used a screwdriver or knife, but according to your forensic team, it appears that an ice pick was used. The mechanic that replaced Reanne Orth's tire said it had been punctured by something resembling a nail, yet no nail was found in the tire."

"You're right, Sergeant Monroe. It does seem too coincidental to be anyone other than the same person in both cases. A call came in earlier." He cleared his throat then continued. "The caller wasn't quite sure what she saw was a crime until she read the article in the paper this morning. Mrs. Stevens, the caller, lives in a high-rise condo directly across from Bradenton Beach. She said she witnessed an unusual situation a few days back."

I interrupted. "Excuse me, sir."

"Yes, go ahead, Sergeant Monroe."

"Did she say what floor she lives on?"

The sound of Lieutenant Gibson's chuckle came across the speaker. "I can see why you're a sergeant. As a matter of fact, I asked her that very question. I know how tall some of those buildings are. She said she lives on the sixth floor with a large balcony facing the park. Apparently she was sitting on her balcony that afternoon enjoying an iced tea."

"Thank you, sir. Sorry for the interruption." I jotted down what floor Mrs. Stevens lived on.

"No problem. Anyway, she said she saw two women and two men come up the path from the beach and walk to the trunk of a green car. According to her statement, they all went to the passenger side of the car, disappeared from sight for a few seconds, and then one of the men opened the back of a white van and put both women inside. The van sped off right after that."

"Did the witness get a make or model of the van, and did the women seem to be struggling?" Billings asked.

"The make and model of the van, no, and as far as the women struggling? I'm guessing that's why Mrs. Stevens didn't realize it was a crime. She said they didn't struggle or make a peep. She assumed they were drunk since one of the men was helping them to the van."

I poured a round of coffee for everyone then sat back down. Jack was busy taking notes.

"Damn it… that was likely the Xylazine," I said.

Lieutenant Gibson spoke up, "Xylazine? I don't think we were told about that."

"Sorry, Lieutenant," I said, "we only knew of it because of Reanne's autopsy. It came up on the tox report. Since you don't have bodies, you wouldn't know if Carley and Gina were injected with the drug or not. In addition to using the flat-tire ruse, these men are apparently injecting the women to suppress them."

The lieutenant groaned.

"This could get out of hand quickly. Once the ladies are in their control, we have no idea if they're being held captive or killed."

Lieutenant Clark said, "We need to hold a press conference and get this up on the news. It sounds like we're looking for two men with a white van that are kidnapping women from beaches, parks, and the like. They're using the flat-tire scenario to insert themselves into the situation as if they're going to help a lady—or in your case, ladies—in distress. That's when the women are hit with the needle. Lieutenant Gibson, did our eyewitness get a good enough look at the men to give us any type of description or age?"

"Sorry, not really, but she said they looked strong and fit. They both had on sunglasses, and they both had darker hair. She thought one had black hair and the other, brown. She couldn't give us anything on approximate age or specific features, though. She said a tree obstructed part of her view."

"Okay, that's a start," Clark said. "We'll check out white vans registered in Grand Forks and Washburn County. Meanwhile, we'll put a profile together and fax you a copy. You can contact the press and set something up. We need to get word out to the public and on TV. As soon as we hear back from you, we'll head to Milwaukee. Let's hold a joint press conference."

"Thank you, Lieutenant Clark—and your crew. I'll call

my contacts at the news stations and see how soon we can set something up. You'll hear back from me within the hour."

Clark clicked off the conference call and looked at each of us. "Okay, guys, at least now we know more than we did. Jade, give Todd and Billy a call. See if either of them can come in for a few hours. I need them to run the van info through the multistate database. Take a ten-minute break, fill up your coffee cups, and let's get a profile together for the press. We'll likely be heading to Milwaukee in a few hours."

"You got it, boss." I went back to my desk and called Todd first.

Chapter 22

"Hot damn! Gina's reserve hit, and the bids are still coming in," Jeremy said. "That calls for a beer."

"I'll get them. Keep refreshing the page. This is exciting stuff, man." Matt left the video room and closed the door behind him.

Jeremy heard Matt's heavy boots taking the staircase up to the first floor. Cage slept peacefully on the rug to the right of the computer desk. Jeremy reached down and gave him a scratch behind his left ear. Matt returned a few minutes later with two cold beers. He pulled up the stool on Jeremy's left and knuckled him in the shoulder.

"Man, we're going to be rich."

Jeremy grinned at his brother. "We've got nothing to complain about. After nearly two years, we're still holding our own. Sure, we stay under the radar and don't flaunt, but that's what's keeping us in business, bro, plus our bank account is growing sizably." He hit the refresh button again.

"How much time is left on Gina's auction?"

"Eight minutes. The last few minutes will likely be the

best. This bidding war will shoot her price up like crazy. She might go for more than ten grand."

"How's Carley's doing?"

Jeremy clicked to the other open tab and maximized the screen. "She's got an hour left. We're pretty close to the reserve on her too. This is what we need, bro—young, hot women. Luckily they don't have tats, either. As soon as both auctions are over and the money is transferred, we're heading to the mall. There are some nice young ladies out there just dying to meet us."

They both chuckled.

"I'll give them dinner after Gina's auction is over."

Jeremy nodded and clicked on the refresh icon again. "Okay, it's down to the last minute. Watch the bidding go crazy now."

They both leaned in closer to the screen. The mouse hovered over the refresh symbol, and Jeremy constantly clicked it.

"Thirty seconds. Look how it's going up, man. Fifteen, ten, five, three—done." He hit refresh a final time and saw the last bid. Jeremy whistled and high-fived his brother. "Damn, she went for twelve thousand bucks!"

They clanked their beer cans together and waited for a confirmation from the buyer.

Jeremy noticed he'd gotten an email alert on his account. He always used a pseudonym as his log-in name, as did everyone that had accounts on the darknet sites. He clicked over to his account and read the email. "Okay, here we go. The buyer is from San Francisco. The money is being wired as we speak." Jeremy sent off an email of his own asking when and where the buyer wanted to receive his merchandise. "We still have an hour before Carley's auction is up. Let's have dinner, get ready to go, and leave as soon as hers is over."

Matt went upstairs to prepare dinner for the three girls. Their meal would consist of bologna sandwiches and apples.

Jeremy turned the corner into the room of cages. His hand slapped at the dark wall until he felt the light switch. He flipped it on. A grin spread across his face as he pulled up a chair to Gina's cage and sat down. "Guess what, Gina? You're going bye-bye in a few days. Somebody from San Francisco just bought you, for a great price I might add. That should make you pretty damn proud. You're worth a bundle to some perv. I bet you've always wanted to see the city by the bay, right? Now you get a free trip to the west coast, except it's permanent."

Gina cried quietly in the corner of her enclosure while Jeremy leaned back in the cracked-vinyl office chair and smirked.

Matt descended the stairs, carrying a tray with the girls' dinner. He set it on the small table and ordered them back while he opened the cages.

"You'll get your bathroom breaks when Carley's auction is done. After that, it's lights out. We're going into town for a while. Liz, you'll meet your new roommates later. It's on you to teach them the rules."

Chapter 23

The profile was complete, and the lieutenant, Jack, and I had just arrived at the fourth district police department. Lieutenant Gibson had several TV news stations there, as well as the journalists from several large daily newspapers. They sat on chairs in the police department's pressroom, waiting for us to begin.

Lieutenant Gibson started by thanking the press for attending. He stood behind the podium, introduced each of us, then read the profile we had put together of the individuals in question. At that point, he had said, we were certain that an abduction and a murder had taken place. He asked for the public's help in keeping a watchful eye for any white van that might have two men in it.

Lieutenant Clark stood and took his turn at the podium. "Ladies and gentlemen, I want everyone to be aware that our two counties are working closely together to try to find these individuals. Anyone that sees a white van, especially in the area of swimming lakes, parks, hiking trails, bike paths, or dog parks, please take down the plate number and call it in to any police or sheriff's department. Do not approach a vehicle with that description. Of course, not every white van you see automatically belongs to the assailant, but it's our responsibility to check that out. Keep in mind, these men use the flat-tire ruse to apprehend females. Please do not let anyone approach you offering to help with a flat tire or any type of car trouble. Call somebody you know, or a local garage, for assistance. There are still two missing females that we fear have been kidnapped by these men." Clark held up photographs of Carley and Gina and gave their descriptions and told where they were last seen. "With the police and our sheriff's department's joint effort, along with the public's help, these criminals will be apprehended soon. Thank you."

Both lieutenants took fifteen minutes of questions from the press. The taped coverage would hit the evening news at six o'clock with a repeat of the broadcast at ten.

After a private sit-down with Lieutenant Gibson and his department where we exchanged our most current information, the lieutenant, Jack, and I headed back to North Bend.

"I think that went pretty well," Jack said. "With a description of the vehicle and the known locations where they strike, the public will be watching closely. The news broadcast will cover all of southeast Wisconsin. Hopefully those two are still in the area, and either we or Milwaukee County will get them soon. The noose is going to tighten around their necks pretty quickly with the public's help." Jack rested his left arm across the seat and looked back at me. "Don't forget, Gibson said he'd have his people call the places in Milwaukee County that paint cars. We should get someone on that too, tomorrow. Any white van that comes in for a paint job should trigger a call to law enforcement."

I checked the time as the lieutenant drove—six o'clock. Once we got back to the station, we'd watch the news broadcast that had been recorded.

We walked into the bull pen at six forty-five. Jamison and Horbeck were gathered around the small corner table with Todd and Billy.

"Hey, guys. We were ready to pack it up, but we wanted to touch base with you three before we left," Todd said.

The lieutenant walked over. "What have you got?"

Billy spoke up. "I checked out the number of white vans registered in North Dakota and Wisconsin. Without a make, model, or year, it's pretty overwhelming."

"What's the count?" Clark asked.

"Between the two states, it's thousands. We don't know if it's a panel van, a work van, a privately registered van, a cargo van, and so on. You get the picture. Sorting through the owners could take months."

Clark groaned. "Okay, whatever happened with the darknet human-trafficking scenario?"

"I took it upon myself to dig further, and I opened up a fraudulent account, just to get beyond the first level. Finding the bad, illegal stuff is tough, like going through a maze. The only places that popped up were in Malaysia and Thailand. I saw them for barely a second before they disappeared. If human trafficking sites were that easy to access, they'd be shut down and busted as soon as they started, at least in the United States. Other countries might not be as diligent in monitoring activities like that," Todd said.

Clark exhaled a deep sigh. "Okay."

I could see the frustration on the lieutenant's face. "Let's take a few minutes and check out the six o'clock news broadcast."

We walked down the hall to the lunchroom, where Jamison turned on the TV. We each grabbed a seat and waited for the taped news to start. I bought everyone a soda, then the broadcast began.

The press conference segment lasted less than five minutes. The only thing we had to tell the press was that two women were missing and two men with a white van were seen putting Carley and Gina inside. The back passenger side tire of Carley's car was flat. That very ruse was used in a previous abduction too. We didn't have a make, model, or plate number for the van. We didn't know what state the men or vehicle came from prior to abducting Reanne. At least we made the public aware, and hopefully they would keep a close watch on their surroundings. That bit of information was all we had.

"Anyone up for a beer?" I asked. I needed a distraction for an hour or so to wind down. If I went home, I'd be alone and thinking of the case, and at seven thirty, I was far too jacked up to doze off on the couch.

Everyone was either committed to family time or too worn out for loud music and a crowded bar. They declined my invitation, but I understood the family thing. They had all put in too much overtime lately, it was a Saturday night, and they should be spending it with their loved ones.

Jack walked out with me to our cars. "You going to Joey's?"

"Yeah, Amber works until closing. We haven't had a lot of sister time lately." I shrugged. "If it has to be at the bar, then so be it. Sure you don't want to tag along?"

"Will you be mad at me if I don't?"

"Nah—I'm good, and I have a really big gun." I patted my side and grinned. Twenty feet away, I hit the button on my key fob, the lights flashed, and my car doors unlocked. "Are you coming in tomorrow?"

Jack opened his car door. "Yeah, for a bit, I have plenty of busy work to do. Maybe you haven't noticed, but I can't see my desk anymore—too much paperwork to file."

"Oh, believe me, I've noticed." I climbed into my car. "If the news broadcast served its intended purpose, we may have leads to check out. See you tomorrow, partner."

Jack nodded.

I took off, ripping through the gears of my Cobra—my pride and joy. I checked the rearview mirror and saw Jack standing with his hands on his hips and shaking his head.

Chapter 24

"I can't believe how stupid we used to be," Matt said as he and Jeremy watched from the mall parking lot. The tall overhead lamps glared down on the cars every hundred feet. They chose a parking spot in a dark corner of the lot. Matt leaned back in the passenger seat, his legs crossed against the dash—unworried. A pair of binos rested in his lap. "Between Carley and Gina, we just made over twenty grand. We were lucky to get eight grand apiece before, and that was for the best, like Melanie." He laughed at the thought of her. "I wonder where she's at. She's probably entertaining her new owner in Morocco by now. I guess it does pay to be a little more selective, though, given the money we made today."

The radio played as background noise, but the brothers weren't listening. Their eyes darted left and right across the lot—looking for prey.

Jeremy nodded and pulled the binos up to his face. He followed a few women to their car then put the binos back down. "We aren't always going to be that lucky, brother.

Sometimes we have to take the good with the bad. In the dark like this, we aren't going to see their features that well, just like those two"—he jerked his chin at the car that was pulling away—"because they looked too old. Tonight, we're going by body language, the way they dress, and of course, if there's more than one. Once they get to their car and are busy loading their bags, we'll pull up on the sliding door side and grab them. It should only take a few seconds, and the cameras won't see anything. The van will be blocking the view."

"That's right, we have to exit on my side."

"You leap out first, and I'll slide the door open. We'll hit them with the stun guns and throw them in. You jump in behind them, and I'll drive us away. Punch them unconscious if you have to. The whole thing will take less than thirty seconds."

"Sounds good to me." Matt pulled his binos up and looked around.

"I only need to get us out of the parking lot's camera range," Jeremy said. "Then I'll pull over, and we'll give them the needle. That should keep them quiet until they're in their new homes."

Matt handed his brother a stick of gum. Jeremy slid the foil out of the wrapper and popped the gum into his mouth. Pinching the wrapper between his fingers, he rolled the foil into a tight ball and flicked it to the floor. They continued to watch the well-lit outdoor café directly in front of them on the opposite end of the lot. A mix of couples, families, and a few young single women filled the tables. The theme appeared to be no theme at all, with a little shabby chic thrown in. The tables looked to be different shapes and sizes, obviously repurposed, and the chairs were mismatched. Strings of lights suspended off the aqua-painted pergola lit the area well enough for Jeremy and Matt to see faces and features with their binoculars.

"Those three sitting together look promising," Matt said.

"We've never grabbed three at a time. That might be too ambitious. I wouldn't want any of them to get away."

"Yeah, you're right. Hey, check out the redhead and the dark-haired chick that were just seated."

Jeremy located the table, then he pulled the binoculars up to his eyes and focused on the two women that had just sat down.

"Yeah, they'll definitely work, and they have plenty of shopping bags too. Now, we just have to wait them out."

Jeremy checked the time—seven forty-five. He watched as the waitress approached the table where the two girls sat. She held the order pad but didn't write anything down. Jeremy moved upward with his binos. He saw her talk, smile, and put the pad back in her apron pocket.

"Hmm… maybe they aren't having dinner after all. That could speed up this process considerably."

After a few minutes, the waitress returned with two beers and set them down.

"Perfect," Matt said. "This should be an early night."

Twenty minutes, four songs, and three commercials later, as they sat patiently in the van, Jeremy and Matt saw the redhead flag the waitress down.

"I think they're wrapping things up." Jeremy reached behind the seat and grabbed the two stun guns. "Here, put one in your pocket. Do you have a syringe loaded?"

"Always, brother. You know what they say about never leaving home without one." He chuckled and noticed the waitress carrying the leather check folder to the table. The redhead put her credit card inside, and the waitress walked away with it.

"You about ready?" Jeremy asked. "They should be coming out in a few minutes."

Matt inhaled deeply and let it out slowly. "I'm more than ready. Let's do it."

They watched the two ladies exit through the wrought-iron gate. The walkway was flanked by decorative shrubbery, most likely to hide the fact that the café was right next to the parking lot. Matt cracked his window a few inches. The sounds of laughter and conversation became louder as the women crossed the sidewalk and stepped down to the asphalt.

The brothers waited and watched—ready to pounce.

"Looks like their car is parked a good distance out." Jeremy waited until he saw headlights flash twice. "That's where you're going? You couldn't have parked in a better spot." He turned the ignition key.

Boot heels sounded on the pavement—clip-clop, clip-clop. Laughter echoed from the left of the van. Jeremy watched the brunette click the key fob again and pop the trunk. He inched closer. "Get ready, bro."

Matt's hand gripped the cool, steel door handle. He'd spring out like an animal released from a cage. Jeremy turned wide with the headlights off. He pulled up along the back quarter panel of the car, blocking the cameras mounted on the building. The young women were clearly unaware of the imminent danger. While busying themselves at the trunk, they didn't look up until the van was on top of them—then it was too late. Both women were hit in the neck with stun guns.

They yelped and dropped to the ground. The women were too far away for anyone to hear them. Matt grabbed the redhead and tossed her into the van. Jeremy slammed the car's trunk with his elbow, making sure not to touch anything, and dragged the brunette to the side door. Matt pulled her in.

"Let's go." Jeremy slid the door closed and jumped into the van from the passenger side, stepped on the gas, and pulled out onto the street. "Hit them with the syringe before they start fighting you." Several sharp turns later, he ended up on a dead-end street and killed the engine. He jumped in the back and pinned the brunette down. Matt nailed her in the neck, then Jeremy grabbed the redhead. She flailed and kicked him. "Hang on a second until I get her to hold still." Jeremy squeezed her face between his hands and turned her head to expose her neck. "Just hit her anywhere. It doesn't matter."

Matt sank the needle into her neck just below her left ear. Her grasp on Jeremy's arms relaxed, and her hands dropped to the floor of the van.

"Man, that girl can fight. I guess it's true what they say about redheads having bad tempers. We'll have to keep our distance from her unless we want our eyes gouged out. She gets the cattle prod from now on."

Matt watched in his side mirror as Jeremy drove. "That went pretty smooth, don't you think?"

"Not too bad," Jeremy said as he rubbed his forehead, "except when Red kicked me with her damn boot. We'll check them out better tomorrow. We may have to take them outside in the daylight to get a good look, but we'll definitely have to dose the redhead first. So far I think we made a good choice." He glanced at Matt and laughed. "Ching-ching… I can hear our bank accounts filling up already."

The long driveway was just ahead, and Jeremy turned in. His headlights bounced off the barn behind the house as he hit ruts and potholes.

"Son of a bitch… what was that?" Jeremy backed up and turned slightly to the right. He hit the brights, illuminating a person running toward the field.

Matt craned his neck. "What the—"

Jeremy yelled, "It's Liz. How did she get out?"

"I don't know—what should we do?" Matt looked back at the floor of the van. The girls began to moan. They're going to be wide awake soon."

"Is there any Xylazine left in the syringe?"

Matt pulled the syringe out of his pocket and flipped on the overhead light. "A little."

"Nail them again. There isn't time to deal with them—we have to catch Liz first."

Chapter 25

Joey's was packed, and the music was loud—just the way I liked it. The cartridge made a familiar hiss when Amber cracked open the can and filled my glass with Scottish ale.

"I'm glad you stopped in, Sis. I wasn't expecting it." She looked around. "Where's Jack?"

"The baby wimped out. He probably had to put a fresh coat of polish on his nails." I looked up and grinned at my sister.

She laughed. "You're wicked mean, and you better watch out. If he ever heard you diss him like that, he'd kick your butt."

"Humph… I seriously doubt that. Want a shot?"

"Okay, but only one. What are we having?"

"Jägermeister." I took a gulp of my ale and waited for her expression.

"Really?" Her nose wrinkled, and she stuck out her tongue as if to gag.

"What, now you're wimping out too? Maybe you and Jack should be brother and sister. Fine, I'll drink both of them."

"I'll drink the crap. Just so you know, I'd rather have a shot of Baileys."

"You're such a girl, Amber. Don't forget, Tuesday night is practice at the range."

She grinned. "I love my gun, and I'll admit, I'm getting pretty good."

"Yes you are, but don't let it go to your head. There's always room for improvement. Are you going to pour those shots or what?"

She set two shot glasses on the bar and pulled the green bottle from the shelf behind her. She poured. I motioned for her to fill them up—no weak shots here.

"Salute," I said as I clinked my glass against hers, and we slugged them back.

"Ugh, that was *so* gross." She wiped her mouth with the back of her hand.

I smiled. "Wimp. How about a menu?"

"Sure thing." Amber turned and pulled a menu from the stack by the cash register. "We're running a special tonight—steak sandwich on a sourdough bun and German potato salad for under ten bucks. I'll even throw in a dill pickle spear."

"Keep the spear, but I'll take the special—medium rare."

"You got it."

My order was up within fifteen minutes. Amber carried the plate over and set it in front of me. She chomped on my dill pickle while she grabbed the utensils that were rolled in a paper napkin and set them on the bar.

"Anything else, Sis?"

"A glass of water would be good."

She nodded.

I looked at the crowded bar as I ate. Wall-to-wall people were enjoying the night without a care in the world. I wondered what it felt like, not taking your work home with you.

Amber set the glass of ice water in front of me. "Here's your water. What's up? You seem distracted."

I smiled. "Nah—I'm fine. Just another case weighing on my mind, that's all."

"The one on the six o'clock news?"

"Yeah, you saw it?" I wiped my mouth with the napkin.

"Sure. I recognized the lieutenant on TV, so I turned the volume up. I hope you guys catch those maniacs."

"If they're still in the area, we will—hopefully sooner rather than later. How about the check, Sis? I think I'll head home."

"I got you covered, Jade. Go home, relax, and give Spaz some snuggles."

I reached over the bar and kissed my sister's cheek. "Love you."

"Love you right back."

Chapter 26

Liz dodged and darted every which way, tripping over dirt clods as she ran wildly. The open field was a dangerous place to be—no cover and nowhere to hide. The van was closing in, and the headlights illuminated her. Every time he saw her, Jeremy floored the gas pedal. Their heads bounced off the headliner whenever he hit a rut or gully.

Matt turned and looked at the back of the van. The two moaning girls rolled back and forth, banging off the sidewalls as Jeremy gunned the vehicle through the field.

"Are you going to run her down or catch her?"

"I'm going to hit her. She's nothing but a liability anyway. Damn it, where did she go?"

"I don't see her." Matt frantically searched the horizon for somebody running. The darkened skies didn't help. He saw a flash of movement. "Over there!" He pointed toward the barn.

"Gotcha. I guess it's your lucky day, Liz. I'm not going to run you down after all." Jeremy cranked the wheel, gunned the van, and headed toward the barn. He slammed on the brakes, shifted into park, and jumped out. "Stay with these two and give them that dose," he yelled as he chased Liz toward the barn.

She squeezed through the barely open double doors and ran into the building, tripping over things as she tried to hide. Jeremy wasn't far behind her. He yanked the doors open wider and stopped, listening for a sound that would give away her location. He needed a moment for his eyes to adjust to the shadowy images of barn beams and equipment that faintly showed up from the flood light in the yard.

"Where are you, Liz? You know it's only going to take me a minute or so to find you, then you're going to be in a world of hurt."

He spun at the sound to his left and pulled back just before the board hit him in the head. She screamed and tried to run, but Jeremy leaped forward and caught her by the ankle. Liz fell face-first on the barn floor and grunted.

"You stupid bitch, you're lucky that board missed me."

Her screeching echoed through the night but only for a split second—dead silence followed.

Jeremy dragged her out of the barn by her leg and headed to the house. He motioned for Matt to follow with the van. Matt backed up to the cellar doors, their usual routine when they brought in new girls. The distance was much shorter, and it was a direct route down the stairs to the cages.

"Is she dead?" Matt asked as he jumped out of the van and opened the sliding side door.

"No, but she'll probably wish she was when she wakes

up. It looks like she's already getting a nice knot on her head. I clubbed her pretty good—she's out cold. I'd like to know how the hell she escaped." Jeremy turned her and took her by the wrists. He dragged her down the cement steps to the basement floor. He flicked on the lights. The other girls were awake and staring, wide eyed. "The first person that tells me how she escaped won't get zapped."

Carley spoke up immediately. "She wiggled the links near the bottom of her cage until some broke. She pressed them open with her feet until she could slip through. She said she's been working on those rusty wires for a month."

Matt smirked. "Good thing she didn't know where the keys were kept. We might have been chasing down all of you."

"You bitch. I can't believe you ratted her out in the blink of an eye," Gina said, staring at Carley. The disgust was written across her face.

Jeremy laughed. "Uh-oh, the besties are at each other's throats. I'll take care of that." He grabbed the cattle prod and nailed Gina in the side three times. She fell over and twitched. Carley looked away. "All right, let's get the new girls down here. First, grab one of those cages and take it around the corner. Liz can live in there, away from contact and communication with the rest. She'll be alone from now on. We'll get rid of the broken cage tomorrow." Jeremy pulled Liz across the room and jammed her into a cage in the darkest corner of the basement. "There, she can't even see the rest of you. She can sit there by herself and think about her actions. Let's go."

They went upstairs and returned a minute later. Each

carried a limp, unconscious young woman in his arms. The women's heads hung, bobbing with the movement, and their mouths gaped open. Jeremy and Matt shoved them into new cages, pulled off their boots, and threw them across the room. Matt clicked the padlocks and secured the gates. Carley and Gina cried when they saw the new girls.

"Don't worry. You won't have to witness this for long. Gina, you're out of here in two days, and Carley, you're gone as of Wednesday. Jeremy, did you even tell Carley where she's going?"

"Sure didn't. I totally forgot. Ready for it? It's pretty exciting." Jeremy taunted her. He despised her anyway since she'd spat at him. "Drum roll, please."

Matt banged his hands against the tabletop like bongo drums and laughed.

"You're going to India, Carley. I've heard there are tons of rats there, you know, kind of like you. It takes one to know one, right? I don't know how well you'll like it there, but you'll figure it out." Jeremy kicked the side of her cage and smirked. "Go to sleep. I don't want to hear a peep coming from this room."

"What happens when they wake up? It's going to be them screaming, not us," Carley said.

"You better be good at explaining the rules. If not, you all get the stun gun." With his forehead pinched tightly in a frown, Jeremy glared at her, then he turned and walked upstairs. Matt followed.

The lights went out, and the room fell into blackness, then the door slammed at the top of the stairs.

Chapter 27

I ran for my phone with nothing more than a towel wrapped around my wet body. I seemed to forget to take my cell into the bathroom when I showered, and that's usually when it rang. I looked at the screen—the lieutenant was calling.

"Hey, boss. What's up?"

"Jade, tell me you're dressed and walking out the door."

"I could, but I'd be lying." I pulled the towel tighter against my cold, goose bump–covered skin.

"I think we have another abduction. Get here as soon as you can. Don't stop for coffee and doughnuts either. The coffee is brewing, and I already picked up the doughnuts. Jack, Billings, and Clayton are on their way. I'm calling Todd and Billy too."

"Roger that, boss. I'll be there in twenty." I clicked the red symbol to end the call and threw on a pair of jeans and a long-sleeved T-shirt. As soon as I got a comb through my wet hair, I pulled it back, gave it a few twists around my hand, and secured it with a clip.

"Amber, honey, I have to go. I'll call you as soon as I can. I fed Spaz and Polly and Porky."

My sister groaned, rolled over to her other side, and snuggled back under the blankets.

"Can I have an acknowledgment?"

"Yeah, I heard you."

"Bye, hon."

She waved with a limp hand peeking out of the blankets.

With a swat at the darkened garage wall, I hit the button and opened the overhead door. I climbed into my car and took a second to regroup. *Got my keys, got my purse, got my phone, and got my gun. Good to go.* I backed down the driveway and pressed the button on the passenger side visor to close the garage door. I turned left out of the Ashbury Woods condo neighborhood and gunned my Mustang down the street. Getting to the sheriff's department would take me seven minutes.

I turned onto Schmidt Road, pulled into the parking lot, and saw Jack walking toward the entrance. Billings's and Clayton's cars were already parked. Jack turned around just before he reached the doors and waited for me.

"Morning, partner. It looks like we're going to be busy. Guess my desk isn't going to see the light of day after all."

"Do you know any more than I do?" I asked as I rushed up the steps to meet him.

Jack grinned. "You know that didn't make any sense, don't you?"

I swatted his arm. "Come on. Let's see what the lieutenant has to say."

We went inside and walked around the reception desk, said hello to Peggy at dispatch, and entered the bull pen through the security door.

The lieutenant, Clayton, and Billing sat in Clark's office, waiting for us.

"Jade, Jack. Maybe we should use the conference room. This office isn't quite big enough for all of us. Todd and Billy should be here any minute too."

We all got up and headed down the hall. Clayton grabbed the coffee pot and a handful of Styrofoam cups when he passed the coffee station.

We went inside the conference room and sat. Todd and Billy had just arrived and followed us down the hall.

"Billy, close the door, please. Okay, guys, here's what we know. Two young ladies went missing last night at Westchase Mall. The car is still sitting in the lot. Silver and Ebert have the area cordoned off, and Dan and Kyle are on the scene, going over the vehicle."

"Was the back passenger side tire punctured?" I asked.

"No, it wasn't. Kyle spoke with the mall security department, and they're going to pull up the camera footage from last night. Hopefully that's going to show us what we need. Todd, I want you and Billy to get out there right now and go over that footage. Get back here with a copy as soon as you can. The head of security is there now. He said he'd have the footage from yesterday available for you guys to view and he'd have that copy ready for you too. Go ahead. Get on it."

"You got it, sir," Todd said. "Is there someone we should ask for by name?"

Clark checked his notes. "Yeah, the guy's name is Bob Shilling."

Todd and Billy got up and left the room.

"Okay, what do we know so far, boss?" I poured five coffees, kept one, and slid a cup across the table to Clark, Jack, Clayton, and Billings.

"The girls are Megan Falk, twenty-two, and Jenna Davis, also twenty-two. They were shopping at the mall, and according to Megan's mom, they left her house at five o'clock. The café facing the parking lot has a receipt for two beers paid by Megan's credit card at eight fifteen. The security guard noticed the empty car sitting in a spot near the end of the parking lot at ten thirty. The mall closes at ten. According to Silver, the security guard didn't call anything in as suspicious."

"I imagine people leave their cars overnight in mall lots all the time, right?" Jack asked.

Clark rubbed his eyebrows. "Yeah, it didn't raise a red flag with security. Cars get ticketed after twenty-four hours of not being moved, though. The parents are the ones that called it in. Peggy patched them through to me. Apparently, neither of the girls slept in their beds last night, nor did they answer their cell phones. I sent Silver and Ebert out to the mall, and that's where they found Jenna's car. They talked to security and found out the car had been sitting there since last night. They thought it seemed suspicious at a closer glance. The car wasn't locked. I told Silver I was sending forensics out there to check it over. We should be hearing from Kyle soon with an update."

I wondered if we really had a crime on our hands. The MO wasn't the same as the others. The girls weren't abducted at a park of any kind. They went missing at night rather than the daytime, and all of the tires were fine.

"Boss, maybe the girls met up with friends and caught a late-night party at someone's house. They could be just sleeping it off."

"Maybe." Clark's phone rang, and he pulled it out of his pocket. He looked at us. "It's forensics. Hello, Kyle, I'm putting you on speakerphone. What can you tell us?"

"Morning, everyone. We went through the car, and nothing looked disturbed inside. Popping the trunk told us an entirely different story, though."

"We're listening, go ahead." Clark sat back down with a heave.

"The trunk is filled with shopping bags, two purses, keys, and two cell phones. It definitely looks like an abduction, sir."

"Damn it. Okay, Todd and Billy are en route. They should be there any minute. Get the car back here to the evidence garage and go over it with a fine-toothed comb."

"Got it, Lieutenant. I'll call the flatbed right now."

"All right. There's nothing we can pursue until we see that video footage. Jade and Jack, get over to Megan's house. Clayton and Billings, you take Jenna's. Find out everything about these young ladies. Learn who were their friends, foes, and anything in between. You need the family's statements and everything they can remember from yesterday. Here are both of their home phone numbers and addresses." Clark tore in half the sheet of paper he had scratched the addresses on. "Get back here as soon as you're finished interviewing the parents. By then, we should have the video footage from the mall."

We pushed back our chairs and filed out of the conference room. Outside, Jack and I took one unmarked cruiser, and Clayton and Billings took another.

"Okay, where are we going?" Jack asked as he turned the key over, slid the shifter into drive, and pulled out of the parking lot.

"Looks like Megan's family lives just this side of Allentown right off Highway 33. Take Washington Street out of town for four miles. That should put us pretty close. I'll give the parents a call to let them know we're coming."

The drive took us fifteen minutes. Allentown was a small unincorporated village due west of North Bend. The mall, on the far west side of North Bend, was only a ten-minute drive from Megan's house.

"Turn here," I said, pointing to my right. "Their house should be the fifth one on the left." I saw the last name on the mailbox next to the driveway. "This is the place."

Jack pulled into the driveway of a cookie-cutter ranch-style house. The subdivision didn't look to be much more than five years old. Although the homes were small and similar, they were all nicely kept up, and the lawns were freshly mowed. The Falks' house was covered with tan vinyl siding and accented with dark green shutters, and the two-car garage took up most of the front facade. Flower beds of daisies and dwarf mugo pines lined the sidewalk, and a fully flowered Russian sage surrounded the lamppost in the yard.

We got out and approached the house. With the drapes spread apart at the front window, Mr. Falk appeared to notice us coming and was at the door before we even knocked. He pulled open the main door and pushed the screen door outward.

I introduced myself and showed him my badge, and Jack did the same.

"Please, come in," he said and stepped to the side so we could enter.

His wife leaned against the wall at the entry to the kitchen with her arms tightly crossed. They both looked worried. She came toward us and extended her hand.

"I'm Mary, and my husband is Roger. Please, have a seat." She pointed at the living room couch. "This is absolutely unlike Megan, you know. She wouldn't be gone overnight without calling. Of course, she's an adult, but she does live under our roof. She respects the rules, Sergeant." Mary sat next to Roger on the loveseat across from us.

"I understand. You told our lieutenant that the girls left here yesterday around five o'clock and they took Jenna's car?"

"Yes, that's correct." Mary took Roger's hand and squeezed it.

Jack spoke up, "Would it be common for either girl to leave their phones or purses in the trunk and to leave the car unlocked?"

Mary began to cry. Roger responded to the question. "Detectives, these are twenty-two-year- old girls. They don't even sleep without their cell phones right next to them. Jenna just bought that car last month. She'd never leave it unlocked. She was very proud of her car and kept it clean and locked at all times, especially someplace like a mall parking lot. Megan always complained about how picky Jenna was with it. She'd park quite a distance from other cars just so she wouldn't get any door dingers."

I stole a glance at Jack. "So it would be unlike either girl to leave her phone or purse behind."

"Absolutely." Mary wiped her eyes with the back of her hand.

"Ma'am, do both girls work?" Jack asked.

Mary nodded. "Jenna has a decent job. She's a medical assistant at a doctor's office. Megan is still in school. She has the summer off, of course. This fall will be her last year, unless she continues on to get a graduate degree. She wants to be a biology professor."

"She sounds ambitious, and they're both responsible? Twenty-two is still young," I said.

Roger looked at both of us. "Megan is very responsible. Jenna has been her best friend since kindergarten, and we aren't her parents, but she seems very responsible too. They're both good girls, detectives."

"Is there anyone who was angry with Megan? Somebody she's mentioned that had a bone to pick with her?"

"Nobody we can think of," Roger said.

"Can we just get a quick list of names? Friends, schoolmates, that type of thing?"

Mary got up and walked into the kitchen. She returned

with a pad of paper and a pen. She and Roger took the next ten minutes writing down every name they could come up with. "This is all we can think of at the moment." Roger tore the sheet off the pad and handed it to me.

"Thank you. You've both been very helpful." I handed them our cards. "Please call if you think of anything more."

We shook their hands and told them we'd be in touch. Mary walked us to the front door, and we left. I called the lieutenant as Jack drove. Clark told me Kyle and Dan were back and going over the car in the evidence garage. He also said Todd and Billy had a copy of the parking lot footage, and they said it wasn't good.

I hung up from the call. "Crap."

"What?"

"Clark said he was told the video footage wasn't good. I didn't take that to mean it was fuzzy footage. I think it's going to tell us exactly what we were dreading all along."

Chapter 28

"Are you ready to go downstairs and check out our new guests?" Jeremy asked when Matt walked into the kitchen.

Matt rubbed his eyes and dragged his fingers through his hair. "Man, I was out for the count. What time is it?"

"Ten thirty. You need to start getting up earlier, dude. I've been sitting here waiting for you since eight o'clock. Didn't you hear those two wailing all night long? I went down there twice and zapped everyone."

"Seriously? I didn't hear shit." Matt poured himself a glass of milk and grabbed a piece of raisin bread. He sat down at the table. "Did you check them out at all?"

"Yeah, earlier. I took breakfast bars down for all of them at nine. They look good, but the lighting is pretty dim down there. We'll give them a quarter dose of Xylazine so we can get them outside and take our time checking them over. I don't trust that redhead."

Matt chuckled. "Yeah, she nailed you good with her boot heel. What did you do with them?"

"I threw both of their boots into the burning barrel.

Those things are dangerous. Finish your milk. We have work to do. I've got to decide what to do with Liz too. I think she should go at a clearance price. It would be a quick way to get rid of her."

Jeremy opened the basement door and headed down. Matt guzzled his milk and jammed the bread into his mouth. He followed behind Jeremy and went directly to the cabinet around the corner and pulled out a new vial and a syringe. He poked the needle through the rubber stopper and drew up a quarter dose of Xylazine. Each girl would get half of that. It would be enough to knock them out for close to an hour.

The screaming echoed off the damp basement walls. Jeremy stuffed two spongy earplugs into his ears. "Damn noise. We'll take care of that in a second. Ready?"

Matt nodded.

They rounded the corner. Jeremy had the cattle prod in his hand. Gina and Carley sat in their cages, their heads facing down and not making a peep. Liz screeched from around the corner.

"I'll be right back." Jeremy set the prod down and got a flashlight out of the cabinet. He walked around the corner, shined the flashlight in Liz's face, and knelt down in front of her cage. "You have quite a lump on your head, Liz. I'll make you a deal. You shut up right now or I take you outside and crack you across the face with a shovel. That will really give you a lump. In fact, you'll likely be dead. I can have you in the ground next to Beth in less than an hour. So, what's it going to be?"

The screeching stopped.

"That's what I thought." He got up and walked back into the main room. "Now"—he cocked his head to the side and smiled—"we have to deal with you two." He picked up the prod and headed for Megan's cage. "You're going first, Red."

She screamed and shook the cage violently. Jeremy stuck the prod through the links and gave her an extra hard zap. Her body arched and stiffened. She fell back, momentarily unconscious.

"Hurry up and give her the needle."

Matt reached through the wires and grabbed a handful of hair. He pulled her closer, then he stuck the needle in her neck and released half of the drug. "She's good."

Jeremy turned and headed for Jenna's cage. "What's your name, sweetheart?"

"Jenna," she said quietly between muffled sobs.

"Well, Jenna, it's nice to meet you." He stuck the prod through her cage and hit her with it. She grunted until she passed out. "Give her the drug."

Matt repeated the same process he had used with Megan. He pulled the ring of keys out of his pocket and opened their cages. Jeremy had already opened the cellar doors.

"Enjoy a little daylight and fresh air, ladies. It's beginning to stink down here."

Jeremy yanked Megan out by her leg and tossed her over his shoulder. Matt did the same with Jenna. They dropped both girls on the lawn behind the house. That corner was hidden from view even though they'd hear if a car came down the driveway anyway. They stood above the women and looked down at them.

"What do you think?" Matt asked. He rolled Jenna over and looked at her arms and legs. "Don't see any tats. That's a good sign."

Jeremy did the same with Megan. "Here's one, but it's a small four-leaf clover on her ankle. Nothing too serious." Jeremy laughed. "Aren't four-leaf clovers supposed to be for luck? You know, the luck of the Irish? Hmm… the red hair, she must really be Irish. Sorry, hon, today isn't going to be your lucky day."

They looked closely at both of their faces, their teeth, and their figures. "I'd say we did pretty well considering it was dark outside," Matt said.

"Yeah, maybe that's the best way to go. Blitz attack in the dark… I like it. They should go for a high price too. We'll be out of here in a month, for sure. Vegas, here we come." Jeremy picked up the limp, rag-doll redhead and slung her over his shoulder again. "Okay, let's get them back in their pens before they wake up."

Chapter 29

We met up with Todd and Billy downstairs in the tech department where they had the video footage ready to go. They sat in roller chairs next to the computer. The lieutenant, Billings, and Clayton were there too. I asked Billings how the interview with Jenna's folks went. He shrugged and suggested we compare notes upstairs later.

"Is everyone ready?" Todd asked. "First I want to say we looked over the mall security footage throughout the common areas. Nobody followed the girls as they shopped. Here's what we have, though, from the café camera facing the parking lot."

We crowded around the computer monitor.

"We were able to narrow things down pretty quickly since the café had the time stamp on the receipt from Megan. Here we go."

Todd pointed out that even though the images were dark, the two women were indeed Megan and Jenna. The footage showed them from the back as they left the café and crossed the sidewalk. The clarity faded in and out with the parking lot lighting as they walked to the car with shopping bags in their hands.

"Everything looks normal so far. Nobody is following them," the lieutenant said.

Todd nodded. "Keep watching."

The ladies were almost across the parking lot, and the car lights blinked.

"That's where Jenna hit her key fob to unlock the car. Watch what happens as they get closer and pop the trunk."

My eye caught the image of a vehicle moving slowly into the frame on the right side of the computer screen. It came from a darkened area of the parking lot. Jenna and Megan had just reached her car and were going to the trunk.

"Shit! It's a white van." I leaned in close to the screen, as did everyone else.

What we were witnessing happened a good distance from the cameras. The fuzzy, blurred footage made it impossible to see the make, model and license plate number of the van. It never came close enough or faced any camera directly so we could zoom in on the plates.

"Watch this. These guys are smart, and they know the exact location of the cameras. The van hides everything that's going on. Nobody exits from the camera side of the van, so we don't know how many people are involved. We timed the footage. From the point where the van stops to where it leaves again covers roughly forty seconds," Todd said.

"You can't see anything happening. The girls put their bags in the trunk, the van shows up then leaves less than a minute later, and when the car comes back into camera view, nobody is there," I said.

Billy agreed. "That pretty much covers it. The only thing we're almost certain of is that this abduction and the Carley and Gina abduction was done by the same crew."

"I wish there would have been cameras at the beach. We could have compared vans. This is obviously a panel van—no side windows. Did Mrs. Stevens mention that—no side windows?" I asked.

Clark spoke up. "I don't know for sure, but I'll call Gibson and find out. Okay, we know these guys are still somewhere in the area. I'd venture to say they're closer to us than Milwaukee. Reanne was found in Washburn County, and now Megan and Jenna came up missing, and they both live just west of North Bend." Clark stood and paced while he rubbed his forehead. "We're going to have to do a county-wide search. Let's get that video footage to the news stations and see if anything pops. There could have been someone at the mall last night that noticed the van in the parking lot. Billings and Clayton, you take care of getting the footage on TV."

Clayton pushed back his chair and stood. "Got it, boss."

"Jade, I want you and Jack at the mall. Find out who was at that café last night. Talk to the hostess, waitress, and customers—interview everybody, even if you have to bang on their doors. Interview the security guard again that drove around the parking lot last night. See what he remembers before the mall closed."

"We're on it, Lieutenant." I jerked my head toward the

door to get Jack's attention.

We went back upstairs to get our necessities. With one swipe and a pull of the desk drawer, I had my cell phone off my desk and my purse out of the drawer. I dropped my cell in the front pocket of my blazer as I slipped it on over my shoulder holster. Jack secured his gun too, grabbed his phone, and we left.

"I'm driving," I said as I took a set of keys from behind the reception desk.

We walked outside, and I pressed the unlock symbol on the key fob. The lights flashed on the second black cruiser in the lot. We got in, and I pulled out of the parking lot. I drove only two miles before I pulled into the Pit-Stop gas station.

"Damn it. Why did I grab the keys for an almost empty cruiser, and why wasn't this car already filled up?"

Jack chuckled and got out of the car. "I'll grab a couple of sodas."

He disappeared inside while I stood at the back of the car, squeezing the gas nozzle and watching the dollars add up. I was glad we weren't heading to an emergency—the car was bone dry.

Jack returned as I waited for the gas pump to spit out my credit card receipt. He climbed in the passenger side, and I got in behind the wheel. He handed me a gooey, nut-filled chocolate bar and a soda.

I grinned. "Thanks, partner." I peeled back the wrapper of the decadent sugary treat and took a bite. "Man, I love these things."

Fifteen minutes later, we were parked at the mall, just outside the café. The timing was good. The café had opened an hour earlier, and the staff had settled into their daily routine. Jack and I approached the hostess standing at the podium. She had already reached for two menus and gave us a welcoming smile. I looked behind me to make sure nobody was standing in line to be seated. I didn't want to hold anyone up, and I didn't want anyone to hear our conversation.

"Table for two?"

I leaned in and flashed my badge. "We'd like to speak to the manager, please."

Her eyes widened. "Oh… certainly, right this way." She motioned for somebody to come and take her place for a few minutes.

The hostess led us down a short hallway opposite the kitchen. A closed door with a plaque that had PRIVATE written across it was directly in front of us. She knocked on it twice. The person on the other side said to come in.

She peeked around the door. "Mr. Hughes, there are two detectives here to see you."

"Detectives? Send them in, Natalie."

He stood when Natalie opened the door wider for us to pass through. I nodded and thanked her. Mr. Hughes looked to be in his late thirties, a handsome man with short blond hair and a neatly trimmed mustache. He had curious but friendly eyes. He was dressed casually, wearing a pair of shorts and a cranberry-colored T-shirt. Behind that closed door and away from the crowd, he looked to be knee-deep in schedules and payroll paperwork. I doubt if he was expecting visitors on a Sunday at noon. He extended his hand to shake ours.

"Detectives, how may I help you?"

I introduced myself and Jack, then I gave Mr. Hughes a condensed version of why we were there.

"Sir, we're going to need to speak with the hostess and waitress that were on duty last night between six and nine p.m. We also need to know any patrons' names that paid with credit cards and the names of anyone that made reservations last night. We'll have to interview them as well."

"Is this about the incident with the car being in the lot overnight? Why is that such a big deal?"

"Sir," I said, "it's a police matter and early in the investigation. We aren't at liberty to discuss much yet, but I can tell you the video footage from the parking lot last night is going to be on the news. All I can say for now is that the girl that car belongs to, and her friend, are missing. So, can we get those names?"

"Of course." Mr. Hughes reached into the stack of receipts from last night and started separating the credit card receipts from the others. "It's only going to help you if their names are on the receipts, right?"

"That's correct, sir. The reservations list will help as well. May I see that while you're working on the credit card names?"

"Certainly." He turned and opened the file cabinet at his back and pulled out a folder containing the current month's reservation list.

"Here's July's list. It goes by week, date, and time. Last night's reservation list is on the top."

"Thank you. If you don't mind, we'll sit on the patio for now and go over the names."

"That's fine. I'll be out as soon as I organize all of the credit card payments with names on them."

Jack nodded as he held the door open for me, and we exited Mr. Hughes's office. Natalie seated us in a shady spot on the patio with a good view of the parking lot. Jack and I stared out, trying to replay in our minds what might have taken place last night.

"The girls exited right there at the gate and crossed the sidewalk. They walked three quarters of the way across the parking lot without incident while they were watched and targeted as prey. As soon as they opened the trunk, the van pulled up, and within seconds they were overcome and thrown in the van." I looked at Jack and rubbed my temples. "They must have been disabled somehow to make the abduction go so quickly." I pondered the event, wondering how it all went down.

Jack spoke up, "Two men can easily overtake two unsuspecting females that are preoccupied with loading bags in their trunk. They didn't need Xylazine at that point. All they had to do was get them in the van then find some secluded spot to disable them."

"Yeah, you're right." I shook my head and thought about how fearful the girls must have been. "Let's see which names on this list actually include phone numbers."

We searched through the list and found thirty names

that had reservations during our three-hour window. Seventeen of those names included phone numbers. I wrote down each name, number, and reservation time. Calling them seemed far more efficient than driving to each house for a face-to-face interview. We'd pay a sit-down visit to anyone that sounded as though they might have seen something suspicious or questionable.

Mr. Hughes met up with us at our table. He gave us the credit card receipts that had names on them. We compared them to our reservations list and ended up with an additional three names. Later we'd deal with those names and the ones without phone numbers on the reservation list.

"Mr. Hughes, we need to speak with the hostess and waitress from last night. Would you mind calling them? We can have a sit-down interview with them as long as we're here anyway."

He nodded. "I'll get right on that. I'll have the waitress bring you a carafe of coffee or a few soft drinks. Which would you prefer?"

Even though we were in the shade, the day was warming up.

"A glass of iced tea would be great," I said.

Jack decided on the same.

"How about something to eat? It's on the house."

I looked at Jack and shrugged.

"An appetizer would be nice," Jack said. "We'll split one. Any type of finger food is fine."

Mr. Hughes said he'd have the waitress put an order in, then he excused himself to make the calls.

I split the list in half, and we began calling. Our approach would be the same with everyone. We'd introduce ourselves, have them acknowledge that they ate at the café last night, and ask if they noticed anybody or anything that seemed suspicious during their dinner or afterward. We'd also include the parking lot and ask if anyone had noticed a parked white van. We whittled away at the list of names with nothing helpful yet. Mr. Hughes returned forty-five minutes later with the waitress and the hostess from last night. He introduced us to both ladies.

"Sergeant Monroe and Detective Steele, this is Jillian, the hostess, and Tina, the waitress. Ladies, please help the detectives with as much as you can remember. If you need anything else, please don't hesitate to contact me."

We thanked Mr. Hughes, and he left. I studied both girls; their demeanor was casual, friendly, and open. Jillian looked to be in her late twenties, tall, slender, and pretty. Her blond hair was in a tight ponytail that fell just past her shoulders. Her makeup was impeccable, and she had flawless golden skin, likely from being a sun worshipper. Tina was cute and short, probably not much taller than five foot two. She appeared to be in her early twenties, at best. Her style was a little edgy, but she was sweet nonetheless. Her hair was spiky and short, and she wore a diamond stud piercing in her right nostril.

Jack motioned for them to take a seat, and the waitress on duty brought each of them a glass of water. We asked the ladies to tell us everything they could remember about Megan and Jenna, even if it seemed insignificant. They both admitted they didn't have very much contact with them since they ordered only one beer each and nothing more.

"I'm pretty sure they were only here for about a half hour. I do remember they had a lot of shopping bags, so I seated them against the wall," Jillian said. "Most of the tables were full, and I didn't want anyone tripping over their bags."

I wrote that down, even though the quantity of bags was already documented from the trunk contents.

"Which table were they sitting at?" Jack asked.

Jillian pointed at two tables away from where we were seated.

"Do you remember their demeanors?" I took a sip of my iced tea as I waited for a response.

Tina spoke up, "They seemed happy-go-lucky. They were joking around about maxing out their credit cards with shopping and how they could only afford a beer. Of course, they were kidding. I guess they weren't hungry, or maybe they ate inside at the food court."

I wrote that down too. "So they left around eight twenty, is that correct?"

Jillian nodded. "Yeah, that sounds about right. We had an eight thirty reservation that sat at the table they had just left."

"Do you remember them actually leaving?" Jack asked.

"Not really," Tina said. "The redhead handed me the check folder, said they were all set, and I took it. I thanked them and took the folder inside. The busboy came out and cleaned up the table since we had that new group coming in ten minutes later."

I tapped the ice cubes in my glass with my straw. "So you don't recall seeing them walk out to the parking lot?" I looked at both ladies. "Either of you?"

They both said no.

We handed them our cards, thanked them for their time, and watched them walk away.

"Want another iced tea?" Jack asked.

"Yeah, I guess. We still have another hour of calls to make."

Between the unanswered calls and the people who ate at the café but parked in a different lot, we came up empty. We had six people left to call on our combined lists. I told Jack I'd be right back and got up to use the ladies' room. He waved me off and dialed another number.

"Jade, I think we have something," Jack said when he saw me heading back to the table. "Grab your purse. We're leaving. Let's make a quick stop inside and thank Mr. Hughes."

"What happened? What did they say?" My adrenaline kicked in—I was ready to go.

"A woman remembers seeing a white van last night. She just lives a few minutes from here."

"Thank God." I gave Jack a hopeful sideways glance.

"Don't plan a party yet. There's probably more than one white van in the area."

I scowled at him. "Did you really say that?"

"Sorry, I'm just amped up."

Natalie led us down the hallway one more time and knocked on Mr. Hughes's office door. We peeked in to thank him for his help and to say goodbye. Jack handed him our cards, and we left.

"Pull up this address on your GPS," Jack said as we climbed into the cruiser. He got in behind the wheel and took off out of the parking lot.

Chapter 30

The metallic clinking and rattling sounds woke Liz. In the darkened corner of the room, Jeremy fumbled with her gate. With the flashlight wedged under his arm, he pointed it at the padlock and stuck the key in, giving it a jiggle and a turn.

"Get out here and don't do anything stupid," he said as he pulled the gate open. On her scuffed knees, Liz crawled out and stood. Jeremy pushed her toward the bathroom. He handed her a clean outfit and told her she had fifteen minutes to shower and freshen up.

"There's makeup in the basket on the back of the toilet. Make sure you put plenty on that bruise on your forehead."

Liz nodded and went inside. Jeremy latched the bathroom door behind her and snapped the padlock closed.

He walked away and gave each caged woman a threatening glance for good measure as he passed by. They were beginning to learn how to keep quiet. Jeremy entered the video room and woke up his computer. He expected several emails to arrive in his inbox. Gina was scheduled to be delivered to her buyer's representative tomorrow, and Carley was leaving her fine abode on Wednesday. Jeremy sat down and scooted in close to the monitor. With his hand on the mouse, he thumbed the roller wheel and checked each email as he went down the list.

"There we go," he said and leaned in to read the first one.

The buyer's rep for Gina was flying into Milwaukee tomorrow evening and would arrive at seven p.m. on a private jet. At seven thirty, Jeremy needed to be at Holler Park Lodge, where the transfer would take place. Jeremy clicked the computer keys and sent off an acknowledgment response and a thank-you. "Easy as pie," he said and moved on to the email about Carley. Her buyer's rep was flying into Milwaukee too, by way of JFK. Since Carley's buyer was in India, they'd have to make several stops along the way for fuel. He also had a private jet. The buyer said to watch for another email on Tuesday with further instructions. Other than driving, a private plane was the only way to transport these women individually.

Jeremy heard Matt coming down the stairs. Matt peeked around the doorway.

"Is it time for Liz?" He had a bottle of water in his hand.

Jeremy checked the bottom right side of the computer screen. "Yeah, she's been in the bathroom long enough. Get her out. Is that water laced?"

"Definitely. I don't trust her after that stunt last night." Matt turned and walked away. He was back with Liz a few minutes later. Jeremy had the video and camera equipment set up and ready to go. He gave Liz a long look.

"Turn around slowly so I can check you out."

She did as she was told.

"Yeah, you look okay. Drink that water, then we'll get started." Jeremy had the auction site up on the computer, but the screen was minimized for now. He would log in after they had completed all of the still shots and videos. Liz had fifteen minutes to stand, swirl, and move around before she'd be half looped. Keeping her somewhat sedated was a wise move. Her photos and video, along with her vital statistics, would be uploaded to the site in twenty minutes.

"Ready to go?" Jeremy asked.

"Yep. Liz, get in that photo booth and start smiling, pouting, and looking hot. You better work it for all it's worth."

Matt began taking pictures of Liz. The auction site allowed five still shots and a minute-long video. They'd set the reserve, click a button after they gave her information and photos one final review, then the bidding would start. Liz's auction would last for five hours, like the rest, but her reserve was set lower. She had been on the auction site several times already without hitting that magic number. This time would be the last—she needed to go.

With Liz, Carley, and Gina gone, they'd have only the new girls left. After they were sold, they'd pack up and head southwest. The joint bank account had hit forty thousand, and it was still climbing. Jeremy never wanted to stay in one place too long anyway. They were perfecting their craft and learning the best abduction methods. Jeremy kept detailed notes, and the blitz attack at the mall was one of the methods high on his list.

"What are you going to set her reserve at?" Matt asked after he returned the stumbling Liz to her cage. He sat down next to Jeremy at the computer as the pictures were being uploaded to the site.

"I'm thinking six thousand." He needed to get rid of Liz and focus on getting as much as he could for the new girls. "Did Jenna ever say what the other girl's name was?"

"Yeah, not to me, but I heard them talking to each other. Apparently her name is Megan."

Jeremy's white teeth gleamed through his grin. "So she truly is an Irish hothead. I'll make sure to include that in her listing. Some guys like the fiery, combative type."

Chapter 31

"The address is right around the next corner on Fairview Street. It should be the third house on the right," I said as I led the way using the GPS. "What is the person's name we're meeting with?"

"I forgot." Jack leaned forward and pulled the notepad out of his back right pocket. "Here, see what I wrote."

I paged through his notepad to the last entry. "Here we go. We're meeting a Diane Evans?"

"Yeah, that's right. This looks like the place." Jack slowed, and I double-checked the address.

"Yeah, this is it. Pull in."

Jack parked, and we exited the cruiser. The neighborhood was nice. The outskirts of town had several newer master-planned communities with clubhouses, pools, tennis courts, and activity directors. This neighborhood fit right in with that description. Most houses were single-story stand-alone or side-by-side condos, and none looked to be more than a few years old.

"I like this area," I said as we walked up the sidewalk.

Jack rang the bell. We heard a small dog barking on the other side of the door.

I laughed. "Hey, at least this one sounds a little less terrifying than the ones in Terrance King's neighborhood."

"You never know," Jack said. "I've always thought it was the ankle biters that were more vicious."

We heard a female voice telling the dog to hush and to go lie down. The door opened slightly, and the woman stuck her leg in the space to block the pup from making a run for it.

"I'm so sorry, one second." She closed the door and reopened it with the dog in her arms. "Skippy loves to escape any chance he gets. Please, come on in."

We already had our badges exposed on the chains around our necks to put her mind at rest. We entered the tiled foyer, and I could see the kitchen and family room just beyond the entryway. Her house looked warm and inviting. We introduced ourselves.

Diane led the way to the kitchen and motioned for us to have a seat at the table next to the bay window. "I just made a fresh pot of coffee. Can I fix you each a cup?" She put the dog on the floor.

"Okay, sure. Thank you," Jack said. He glanced at me, and I nodded. "Black for both of us."

Diane set a trivet on the table and placed a thermal carafe on top of it. She brought over three brown ceramic mugs.

"I drink mine black too." She reached down to pet Skippy, who was sitting at her side. "What can I help you with, detectives?"

Jack started while I pulled out my notepad. "May I call you Diane?"

"Sure, that's fine."

"Okay, Diane, I understand you were at the mall last night? Did you go to Chew, the café with the outdoor patio facing the west parking lot?"

She nodded. "I was there with my daughter but only for ice cream. We were shopping prior to that for a birthday present for her best friend. My daughter, Anna, is seven."

"Okay, do you know what time that was, and how do you remember a white van specifically?"

Diane looked up for a few seconds as if she were thinking. "We didn't go to the mall until after dinner and the dishes were cleaned up. It was right around when the news came on, so I'd say six o'clock, give or take a few minutes."

"Great." I wrote that down. "And the white van?"

"Well, Anna and I have always played road games. Yesterday we were looking for out-of-state license plates. I told her if she found one, I'd buy her an ice cream cone for dessert. Wouldn't you know it, when we pulled into the parking lot, I was right behind a white van that had his left-turn blinker on. He was waiting for the traffic to pass." She grinned. "Anyway, Anna noticed the van's plates and yelled out. She was so excited knowing she'd get an ice cream cone out of it."

I smiled. "Where were the plates from?"

"Montana. They were really cool plates too, with a ghost-town scene."

"Would you happen to remember any of the numbers or letters on the plates?" I looked at her hopefully.

Diane rubbed her forehead as if that would spark her memory. "Um... um... oh yeah, there was an AE on it because Anna mentioned it was her initials."

"That's a big help. Do you remember anything about the van itself, like bumper stickers, rust, dents, or even the people in it?"

"I didn't see the people in the van, and as far as dents, rust, or bumper stickers, no, I don't think so."

"No, there wasn't anything like that, or no, you don't remember if there was?" Jack asked.

"Sorry, I don't remember if there was. We commented on the plates, the van turned left, and we went right."

"Were there back windows that you can recall?"

"I don't think so. I'm pretty sure the back was solid."

"You didn't see the van again while you were there, did you?"

"Nope. We parked, shopped, and had ice cream. We left for home around seven forty-five."

"Okay, you've been very helpful, Diane," Jack said.

We handed Diane our cards and asked her to please call if she remembered anything else, then we left.

I got into the passenger seat and called the lieutenant as Jack drove. He picked up on the third ring.

"Hey, boss. We may have a lead."

"Good, because we really need one."

"We just interviewed someone that was at the mall last night. She remembered a white van with a Montana plate that had a ghost town on it, and the letters A and E were in the plate number. That's all she remembers. Oh, and there weren't any windows on the back doors."

"That's something. I'll get Todd and Billy on it right away and add that information for the news anchor to mention on the broadcast. Anything else?"

"Not so far. Do you want us back or should we interview the security guard again from last night?"

"Yeah, do that for sure. The head of security is Bob Shilling. He'll have the address and phone number of the guard that patrolled the parking lot last night."

"Got it, boss. I'll update you after we talk to him." I hung up, and Jack drove us back to the mall.

Inside, we headed to the security office and knocked on the glass door. The man behind the first desk looked up and motioned for us to enter when we flashed our badges. Jack pushed the door open, and we entered the room.

A bank of computer monitors lined the back wall. Split screens on each one showed the mall from the inside, in each corridor, and outside, along the building and the numerous parking lots. A long counter facing the monitors was equipped with computers and six roller chairs. Four individual desks took up the rest of the room.

"Officers, how can I help you?"

The portly man pushed back his chair and stood. He turned down the volume on the radio next to him on a short filing cabinet, then he extended his hand and gave ours a strong shake. A thin ring of graying hair was all that remained on his head, and he had a gray mustache. He wore thick black bifocals, and a god-awful lime-green tie adorned his short-sleeved white shirt.

"Are you Bob Shilling?" I asked.

"Yes, ma'am, that's me."

"Nice to meet you, Bob. We're here because we need the name, phone number, and address of the parking lot security patrol from last night. I guess you spoke with him after that car was left in the parking lot overnight, but none of our officers have talked to him yet."

"That's correct. Once your guys arrived earlier, I called the patrol officer and did a phone recap with him. He said he was just going by protocol."

"Which is?" I asked, even though I already knew what he was about to say.

"Ticketing the car after twenty-four hours. Cars are left overnight often. It's never raised a red flag before."

"I understand. We'll still need to speak with that security guard."

"Sure. Give me a second, please." Bob opened the file cabinet behind his desk and pulled out a folder. "Here we go."

He handed me the file. I wrote down the security officer's name, phone number, and address. "Thank you, sir. Here are our cards. If you think of anything else, please call us. We appreciate your help."

I closed the glass door at our backs, and we left the building. We walked through the parking lot back to the cruiser.

"So where does this dude live?" Jack asked.

I opened my notepad. "Let's see. His name is Ollie Miller, and he lives on the south side of town. Actually, he only lives a few blocks from me. I'll give him a call."

Chapter 32

Jeremy sat near the barn on the bench seat of the splintered, paint-bare picnic table. A half-dead basswood tree hung above his head and threw shadows across the yard. He drank a Mountain Dew as he stared out at the overgrown weed-filled land to his south. The screen door slammed, causing him to instinctively turn his head that way. Matt and Cage were walking toward him. Smoldering embers kept the burning barrel hot, and smoke threaded up to the still sky.

"What are you burning?" Matt asked as he passed the rusty fifty-gallon drum. He threw a bright orange Frisbee, and Cage took off after it.

"The damn boots. Those girls will wear what we give them to wear, something suitable like nothing on their feet at all. That will help keep them from running." Jeremy got up and chased the Frisbee. He gave it a fling across the yard. Cage jumped and caught the plastic disc in mid-air. Jeremy looked at his watch. "Liz's auction ends in a half hour. Guess I should get back downstairs and see how it's going."

"I checked ten minutes ago."

"And?"

"And she still had three hundred bucks to go before the reserve would hit."

"Damn it. If she doesn't sell this time, she's going in the ground next to Beth. Six grand isn't asking too much for her. Sundays are slow, but I guess we'll see."

Matt picked up the disc and gave it another hard throw. Cage was on it in no time. "What about the two new girls? Are we going to wait until next weekend before we list them? That's a long time."

"Nah—I'll put them on a three-day auction. We'll start it first thing Thursday morning so it ends Saturday at midnight. They should do well. We'll start packing up after that."

Jeremy whistled, and Cage ran toward him. "Come on, boy, get back in the house."

They walked down to the basement, where Matt handed each girl a banana and a bag of chips through the wires of their enclosures. "Back up so I can put water inside."

Jeremy leaned against the doorway to the video room and watched as each girl slid to the farthest corner of her cage. Matt opened the gates and passed bottles of water through.

"Why are we here? What are you going to do with us?" Megan asked, choking back the tears.

Matt looked toward Jeremy and grinned. He sat down on the chair across from the cages and cocked his head. "Really? Come on, Meg. You look like a smart young lady. What do you think we're going to do with you? I'm sure you ladies have had a lot to talk about, haven't you?" Matt got up and walked around the corner. Jeremy handed him the baby monitor from the top of the jelly cupboard. "Do you know what this is, Megan?" Matt asked when he returned to the chair.

"Yes." She burrowed her head against her chest and quietly cried.

"Yeah, that's what I thought. We listen to all of your conversations down here. Remember that. You and Jenna are going to be long gone in a week or so, so I'd suggest you enjoy our company while you can. You never know what kind of freak is going to snap you up at your auction." He smirked and walked away.

"Come on, let's check the bids," Jeremy said. "The auction is going to end in a few minutes."

Matt joined Jeremy in the video room and closed the door at his back. They both sat on roller stools and scooted in closer to the screen.

Jeremy hit the refresh icon. "Five minutes left, Liz. Your life is hanging in the balance. Either someone is going to save you or you're doomed to be worm food."

At the two-minute mark, the reserve button illuminated green.

"Check it out, man. She hit the reserve—sweet!" Matt high-fived his brother, and they both leaned back and relaxed with a sigh. "Anything in the next two minutes is pure bonus."

The bidding ended, and Liz went for seven thousand dollars to somebody in Tennessee.

"That's cool," Jeremy said. "I bet they'll just drive here to pick her up. It can't get much easier than that."

Jeremy confirmed that the seven thousand dollars was deposited in their account, powered down the computer, and they walked out. Matt hit the wall switch and closed the door behind them.

"You're sold, Liz. Guess you aren't going in the ground after all," Jeremy said as he reached for the handrail and went upstairs.

Matt headed for the kitchen. He pulled the handle on the freezer door and knelt down to look inside at their dinner choices. "Feel like a pizza?" he asked.

Jeremy had just settled on the couch and reached for the remote. Cage jumped up, spun a few times, and found a spot in the corner.

"Comfortable?" Jeremy patted Cage's hindquarters, held down the channel selector with his thumb, and began scrolling through the stations. "Yeah, pizza sounds good. What the hell?" Jeremy sat up straight and hit the pause button. "Shit—Matt, get in here."

Matt looked around the doorframe. "What's wrong?"

"Sit down and watch this. This just came on the news."

Matt sat on the chair next to the couch, his elbows resting on his knees while he leaned forward. With the remote in his hand, Jeremy rewound the news to where he'd started watching it. He hit Play. The anchorman explained that the video on the screen had been captured last night at the Westchase Mall in North Bend. The image showed two women loading their trunk with shopping bags, then a white van came into view. It stopped at the car, blocking the camera, then sped off less than a minute later. The women were gone, and the car remained. Jeremy was thankful that the video was somewhat grainy. The anchor went on to tell the viewers the names of both girls, then a split screen showed their faces. After the commercial, the anchor said they had just received more information on a white van seen at the mall yesterday. He said this particular van had solid back doors, Montana plates with an A and an E in the number, and the background of the license plate was a ghost town. The anchorman went on to explain that although that might not be the same van as in the video, anyone who saw this van should call the Washburn County Sheriff's Department immediately.

"What's this?" Jeremy's back stiffened, and he wrung his hands. His forehead furrowed so that his eyebrows almost touched. "Now they're showing a taped segment from the night before too? We totally missed that one. Son of a bitch, there's that sergeant from the bar I told you about. See the chick sitting on the right side of the podium? That's the one who was the sister of the bartender at Joey's. I'll be damned. She must be important to be sitting in on that press conference. Damn it to hell, she knows my face too." Jeremy threw the remote across the room.

"So what if she knows your face? She doesn't actually know who you are. You were just another person getting two beers at the bar."

"Right, but I talked to her." Jeremy ground his fists into his eyes.

"If we're never caught, it's a moot point, dude," Matt said.

"Okay, I have to think about this. First off we have to paint the van and steal some local plates. We'll get the paint tonight. Daylight is too risky. See where the next largest town is north of here."

Matt did a Google search on his phone. "We'll have to go to a superstore that's open late. Everything else closes early on Sundays."

"Yeah, let's go. We'll hit a few of them. You'll go in and get paint at one, then I'll go in and get more at another. Put a baseball cap on and cash only. So where are we going?"

"There are two big-box stores in Deerfield, about ten miles north of here. I'll grab the flashlight and some tools. We'll need them for the license plates. I guess the pizza can go back in the freezer for now."

Chapter 33

Jack and I had just wrapped up our interview with Ollie Miller. He told us his routine was to walk the mall interior for a two-hour stretch, then he patrolled the parking lot in his security car for the same amount of time. He went back and forth regularly for the length of his shift except for a half-hour lunch break in the food court at seven thirty. All of the security guards did it the same way, according to him.

We thanked him, got in the cruiser, and left.

"Okay, so Ollie's shift is from three until eleven, and he always starts inside. That means he was outside patrolling the parking lot from five to seven and then again from nine until eleven. He never saw the van outside, just like he said." I watched as cars whizzed by from both directions. "Okay, you're good to pull out." Jack turned left and headed east. I continued with my train of thought. "The girls were abducted just after eight fifteen. The first time Ollie noticed the car sitting there was after the mall closed and the parking lot emptied out. He doesn't know anything—another dead end."

Jack groaned and raked his fingers through his hair. "Give the lieutenant a call. Maybe Todd and Billy got a hit on the plates. The news must have aired the segment already too."

"Yeah, good idea." I dialed the lieutenant's office phone. He answered right away. "Hey, boss, anything on the plates?"

"Yeah, they were reported stolen several months ago. The news just aired the segment about the girls and showed the mall footage. Guess we jumped the gun on the plates, but if our perps are stupid enough to leave them on the van, it could still help us identify the vehicle."

"True, but that sucks. They sure know how to cover their tracks."

"We'll get them, one way or another."

"I know that, boss. I never doubted it. Jack and I are heading back. We'll see you in a few."

Jack pulled into the lot and parked the cruiser. We went inside, and I handed the lieutenant my gas receipt from that morning.

"Isn't there a designated person that's supposed to keep the cruisers full of gas?" I asked with a huff.

"Yeah, I'll get on them tomorrow. Do you two want to watch the news footage from earlier?"

Jack spoke up, "Sure, why not? Jade, do you want a soda?"

"Yes, please." I walked into the break room and plopped down at the long lunch table facing the TV on the wall. Jack dropped two quarters into the vending machine, hit the button for root beer, gave the machine a swift kick, and two cans dropped out. He turned and grinned while I shook my head.

"Someday you're going to get busted, mister."

"Not unless you rat me out." He carried the cans over and sat down next to me.

I clicked on the TV to the recorded news segment from earlier. We watched it together as we drank our sodas. Anyone that might have been parked in that vicinity could have seen the van sitting at the back of the lot. Hopefully, that news segment would spark a memory for somebody and they would call in details that we could use.

I turned off the TV after the news segment, and Jack hit the light switch. We walked the hallway back to the bull pen.

"If there's nothing else, boss, I'm going to head home. It looks like everyone else is packing it in too."

"Yeah, go ahead and get out of here, Jade. I'll update Jamison and Horbeck when they get in. All of you have put in a full weekend, and I appreciate it. Get a good night's rest. Tomorrow starts a brand-new week."

I groaned. "Don't remind me."

Jack and I walked out to the parking lot. Billings and Clayton were right behind us.

"Good night, guys."

"Night, Jade. Night, Jack. See you in the morning. Don't forget, that new ME is starting tomorrow. I'm sure Jason will bring her upstairs and introduce her to everyone."

"Do you know her name?" Jack called out.

"Um, I think her name is Leona something," Billings said.

"Leona? It sounds like she's seventy years old."

I elbowed Jack. "Be nice. We'll find out for ourselves tomorrow. Go home and get some sleep."

"Yes, Mom. Good night."

I watched as Jack drove away, then I got into my own car and left. I drove through town, heading south to my new condo, my cathartic place. Occasionally I sat on my deck late at night with a glass of wine. I needed that time to relax before bed, to wind down and look off into the deep woods ahead of me. The quiet kept me grounded. My job was hectic lately, but it was what I'd signed up for and what I loved. It kept me on my toes, and I couldn't imagine anything else I'd rather do. Taking down the bad guys was in my blood, something I'd wanted to do from early on. My pop instilled that in me as a teenager. I never took anyone's guff, not then and not now.

My car idled at the red light at the intersection of South Main and Highland. Ideas bounced around in my brain about ways to capture the villains that were abducting these innocent young women. I could only imagine how frightened they must be, and it fueled my need to catch these men quickly. Tomorrow, we would recap everything we'd done so far and plan new tactics. Hopefully the news broadcast would bring in fresh leads too.

A flash of white zapped me out of my thoughts and back into the present. A white van just passed through the green light, heading west on Highland. I quickly looked over my shoulder to make sure nobody was in my blind spot and pulled into the right lane. Being off duty and in my personal car didn't give me the right to pull over any random van just because it was the same color as a vehicle we had a BOLO for. I spun around the corner and followed three car lengths behind, my pulse racing. The van turned into a subdivision near the hospital. I continued behind it, inching up closer to check the plates. I knew by now the criminals we were after could have easily swapped out the plates with another set of stolen ones. The van turned again and pulled into a driveway. I slowed down and waited along the curb with the house in plain sight. Relief and disappointment swept across me when I saw a man, woman, and three kids get out and walk up the sidewalk to the front door. I pulled away from the curb when they went inside, then I headed for home.

Chapter 34

"Here's the list of things for you to get. Fifty bucks should cover it." Jeremy parked the van a half block away from the store entrance.

Matt clicked on the overhead light and looked at the sheet of paper. "Okay, five cans of primer and a roll of masking tape."

"Yeah, that's it. I'll get the paint and a roll of paper towels to cover the windshield and door windows at another store. Keep your head down and the baseball cap on at all times. Make it fast. Walk tight along the building where the cameras can't see you. I'll scope out the parking lot while you're inside. If I see a vehicle parked far enough away without cameras close by, we'll swap the plates when you come back out. Oh yeah, add work gloves to your list—two pair of large ones. Call me when you're coming out. I'll be on the far right end of the lot."

Matt nodded and exited the van. Jeremy waited until Matt was inside the building then began to troll the outer edges of the parking lot. He wasn't having any luck.

Cameras were attached on the tall light poles scattered throughout the lot. He'd have to come up with another plan.

He parked along the right side of the lot across the street from the store. Jeremy waited for fifteen minutes, then his phone rang out.

"You done?" Jeremy continued to check the side mirrors as he talked.

"Yep, I have everything. No problems. I'll be out in a minute."

"Good." Jeremy hung up and watched the lit entryway to the store.

Matt exited and hugged the side of the building as he walked. He crossed the street and climbed into the van, then Jeremy took off.

"We aren't swapping the plates here?"

"Nah—there's cameras every fifty feet. Let's go to the next store. I'll get the spray paint, then we'll find a quiet residential street, someplace dark to snag different plates." Jeremy drove seven blocks to the next superstore and parked the van just outside the lot. "Keep your eyes peeled for trouble. I'll be back in a few minutes."

He got out and stayed in the shadows. He was gone for barely ten minutes. Back at the van, he tossed the two plastic bags full of spray paint and paper towels into the back and climbed in.

Matt turned the radio on and scanned the stations, trying to find one that wasn't playing commercials. He settled on a country station and tapped his fingers on the dash while Jeremy drove, skirting the outer edge of the parking lot. Jeremy noticed Matt staring out the side window at families exiting the store. Kids rode the bottom rail of the carts, squealing as they zoomed through the parking lot and heading toward parked cars. They both chuckled.

"It's gotta be nice."

"What's that?"

"You know, to be a kid. No cares, no worries—having decent parents. That sort of thing."

"You getting sentimental on me, bro?"

Matt smirked. "Nah—just wondering what it feels like, that's all."

Jeremy turned down the radio. "Maybe we'll both have kids someday." He glanced across the van at Matt and laughed. "Or not. Come on. We have to focus. There's bound to be exactly what we need parked along the curb somewhere. Look for a quiet residential neighborhood."

He pulled out onto the busy street and drove a few more blocks. Large overhead lights illuminated the area, and retail stores lined both sides of the street. Jeremy looked down every side street and finally turned right. A quiet, older neighborhood lay ahead. With his neck craned, he looked up through the windshield and grinned. "Hope Street—a fitting name. I hope we find a car parked along the curb, away from streetlights. He continued on until the street intersected with Melody Lane. A pickup truck sat at the last house on Hope Street. Two cars filled the driveway, making it nearly impossible for the homeowners to see anything the brothers might be doing out on the street. The drapes on the front window of the house had already been closed for the night, and the porch light was off.

"This is about as good as it's going to get," Jeremy said as he turned the van around and stopped about fifty feet behind the truck. "Grab the tools and the flashlight. We'll remove the truck's plates and get the hell out of here. We can stop somewhere else and put them on the van."

The brothers exited the van and quietly closed the doors. They stayed in the shadows as they approached the truck. Jeremy went to the front, and Matt went to the back. Each with a screwdriver in hand, it took only a minute to remove the plates. Jeremy looked around, making sure the coast was clear, and crept back to Matt.

"Aren't you done yet?"

"This damn screw is stripped."

"I'll work on it. Get a cutter out of the van. If we have to cut the plate around the screw, we will. We have to make this quick."

Matt scurried off and opened the back of the van. A toolbox sat inside just for these types of situations. He ran back, staying low to the ground. Jeremy took the cutter and split the plate around the screw. With his gloved hand, he gave it a yank, and it came loose.

"Let's go." Back in the van, Jeremy drove a mile farther until he found a dead-end street. "This looks good. Take the front plate and make it quick."

They exited the van for the last time until they reached the safety of the farm. The plates on the van were removed, and the replacements were installed.

Jeremy climbed back into the driver's seat while Matt threw the old plates in the back of the van.

Matt pulled his gloves off and slapped his hands together. "One job down and one to go."

Jeremy nodded. "Tomorrow we'll get up early and paint the van. It needs to be dry, and it has to look good before we hit the road with Gina." He checked the side mirrors and pulled away from the curb. "Now let's get the hell out of here."

Chapter 35

I sat at my desk with a fresh cup of coffee cradled between my fingers. The scented steam rose and dispersed above me. Stacks of paper were spread around me, and more files than I cared to admit needed to be put away. It didn't take long for my desk to become a rat's nest of things to catch up on. I came in early just to get a head start on that project. I looked around the bull pen and realized everyone else's desks looked just like mine. One by one, our detectives came in and plopped down on their chairs, giving their own workspace a disgusted headshake.

"How did this much crap end up on my desk?" Jack asked. "Did you sneak your stuff over here before I walked in?"

"Yeah, you busted me—that's exactly what I did. Did you notice all of our desks look the same? I just happened to come in early to address this very problem before the bull pen starts looking like a hoarder's house."

Billings walked through the door. "I think it's too late for that, Jade." He headed to the coffee station and poured himself a cup.

"Well, maybe we ought to take thirty minutes and straighten our desks up before the mice take over the room."

Jack nodded and pulled the garbage can closer to his chair.

"Doesn't the new ME start today?" Clayton asked as he balled up a piece of waste paper and launched it toward Jack's garbage can. "Ta-da—three-point shot. Not bad, if I do say so myself."

I laughed. "You shoot like a girl. I can do that with my eyes closed. And yes, the new ME does start today. I'm sure Jason is relieved. He's had a lot on his plate lately."

"What's her name—Leona?" Jack asked with a smirk, glancing at the door to make sure it was closed.

"Actually it isn't. I asked Jason again, and he said her name is Lena. Lena Wentworth—nice name. It sounds strong. I'm anxious to meet her."

"What's her deal?" Billings asked.

"I have no idea what her *deal* is other than she's from Indianapolis and she's the new ME. Why don't you get acquainted with her over lunch, Billings, and interrogate her?"

His face turned red, and I grinned.

The door opened again, and we all looked up. Jason entered with a petite blond woman who looked to be around forty years old. She had a friendly face and an instant smile—I liked her already.

"Everyone, I'd like you to meet Lena Wentworth, our new chief medical examiner. Lena, this is Jade Monroe, our sergeant detective. Her partner, Jack Steele, is right there."

Jason pointed, and Jack stood and shook her hand. "These are detectives Chad Clayton and Adam Billings. I'm sure you'll get ribbed sooner or later by everyone, but they're a fun group and very loyal to each other."

We all shook Lena's hand and welcomed her to the fold.

I gave Billings a sideways grin and invited Lena to have lunch with us later. We could all get better acquainted, hopefully over an enjoyable, relaxing meal.

Clark came out of his office and welcomed Lena to Washburn County with a firm handshake. He had already met her last week, but today was her formal introduction to everyone.

"If we're still around when Jamison and Horbeck come in, I'll introduce you to them too. Eventually you'll get to know all of us," Jason said.

Lena smiled and spoke up. "It's nice to meet all of you, and I'm enjoying North Bend so far. It's a far cry from Indianapolis, but I really like the small-town feel. I'm sure I'll settle in just fine."

"Okay, we'll see you guys at lunchtime. If nothing comes up between now and then, we'll come up at noon," Jason said.

We waved as they walked out, then we got back to cleaning off our desks.

"So?" Jack said.

"So what?" I asked.

"Don't be coy. What do you think of her?"

I chuckled. "I think she seems sweet and friendly. We'll see how she is in the field when the time comes. What do you guys think?"

Clayton, Jack, and Billings looked at each other and shrugged—then nodded.

"Yeah, she seems all right," Billings said.

"Okay, ladies, what's the plan for the day—after you straighten up your workspaces?" Clark asked as he stood against the doorframe to his office. He looked back and groaned at his own desk.

"Hopefully some calls will come in about the news coverage from last night. I think the local channels are going to air the footage again at noon, six o'clock, and ten tonight, boss," I said. "If we don't get any leads from that, I think it's time to move on to plan B."

"Canvassing the area door to door?" Clark asked.

"Yeah, I think so. I'm sure Todd and Billy can help us set up a perimeter around the area where Reanne was found. Five miles or more, I'd say. Speaking of Reanne, shouldn't we release her body to her parents?"

Clark tugged on his left earlobe. "Yep, it's time. I'll double-check with Jason to make sure he has everything completed. He and Lena can finish up the official paperwork today, get the death certificates for the family, and arrange transport. Jade, call her folks and give them a heads-up. They need to let us know where they want her body transported."

"Got it, boss, I'll get on that right away." I filled my coffee cup, topped off everyone else's, and sat back down at my desk and dialed Reanne's mom, Charlene. "Hello, Mrs. Orth. Sergeant Monroe calling from Washburn County. How are you doing?" I grimaced at the foolishness that always spilled out of my mouth when speaking to family members of a deceased person. I never seemed to have the right words. That was definitely something I needed to work on.

"Hello, Sergeant Monroe. I guess we're just trying to get by one day at a time. We'd like to set up a funeral service for Reanne, though."

"That's why I'm calling, ma'am. We can release Reanne's remains to any funeral home you'd like. Have you and Mr. Orth contacted anyone yet?"

"Yes, we have. We'd like her sent to Abraham and Miles Funeral Home here in Grand Forks."

I wrote that down. "Mrs. Orth, have you decided how many death certificates you'll need? We can send them along with the driver."

"Um… just a second."

I heard her voice crack over the phone as I waited.

"I'm sorry, I guess I'm still very emotional. Does five sound right?"

"Yes, five should do it. Sometimes people need more when there are insurance, homes, debts, and so on to deal with, but in Reanne's case, five should be enough. Our medical examiner is probably finished with the paperwork and can set up transport anytime you like. Why don't you check with the funeral director and get back to me on that?"

"Okay, I should know sometime today. Can I call you back at either of the numbers on your card?"

"Yes, ma'am, and if I don't answer on my desk phone, feel free to call my cell. Again, Mrs. Orth, you have the

Washburn County Sheriff's Department's condolences."

"Thank you. Goodbye."

I hung up and took a deep breath. My desk phone rang not more than a minute later. John from upstairs was calling.

"Hey, John, what's up?"

"Morning, Jade. Apparently there are a few meth lab rats up here that want a face-to-face with you."

I laughed. "Sounds like you've been talking to Jack. Hang on a sec." I turned to Jack. "Hey, partner, do you want to go upstairs with me and have a heartfelt conversation with a few lab rats?"

"Hell, yeah. What do they want?"

"No clue. What do they want, John?" I grinned at Jack as I listened.

"They said they have important information for you, for a price."

"Really? We'll see about that. Link them up. We're on our way. Who are we talking to?"

"Frankie Freeman and Ryan Boesch."

"Awesome—two smart-asses that are going to make my morning. We'll be right there."

Jack pushed back his desk chair and stood. I joined him at the door, and we headed upstairs with fresh cups of coffee.

John met us after we signed in. "They're in the cafeteria, anxiously awaiting your arrival." He gave me a wink.

"Do you have their sheets? I'd like to see what's on the table."

"Sure, one second." John reached across his desk and handed me both files. "I figured you'd want to take a quick look."

"Thanks. Jack, aren't these the same two that didn't have anything to say to you a few months back?"

"Yep—Frankie and Ryan, the very same two. Now they remembered something?" Jack rubbed his chin. "That's interesting. Their sentencing date must be getting close."

I flipped a few pages. "Yeah, here it is. They're both charged with manufacturing meth with intent to sell. These are the same guys from the lab in Newburg, right?"

"Yep. They had quite an operation going," Jack said. "Shall we?"

"Yeah, let's see what they know."

We walked into the cafeteria. Both men sat, linked to the lunch table near the door. A one-way window faced the cafeteria, and the guard station where John sat was on the other side of the glass.

"Boys," I said, "I hear you have a song to sing. Let's hear it." Jack and I took a seat across from them.

"Not until we get a deal," Frankie said, sneering.

"Let's go. I don't have time for this crap." Jack began to stand.

I got up too.

Ryan called out, "Wait."

"Is there something you want to tell us?" I looked at my watch. "We have a busy day ahead. Talk now or go back to your cage."

"We want a deal, though—fewer charges. We're looking at ten to twenty."

"Yeah, I know. It sucks to be you." I cocked my head. "Do you have something to say or not?"

Frankie spoke up. "We have two names. They just started up a new lab outside of town, and it's big."

"We're listening," Jack said. He propped his hand under his chin and leaned forward.

I took out my notepad. "Just so you know, boys, if this intel is a bunch of bs, I'll personally make sure you get the maximum sentence. I'm not about to waste my time with two punks like you."

"It's real. Okay, the new lab is at a farm out on Granville Road."

"We need an address."

"I don't have an address, but I have a description and the names. Abe Negrete and Don Simmons are the guys who fund the labs. It's a nonstop operation, and they run labs all over the state. If one closes down, like ours did in Newburg, they start a new one. They don't do any cooking themselves. They find the locations, pay for everything to get the labs going, and then have their minions make the meth and distribute it."

"Minions as in guys like you?"

Frankie stared at me, his fists clenched under the chains.

I smiled. "And how do you know all of this?"

Ryan spoke up, "We do have visitors, you know. They keep us up to date on what's going on out there."

"That's real kind of them. Now what about that description?" Jack said. He took a sip of coffee.

"The farmhouse is red with a black roof. The barn

matches it. There's a white fence at the front of the yard. They make the meth in the barn since it's set back from the house."

"Smart. In case some fool blows the place up?"

Frankie smirked. "I guess."

"Who lives in the house?" I asked.

"The cookers. I heard they work around the clock and take shifts to eat and sleep. Ryan and Abe check on every lab a few times a week."

I looked at the analog clock above the door—nine o'clock. We could round up a few deputies to go with us to check out their story. "Is this farmhouse north or south of Linden Road?"

"It's north," Ryan said.

I closed my notepad and slid it into my back pocket. "How many cookers were at the house you two got busted at?"

Ryan looked at Frankie, his right eyebrow arched. "I don't know, maybe ten in all, but we weren't always in the lab at the same time."

"Is that about the normal number of people?"

"Yeah, ten to fifteen if they're working around the clock," Frankie said.

"Okay, boys, thanks for the info. We're going to check it out."

"What about our deal?"

I looked at Jack. "Did you offer them a deal?"

"Nope—did you?"

"Hell no—never have, never will. Have a nice day, ladies."

I heard Ryan call me a bitch as we exited through the door. I thanked John, and we went back to the bull pen.

"I'm going to talk to Clark and see if he wants us to check it out. It *is* out of the city's jurisdiction."

Jack nodded and went back to clearing his desk.

I knocked on the door, and the lieutenant looked up from his paperwork. He waved me in.

"Jade, what's up?"

"Jack and I just talked to some of the meth cookers upstairs. They gave us some intel we ought to check out."

"Do you think it's legit?"

"If it is, it will be worthwhile. They gave us names of two of the bigger players, if they're actually real people. I'll pull their names up and see if they have rap sheets. The boys gave us the location of a lab that recently started up on Granville Road. I'll look on Google Maps first to see if the place really does exist."

"So what was their motivation to sing?"

I laughed. "They thought I'd bargain with them. If their story is bs, they're going to be in a world of hurt. I already told them that."

Clark glanced at the clock on the wall. "You do have time on your hands. Okay, grab Jack, Silver, and Donnelly and go check it out. Watch yourselves—those types are sketchy—and surveillance only. We have to know if they're actually cooking. If they are, we'll hand it off to the DEA, especially if there a lot of people involved. Be careful out there."

"Will do, boss, and I'll keep you posted."

I had Jan dispatch Silver and Donnelly back to the sheriff's department. Meanwhile, I went downstairs to have Todd pull up the names Abe Negrete and Don Simmons to see if either of them had outstanding warrants. If they were as smart and discreet as the boys upstairs made them seem to be, they wouldn't have any sheets at all. They'd be flying under the radar, as invisible as ghosts.

"Hey, Todd, can you pull up both of these names for me? I want to see if they're in the system for any felony drug charges."

"Sure thing, Jade, give me one second here." He powered up his computer and waited until the screen came to life. "Have you guys met Lena yet?" He logged in to the database system.

"Yep and I like her already."

Todd nodded. "Yeah, she seems cool. Here we go. Okay, first name." He looked at my notepad and typed in Abe Negrete. Nothing came up in Wisconsin. "Next name."

"It's Don Simmons." I waited.

"Nothing on him either. These are listings only for Wisconsin, though. Both names come up in the nationwide database but not under anything drug related, and they might not be the same people anyway."

"Got it. Either they're fictitious names for the guys that run these meth labs or they actually know how to keep their hands clean. Oh, as long as I'm down here, can we check on Google Maps for a farmhouse on Granville Road? I guess it's north of Linden Road. Supposedly, it's a red farmhouse with a matching barn. Both have black roofs, and there's supposed to be a white fence along the road. That's all I know. Granville ends at Highway C, so between Linden and C is about a two-mile stretch."

"Yeah, sure, I'll pull it up."

Todd zeroed in on the intersection of Granville and Linden Roads and began the search. I pulled up a chair and leaned in close to the computer monitor, staring at the satellite image. He zoomed in and headed north on Granville, checking every farmhouse along the way.

"There's a farmhouse and a barn with black roofs." I pointed at the screen to the farm I wanted him to zoom in on.

"Yeah, I got it."

"Okay, can you switch it to street view so we can take a look?"

"Sure can."

"Hmm… the house is white and the barn is red. How often does Google update these images?"

"I think it's every five years, and they're doing it this year. They may not have gotten to the rural areas yet. There is a white fence out front, though," Todd said.

"Uh-huh, I see that. The house could have been painted since this street view was taken."

"Yeah, it definitely could have been. Is that it, Jade?"

"Yep, that should do it. Thanks a lot." I patted Todd's shoulder and walked out through the glass doors. I went back upstairs and worked on my desk disaster while I waited for Silver and Donnelly to arrive.

"What did Todd know?" Jack asked. He passed the

garbage can to me.

"Neither of the guys our meth rats mentioned have sheets, and the farmhouse is a maybe. It looks like the right description except the house is white."

"Maybe the street view hasn't been updated lately."

"Yeah, we thought the same thing. We got the okay from Clark to check it out—surveillance only, though—just to make sure they're actually cooking."

"I agree. Donnelly called while you were downstairs. They're just a few minutes out."

I nodded, pushed back from my desk, and got up. I rapped on the lieutenant's half-opened door and peeked through. "We're heading out, boss. The lead could be legit."

"Okay, update me when you get there."

Chapter 36

I explained the situation to Donnelly and Silver as the four of us walked to the unmarked cruisers.

"When we get close to the farm, we'll surveil the layout and situation first. According to Google's satellite image, there's a long dirt path leading in from a neighboring road. I'm sure it was a tractor path from days gone by. Anyway, let's drive by the house first, make sure it's the right place, and see if we notice any activity. We'll enter from the dirt path if everything's a go and walk the final quarter mile in." I popped the trunk with the key fob. "We're wearing vests just in case, so check your trunk and make sure there are two vests inside."

Jack checked our trunk, and Silver checked theirs. I climbed into the cruiser that was parked next to the one Donnelly and Silver had. I lowered the passenger side window.

"Just follow my lead. We're using a different channel frequency today in case they have scanners. I'll let dispatch know, and keep your cell phones handy too. I'll call you,

Silver, when we're close."

Donnelly nodded and climbed in behind the wheel of their car. They followed us out of the parking lot, and we headed east. The farm was about fifteen minutes away.

My cell phone rang as Jack drove. I pulled it out of my pocket and looked at the screen—Charlene Orth was calling back.

"Mrs. Orth, hello."

"Sergeant Monroe. I spoke to the funeral home, and they told me they have next Saturday open. Most of Reanne's friends and our family are local, so there's no need to delay the service. I'm sure Saturday will work out, so I told them okay. The funeral director is meeting with me later today to go over the details."

"That sounds fine. I'll have our ME arrange for Reanne's transport. She should arrive at the funeral home no later than Wednesday. If you wouldn't mind, Mrs. Orth, I'd appreciate it if you'd just text me the name, phone number, and address of the funeral home. I'm not at my desk right now."

"Okay. Please give me a call when you have it arranged."

"Will do. It should be sometime later today. Thank you for calling. Goodbye."

I hung up and looked to my left at Jack as he drove.

He turned toward me. "What?"

"Just thinking. Today is Monday. Wouldn't it be nice to have these cases wrapped up by the weekend? What would you do with a weekend to call your own?" I could almost see his wheels turning.

"Hmm... wow, that sounds nice. I'd probably get my brothers on board and head to our cabin in Hudson. Maybe we'd do a little fishing and probably a lot of drinking."

I laughed. "Sounds like fun. Hopefully that will happen sooner rather than later. We'll start knocking on doors tomorrow. Four girls are missing for sure, and I can't even imagine what they're going through."

Jack gave me a concerned look. "That's if they're still alive. This looks like Granville Road coming up." Jack slowed the cruiser.

"Okay, turn left. I think we have about half a mile before we intersect with Linden. From there, we continue north on Granville until we see the place. According to Google Maps, the farm that fits the description is on the right side of the road."

"Got it. Why don't you call Silver and tell him we're getting close."

I nodded, hit the phone icon next to Silver's name, and waited for him to answer. He picked up before the second ring. "Hey, Aaron, we're getting close. We'll drive by slowly in front of the property. I'll stick my arm out the window when we pass the place. Keep your eyes peeled for any activity at the location. Then we'll go to the next intersection and pull over to discuss the situation."

"Got it, Jade, we'll be watching."

Jack continued north for another three quarters of a mile.

"Okay, there's a farm coming up on the right. Slow down a bit."

Large trees hung over the road and cloaked the front of the house in shade. I didn't have a good visual yet. We were almost on top of the property before I saw a white fence, then the red house. With my index finger already on the window button and waiting, I quickly pressed it and stuck my arm out. Within the short few seconds I had, I scanned the property and saw four cars parked next to the house. I didn't see anyone outside, and then the house was in our rearview mirror. I spun in my seat, trying to see behind us for any additional details. "Did you see anything besides the cars in the driveway?" I asked, looking at Jack.

"Not really. It isn't like we can stop and have a leisurely look around."

I hoped Silver and Donnelly would have more to add after they passed by. We met up the road on a dead-end lane. Jack pulled over, and Donnelly slid his cruiser in behind us. I opened the passenger door and grabbed my sunglasses from the console.

"Did you guys see anything else besides the four cars?" I got out and slammed the door behind me.

"Yeah, didn't you see the dogs?" Silver asked.

"Damn it, dogs?" I rubbed my left eyebrow. "How many?"

"I saw two for sure standing at the screen door."

"Big or small?" I groaned.

"Unfortunately, big. Couldn't tell the breed since they were crowded together behind the door, and I didn't have time to study them. All I know is that they looked big and they were both black."

"Great. They could be Labs. I hope to God they aren't Rotties. With any luck, they'll stay in the house. If they do, they won't notice us coming in from the back. You didn't happen to see any garbage cans or piles of trash, did you?" I asked.

"Nah—we only had a few seconds to see what we did. The curtains were all drawn, though," Silver said. "The house and grounds looked unkempt. Doubt if they're the owners. This has to be the right place. No pride in ownership because they're renters, two large guard dogs, and curtains closed in the daytime."

Jack spoke up. "Yeah, I saw that too. They aren't cooking in the house according to our jailbirds, but they may be sleeping in shifts and want to keep the house dark. I did see the NO TRESPASSING and PRIVATE PROPERTY signs at the end of the driveway, though. That's a sure indication they don't want company. They could be armed and paranoid—the worst combination."

"I didn't catch a whiff of any chemicals, but the barn is set back from the road. Okay, boys, are you ready to check this out?"

Donnelly nodded. "Lead the way, boss. We'll be right behind you."

Jack and I climbed back into the cruiser and headed for the next road to the east. We'd make three right turns at each intersection until we were at the backside of the property.

We reached the tractor path that led to the long-forgotten field. From the way the layout looked from the satellite image, the path ended about a half mile in. The west side of the field had a natural rise and a row of trees and bushes, then it gradually sloped down to the barn and house beyond that. We turned in and drove slowly so we wouldn't create a dust cloud. Our approach needed to go unnoticed. The path was bumpy and riddled with large rocks and potholes anyway. It looked as though nobody had driven on it for years.

A pile of empty chemical bottles, cans, and pill bottles, along with the smell, would definitely give this crew away if they were cooking. With any luck, we'd see something through our binoculars to substantiate the jailbirds' claims. I'd never get our local DEA involved unless we knew for sure what was going on. This crew could possibly lead to the ringleaders of the statewide meth problem. We'd find out more once we got closer.

Jack stopped the car just at the point where we saw the roofline of the barn. That was close enough. I got out and motioned for Donnelly to stop. I made a quick call to Clark to tell him we were at the location. I'd update him again once we knew what we were dealing with.

"Okay, guys, this is as far as we go with the vehicles. Let's head to that tree line and check out the house and barn with our binoculars. With the tree cover at that ridge, they won't see us even if they are outside."

Jack, Donnelly, Silver, and I put on our vests, strapped on our weapons and our shoulder mics, and hung our binoculars around our necks. We crouched down and took off for the tree line. Once we were in place and had a good visual of the barn and house, we sat on the ridge behind scrub brush and surveilled the situation.

The wind caught in my hair and swirled it across my face. I pulled the elastic band off my wrist and tied it back, then I sniffed the air. "Smell that?" I whispered. "The wind is blowing this way. Somebody is up to no good. It smells like skunk."

The guys nodded, and we settled in to watch the house and barn.

"I see a dump site," Jack said.

"Where?" I asked.

"Look to the far right of the barn. Go beyond that for about thirty feet. You'll see a pile of rocks then a gully. Look closely at that gully. It's filled with chemical cans, plastic canisters, tubing, and bottles."

We turned our binoculars in that direction. With my fingertip, I barely touched the diopter between the eyepieces to adjust the focus.

"Sure as shit, there it is. See any movement anywhere?"

"Not yet," Silver said. "It seems awful quiet at the house."

"Yeah, there are probably a handful of people in the barn, and the rest are likely sleeping. We need to move in and see what's taking place in the barn. There are definitely signs of a meth lab littered about, but we have to see for ourselves if they're actively cooking. Are you girls up for it?" I grinned at each of them.

Jack snickered. "I only see one girl here, and she's talking a lot of smack."

"Yeah, I tend to do that when we're facing trouble. Jack, you and I will take the left side of the barn. Silver, you and Donnelly take the right. We need to find windows and try to get a look inside without being seen. Peeking in through the barn doors not only puts us in a vulnerable position but there's no cover from the house either. Remember, this is surveillance only."

"Yes, Mom, and don't forget about the dogs," Silver said.

"That's right, those damn dogs. Everywhere I go, there are dogs. What's wrong with cats?"

Jack whispered, "I don't think cats give a crap about intruders or anything else for that matter. They just want to be left alone. You guys ready?"

I looked at Silver and Donnelly then nodded. "Let's go."

Jack and I scurried down the hill, trying to stay out of view of the windows on the back of the house. Donnelly and Silver did the same while they hid behind brush and rock piles. Once we reached the barn, we would lose sight of each other, and we'd have to depend solely on our shoulder mics for communication. We didn't want anybody to hear us, so our use of them would be limited. For now we were going by hand signals. We reached the back of the barn, and so far we hadn't been seen. I motioned that we were going ahead. We all needed to hug the sides of the building and move quietly and slowly.

I whispered to Jack as we slinked forward, "There's a window coming up close to the front of the barn. What do you want to do?"

"I'll take a look. I'll go under the window then take a peek, looking back into the main part of the barn. Keep your eyes and gun pointed at the house. You never know if these people are only cookers or paranoid tweakers too."

I nodded and kept a vigilant watch on the farmhouse. It stood about fifty yards in front of us. I whispered into my shoulder radio and asked Donnelly how it was going on their side.

"So far, so good, Jade. We haven't seen any movement yet, and we're approaching a window now."

"Jack is taking a look on our side. Hold off until I get back to you."

"Roger that. We'll sit tight."

Jack scurried under the window in front of us. I nodded and kept my gun drawn at the house, my eyes darting from the farthest left window to the back door. That was all I could see of the house without stepping out into the open. Jack stood alongside the rotting frame of the barn window and moved his face slowly closer to the dirty glass panes. He peeked in then quickly pulled back.

"Okay, there are a handful of people inside that I can see, and they're definitely cooking. Chances of them having guns are slim. They'd probably blow themselves up if somebody shot a weapon."

"Well, the same goes for us. Let's get out of here. We have the proof we need. We'll hand this off to the local DEA and let them close shop here and track down the big boys."

"Yeah, tell Silver and Donnelly we're moving out."

We knelt down along the barn, and I called Donnelly

again on my shoulder mic. "Jack saw a handful of people in the barn, and they were definitely cooking. Are you guys able to get a few shots of the dump site with your cell phones?"

"Yeah, I think so," he whispered. "It's just past the pile of rocks, I'd say not more than thirty feet from us."

"Be careful. There isn't any cover between the barn and the house. Get a few images if you can for proof, then head up the hill. It's time to go."

"Okay, that works for us. See you in a few minutes."

Jack and I stood and began backing up, still hugging the side of the barn. A noise came from the house. Jack raised his hand for me to hang tight. He inched forward to take a peek around the corner. I heard the screen door open and slam closed.

"Shit, somebody must have seen us. They let the dogs out, and they're coming this way."

I heard the barking getting closer to where we stood. "What should we do? There's no place to hide."

"Run for the milk house, Jade. It's the only place to take cover."

"We can't. The safest place is here against the barn. If the people inside the house are armed, we'd be sitting ducks out in the open like that. They won't take the chance of shooting up their meth lab. If the dogs attack, we'll have to give them a hard kick. That might scare them off. If not, they're going to get one between the eyes. Come on. Let's make a run for it. Try to stay behind the barn."

We ran as fast as we could. We stayed low and zigzagged

when the gunfire started. The rise and tree line were still fifty yards away. I looked up and saw Donnelly and Silver cresting the hill. I knew they were safe. Gunshots sounded behind and around us. They were dangerously close. Donnelly and Silver returned fire, trying to give us a chance to reach cover.

The sudden pressure threw me forward and knocked me to the ground. I grunted as my face slammed into the dirt.

"Jade! Son of a bitch, you're hit."

I couldn't speak for a minute. The wind was knocked out of me. Jack crouched low and ran to my side.

"Thank God, they only hit your vest! Holy shit, brace yourself."

My lungs finally filled with air, and I screamed out when one of the dogs reached me and grabbed my ankle. It sank its teeth into my leg and shook it violently. Jack leaped up and gave the dog a strong kick to the head. It yelped and backed off, giving Jack just enough time to pull me away. He shot at the ground next to it, and both dogs ran back toward the house.

"Jade, can you stand? We have to run. We've got to get to that ridge."

I was still writhing in pain but nodded.

Bullets sprayed around us and hit the ground not more than a few feet away. Dirt clods exploded like land mines. The shots were likely from multiple shooters, but the return fire from Donnelly and Silver was even more intense. We needed to get over the rise and behind the tree cover to safety.

I saw Silver crouch and run toward us. We were only twenty yards from the ridge. Donnelly continued the rapid-fire shots at the house. Aaron grabbed my right arm, Jack had my left, and they pulled me over the hill.

Jack ran for our cruiser parked back on the path and pulled it closer to where we were stationed. He jumped out and helped me as I hopped to the car, blood dripping off my foot. Jack found the first aid kit, then he pulled my shoe and sock off to assess the damage. He shook his head and wrapped my bleeding ankle tightly with gauze and an ACE bandage.

"Jade, I want you to lie down in the backseat and stay put. Call for backup. I have to help Donnelly and Silver." The radio crackled as he handed it to me. "Tell Clark we need assistance ASAP. Let him know you're injured and we're taking on gunfire."

"Jack, wait. Take my gun. You'll need it."

He grabbed it and nodded a thanks. I watched as Jack ducked down and ran back to the ridge. I made the call to dispatch. "Jan, we're taking on live rounds, and we don't have much ammo left. I was hit in the back of the vest, my ribs may be injured, and a dog got my ankle pretty good. Tell the boss we need backup, now. I think teargas is the only way to get those people out of the house and barn. I have no idea how many individuals we're dealing with. Clark knows the location on Granville. We're in the field on a ridge behind the barn."

"I'm on it, Jade. I'm dispatching an ambulance too. I'll have someone at your location in less than ten minutes.

Don't be surprised if the lieutenant shows up with a SWAT team. Stay safe."

I clicked off the radio and closed my eyes. My ribs ached, my ankle throbbed, and all I could hear was gunfire. The sound of sirens approaching and people yelling filled my head—then silence.

Chapter 37

I opened my eyes and saw Amber and my mom sitting in two chairs next to a bed that I was lying in.

"What the heck? Where am I?"

"You're in the hospital, Jade. How are you feeling?" Amber asked.

"I don't know—I'm groggy. I feel like I'm doped up."

My mom wiped her eyes. "Yeah, that's because you are. You were coughing up blood. Apparently your ribs and lungs are bruised from the impact of the bullet that hit your vest. You also have fourteen stitches around your right ankle. Your shoulder might be sore too. You were given a tetanus shot because of the dog bite. Honey, you're lucky to be alive."

I gave her a weak smile. "But I am, Mom, and that's what counts." I groaned at the flash of images coming back to me. "What happened at the farm? How are Jack, Donnelly, and Silver?"

I looked at the door and saw Jack standing in the hallway beyond the glass. He was smiling at me. I waved him in.

"Jack, thank God you're okay. How is everyone else? What happened? Mom, Amber, can you give us a few minutes?"

"Sure, Sis. Come on, Mom. Let's grab a snack in the cafeteria."

I watched as they walked out and closed the door behind them. "Jack, what happened?"

He pulled the chair closer to the bed and reached for my hand. "You blacked out, partner, but we got the bad guys. I'm so thankful you're going to be all right. The doctor wants to keep you overnight for observation, then you'll be released tomorrow. Light duty only, he said." Jack laughed. "Apparently that doctor doesn't know you well. I'm pretty sure Clark is going to make you stay in the bull pen for the rest of the week. He reminded you of how messy all of our desks are, but I have a feeling you don't remember talking to him."

"He wouldn't dare do that to me!"

Jack chuckled. "Anyway, you're going to be wearing an elastic band around your ribs for a while, and you might have to wear a boot. Your foot is stitched and bandaged, and I doubt if your shoe is going to fit."

I pulled the blanket back and looked at my right foot. It was wrapped so much that it resembled a club. All I could see were my toes. "Shit, that mutt must have got me good. I'm glad it's my right foot, though."

"Yeah, why's that?"

"How could I push the clutch in if it was my left foot? Okay, so fill me in."

He smirked. "You never take a break, do you, Monroe?"

I pushed the button to raise the back of my bed, then I winced. My ribs hurt. "So, what happened?"

"The ambulance, Clark, Billings, Clayton, two more deputies, and a SWAT team showed up. They needed the tactical team to clear the buildings. They threw teargas grenades in the house and barn. After it was all said and done, there were seven people in the barn and nine in the house. They had quite the operation going on—it was the real deal, Jade. We couldn't have corralled them ourselves with just our service weapons and one extra magazine each. Two guys came out of the house injured. We're assuming they were the ones firing on us. Between the fingerprints on the guns that were seized and the slug we pulled out of your vest, we'll figure out who was shooting at us. They'll get extra charges filed against them for shooting at law enforcement officers. They'll be lucky if they ever see the light of day again."

I nodded and squeezed Jack's hand. "You saved me, Jack. You and Silver got me to safety. I'm so thankful to both of you."

He smiled at me. "No sweat. That's how we roll."

I weakly punched his arm.

"Whoa… careful there, woman."

"Whatever… then what happened?"

"And then Clark called the local DEA division. They took over the scene. With any luck, the meth cookers in our area are going to be a thing of the past. It's a good possibility, thanks to the number of people arrested, that somebody is going to start singing and pointing fingers at the big players."

"That's good, but we made quite a mess of the day, didn't we?"

"Not at all, and I don't even want you to think like that. We got a bunch of drug pushers off the street and out of our county. It was a good day, except for the part where you got hurt."

"I'll be okay in a few days. We have a lot to do, Jack, and I don't have time to be lying around having a pity party for myself. We have some serious bad guys to take down."

"We will, but for tonight and the next few days, you're going to take it easy." Jack kissed my forehead. "Get some rest and call me when the doctor releases you tomorrow. I'll pick you up."

"You sure?"

"Absolutely. I know you'd head to the station anyway, and I'm not about to let you drive yet." He started for the door.

I smiled. "Hey, Jack."

He turned back toward me. "Yeah?"

"Can you hand me the remote?"

He shook his head, then he handed me the TV remote. "You're something, you know that? Have a good night, partner. Oh and by the way, I took care of everything with Charlene Orth and transporting Reanne's body to Grand Forks. Jason and Lena have it all under control."

"Thanks, Jack." I watched him walk out and close the door behind him.

Chapter 38

He yelled down the stairs, "Is she ready to go?" Jeremy looked at his watch and paced back and forth in the kitchen. They needed to be on the south side of Milwaukee in just over an hour.

Matt answered from the basement, "Yeah, back the van up to the cellar doors. We're coming out that way."

Jeremy went outside and moved the newly painted van. He unlocked the outer wooden cellar doors and let them bang against the ground. He opened the back doors of the van and noticed the paint was still a little tacky in some spots. He reminded himself not to lean against the vehicle.

Matt grunted as he climbed the stairs with Gina tossed over his shoulder.

"What the hell? You gave her a dose?" Frown lines creased Jeremy's forehead.

"Don't worry about it. It was just a small amount. This bitch is way too feisty to sit in a cage in the back of the van for forty-five minutes. She'd be screaming the entire way."

"Yeah, you're right. Watch the van. It isn't completely

dry. Too humid today, I guess."

Matt nodded and shoved Gina into the cage, then he padlocked it. "Let's go." He slammed the cellar doors and locked them. "Do you know how to get to Holler Park?"

"Yeah, it's already programmed into my GPS." Jeremy climbed in behind the steering wheel. Matt rode shotgun and cracked open two bottles of water. He handed one to Jeremy as he turned left out of the driveway.

"What's the guy's name we're meeting at the park?"

"Mr. Johnstone. We're supposed to call him when we're five minutes out. He said he'll be in a red van near the lodge. How long will Gina be out?"

"Not long. I only gave her enough to keep her quiet until we get there. She'll still be groggy when we hand her over, but that's better than her yelling for help. I don't trust that girl."

"Yeah, I hear you." Jeremy rubbed his forehead, recalling the time she kicked him in the head.

They were on the interstate heading south fifteen minutes later.

"We should get an email from Carley's buyer tomorrow, and Liz will be gone by the weekend. Everything is going exactly as we planned, and the bank account is getting fatter by the day."

"Don't forget to list Megan and Jenna on Thursday for their three-day auction." Matt rubbed his hands together. "Those two should do well."

Jeremy grinned at his brother. His smile almost touched the deep dimples situated in the middle of his cheeks.

"That's what I'm counting on."

The clicking of the right blinker told Matt they were getting close. Jeremy checked the side mirrors and pulled over to the far right lane. He exited the freeway onto Layton Avenue at seven fifteen.

"We're almost there." He handed his phone to Matt. "Call Mr. Johnstone's number. Holler Park looks pretty small according to the website, even though it's secluded. We have to know if other people are there."

"Sure thing." Matt hit the green telephone symbol next to Mr. Johnstone's name and waited. "It's ringing," he said. "Hello, Mr. Johnstone. We're almost there with your merchandise. I have you on speakerphone."

"Hello, gentlemen. I'm at the park, and so far I'm the only vehicle here. If we make the transfer quickly, I think we'll be fine."

"That sounds good. Do you have something rigged up for transport?" Matt asked.

"A set of chains."

"Good enough. We have a little something extra to give you if you need it. We'll be there in five minutes."

"Very well, and what vehicle am I looking for?"

"A black van," Jeremy said.

Jeremy turned off Layton onto South Sixth Street. The park entrance was just ahead on his left. He checked the surroundings through the windows and mirrors— everything seemed quiet and normal. He pulled in at the green park system sign. Tucked in next to the lodge was a red van. No other vehicle, bicycle, or person was there. The timing was good. Most people were home, finishing off their evening meal, and relaxing in front of the television set. At seven thirty on a weeknight, the park was completely empty.

Jeremy backed the van in next to the other one. The rear doors of both vehicles were nearly on top of the pond behind them. Even if somebody happened by, they wouldn't be able to see what they were up to.

Mr. Johnstone exited his van. Matt and Jeremy did too. Introductions were made, and the three men walked to the back of the vehicles, where they opened the doors. With their heads on swivels, each man checked his surroundings regularly. Matt pulled out the key and unlocked the cage.

"She's coming around. Would you like us to give her another dose or do you want to do it later?"

"Go ahead. It's probably easier while she's still groggy."

Matt agreed and gave Gina another poke with the needle. He instructed Mr. Johnstone to give her only small doses at a time if he wanted to keep her sedated for the trip. Too much at once would do her in permanently.

"I understand."

Matt opened the cage and pulled Gina out by the legs. Jeremy hooked his hands under her arms, and they lifted her to the other van. Mr. Johnstone grabbed the back door and, with a grunt, stepped up on the bumper and pulled himself inside. He fastened the arm and leg chains to Gina and snapped them closed.

"That should do it," he said as he wiped his hands on a rag that was in the back of the van. "Nice doing business with you both. We'll be in touch once I arrive back in San Francisco and Mr. Black has possession of her. I'm sure he'll be pleased."

Matt closed the back doors of both vans and handed Mr. Johnstone the syringe. The men shook hands and parted ways.

"Easy as pie, once again," Jeremy said as he pulled out of the parking lot. "Feel like stopping for dinner somewhere to celebrate another successful transfer?"

"Sure, why not?"

Chapter 39

"Take it easy, Jade."

"I'm not an invalid, for Pete's sake."

"Well, yeah, you sort of are. Anyway, it's hospital protocol. You have to be released in a wheelchair, so just deal with it. Seriously… women."

I shot Jack a dirty look. "I need to get to work."

"That's where we're going. Now let me help you get in the car."

Jack opened the passenger door and pushed the wheelchair as close as possible to the seat. He lifted the footrests and extended his hand to help me up.

"You do know I can do this myself, right?"

"Yeah, I know. I just wanted to be a gentleman, that's all."

I saw the disappointment in his eyes and immediately felt like a jerk. I raised my arm so he could help me into the car.

"Thanks, Jack."

"No problem."

I watched as he closed the door and pushed the wheelchair back into the hospital vestibule. He walked around to the trunk and put the crutches inside, then he opened the driver's door and got in.

"I'm sorry for trying to act tough. I really do appreciate your help, partner."

He smiled. "Did they feed you lunch?"

"Now that you mention it, no, they didn't, and I'm starving. How about Toucan Grill?"

"You sure?"

"Yeah, easy parking and we can sit outside. The sun will feel good, and I'll only have to hobble for fifteen feet. Damn crutches. I hate the things."

Jack pulled out of the hospital's parking lot. We had five minutes of highway driving, then we'd exit on Washington Street. Toucan Grill was just a few blocks away on North Main.

"You won't need them for long. As soon as the initial swelling goes down, you can put pressure on the walking boot. I bet you'll only use them for a few days."

"Good, because we have a lot of door-to-door interviews to do."

"Ja—"

I interrupted, "Don't 'Jade' me, and don't try to talk me out of it. I'm going on the interviews."

Jack huffed and pulled into Toucan's driveway then parked the Charger. He opened his door, got out, and popped the trunk. He came around to my door, opened it, handed me the crutches, and then walked away.

I laughed. "Okay, fine, you can help me a little."

We sat at a picnic table with the sun on our shoulders. It felt good, and the warmth was as soothing as a hot bath. The waitress came out and greeted us. She looked like a high school student, likely working part-time during her summer break. Her blond hair was pulled back in a high ponytail. She reminded me of a younger version of Elise, my yoga instructor, and one of Doug's victims. Her nametag had Emily written across it.

"Hi, Emily. We'll start with two medium iced teas. Give us just a few minutes more on the lunch order," Jack said.

She nodded. "Sure. I'll be right back."

She returned a few minutes later with our beverages, two straws, and two napkins. She took our order then left.

"Hear me out before you interrupt—deal?" Jack said.

"Deal."

"Let's see how your foot feels by Friday. If you can put weight on it with the boot, we'll start the door-to-door interviews. We may have to work on Saturday, but realistically, that's when most people are home. We can hit twenty residences, but if everyone is at work, we'll just have to do it over again anyway. Between now and then, we'll have a group sit-down to remind ourselves of who we think we're looking for, we'll set our area perimeters, map out the grid of the roads and houses and then divide up the area with Clayton and Billings. I'll even touch base with the boys in Wausaukee County and see if they want to get on board. The killer could just as easily have come from their area to dump Reanne right at the county line."

"That sounds logical to me."

Emily brought our burgers and fries out and refilled our glasses of tea. She placed ketchup, mustard, and extra napkins on the table. I thanked her, and she walked away.

"Have there been any leads coming in from the news segments?"

"No… at least nothing legitimate. There are always the idiots who call in phony leads. I've never understood why people do things like that."

"Yeah, who knows? If they had the slightest idea of the pain those families are going through… So, we can get started as soon as we get to the station?"

"Sure, as long as you don't overdo it."

"I won't—I promise."

Chapter 40

"What happened to my car?" I noticed it wasn't in the parking lot when Jack pulled into the station.

"I had Amber pick it up last night and take it back to your house."

"Why?" I looked at Jack suspiciously.

"Do you want your foot to heal sooner or later?"

"Sooner." I put on a fake pout.

"Then you aren't going to drive for a while. When the swelling goes down, you get your car keys back."

"You took my car keys?" I shot darts at him with my eyes.

"Are you serious right now? We need you at work, Jade. If you don't do as the doctor instructed, your recovery will take longer. Don't argue with me. Look at it as being pampered."

"Right, and that's just the type of girl I am, someone who needs pampering." I snickered. "Will you pull up to the front door and help me out of the car?"

We both laughed.

Jack parked the car while I waited at the steps. Figuring out how to maneuver the steps with crutches to get in and out of the sheriff's department would be tricky. I was lucky to have Jack as a partner. He was willing to drive me to work and back home every day, and he'd help me get in and out of the building each morning and night. I'd leave it up to someone else to go upstairs to the jail or down to the coroner's office, crime lab, or tech department for now. I was hopeful that by Friday I'd be walking on my own without assistance, even if it was with a medical boot.

Jack instructed me to put my arm over his shoulder and use the crutch on my left side. He'd be the crutch for my right side. It was either that or be carried in and out of the building. I'd figure it out and fast.

Inside, Jan offered her condolences and welcomed me back as I hobbled around the reception desk with the crutches and entered the bull pen. Jack held the door open as I crossed through. My desk held vases of flowers, and Get Well Soon balloons swayed from four-foot lengths of colorful ribbon. Everyone sat in the bull pen, waiting for me to enter. The table at the back held doughnuts and cookies, and a fresh pot of coffee was ready to be poured.

"You guys are all too sweet. Thanks." I smiled at their thoughtfulness and asked Clayton to put two French crullers and a cookie on a plate and bring it to my desk.

"You got it, Jade."

Clayton filled the plate and poured me a cup of coffee too and delivered both to my desk.

Jack piped up. "Don't get used to it. Remember, you

don't want to be pampered."

"Maybe a few days won't hurt." I took a big bite of the doughnut even though we had just finished lunch.

At one thirty, Clark called a meeting for all of us in the conference room. I hopped down the hall and sat in the first chair I reached when I entered the room. Lieutenant Clark, Jack, Clayton, Billings, Dan, Kyle, Todd, Billy, Jason, Lena and I were in attendance. Clark wanted Lena on board just because she hadn't sat in on any of our meetings yet.

Billings brought the pot of coffee and cups in for everyone.

"Okay, it looks like Friday is our target date to start canvassing neighborhoods. Jade, if your foot isn't up to par to do much walking, we're going to have to take this on without you."

I nodded, and I didn't like it, but I understood. This investigation wasn't about me, and I couldn't make anyone wait until I was ready to join in. Either I was on board to begin on Friday or I wasn't, but I was hoping for the best.

Clark continued, "Everything needs to be planned. So far, other than the woman in Milwaukee who actually witnessed the abduction of Gina Sansone and Carley Donovan and mentioned they were put into a white van by two men, and the woman at Westchase Mall who said the van had Montana plates, which turned out to be stolen, we have nothing." He rubbed his chin. "None of the TV news segments produced viable leads, so we're back to square one. Milwaukee PD hasn't received any additional leads either. Since most of the incidents happened in our jurisdiction, it's up to us to pursue these individuals. Until we have proof that they've moved on, we're going to assume they're still in our area. Okay, the floor is open. Let's start putting this together."

"We need to remind ourselves of the physical and lifestyle description of the suspects," I said. "We probably should have the white board and notebooks and pens for everyone in here."

Clark gave Billings a nod. "Adam, can you get those things for us?"

"Right away, Lieutenant." Billings pushed back his chair and headed to the door.

"Sorry, Billings, I'd do it myself since I'm closest to the door, but I'm kind of incapacitated right now. Catch me next time."

Everyone laughed.

"Okay, I want a graph with a five-mile radius of where Reanne was found. Does anyone have anything to add to that? Do you think five miles is too close, too far? Any ideas, input?"

Jack spoke up. "That sounds like a good start. I think a perp would feel relatively safe dumping a body within five miles of his location."

Clark nodded. "Okay, Todd, you and Billy set that up. Make sure you have the street names and each residence shown on the graph. Once you have it put together, let us see it. If there's nothing additional to include, we'll need a handful of copies. Make sure the copies are large enough to read. These detectives have to be able to see every street name and address clearly. I don't want them doubling back because they missed something."

"Yes, sir, anything else for us?" Billy asked.

"Not that I can think of right now." Clark nodded, and Billy and Todd left the room.

Jason spoke up, "Sir?"

"Jason, go ahead. You've got the floor."

"I think we could assume the perp lives on a farm or at least a residence that isn't near any other homes. With the amount of burn marks, scuffs, and muscle atrophy on Reanne's body, it appears they held her over time. She'd have to scream now and then out of pain, fear, or frustration."

"Good point, Jason." Clark wrote those notes on the white board. "So it's probably safe to say we wouldn't find our perp or perps at a country subdivision. That's especially true now that they have other women."

"They could always back into a garage and close the overhead door to bring the women in the house," I said. "Who would see anything?"

"That's also true, but I believe these guys would want to have more privacy than that. For now we'll focus more on the country homes that have a few acres of empty land around them. God knows there's plenty." Clark reached across the conference table and grabbed the gold thermal carafe. He topped off each of our cups. "What else?"

Clayton spoke up. "What we do know is there are likely two men. They must be strong enough and quick enough to overtake multiple women at a time."

"But the women are subdued," I said.

Clayton ground his fists into his eyes. "Yeah, I forgot."

"We know they must be similar in age to Carley and Gina and possibly attractive. Why would two beautiful girls give them the time of day otherwise? They also know where young people hang out."

"That's right, Jade. Okay, the woman in Milwaukee said she saw two men, possibly with darker hair. They're probably anywhere between twenty and thirty years old. They have, or had, a white van. They know where young people hang out, and they likely aren't from this area. Oh, and they found a way to get Xylazine, but that got us nowhere. These guys are smart and know how to stay under the radar. We have to dig deep, people."

Todd and Billy returned with a large map printed out of the area where Reanne was found. They spread it out across the conference table, closer to me, so I wouldn't have to hobble over to take a look.

"This is what a five-mile radius gives us. Keep in mind, half of this map goes into Wausaukee County since she was found on the county line."

Clark wrung his hands. "Damn it, that's right. Okay, extend our side of the county line to go out ten miles. I realize these guys aren't local and don't give a flying fart about county lines. They probably aren't even aware of the location they dumped Reanne. It was just a quiet country ditch." Clark shook his head. "Go ahead, guys. Sorry about my oversight."

"Speaking of Reanne, she's already on her way back to

Grand Forks, right?" I asked, directing my question at Jason.

"Yep, she should arrive tomorrow morning. We sent along five copies of her death certificate with the driver, just like you asked us to."

"Thanks, Jason. So, what do you guys think of me footing the bill for lunch, excuse the pun, for our jailbirds for the rest of the week? Those two snitches did give us important intel about the meth lab and got nothing in return. They could order lunch off the delivery menu from Jimmy's Quick and Tasty, good through Saturday. It's something anyway."

Clark nodded. "Yeah, go ahead. We'll all pitch in and pay for it."

Todd returned to the conference room, carrying the final draft of the map with a ten-mile radius around the location where Reanne was found. Billy was right behind him.

"How's this?" Todd asked as he and Billy spread the map across the table.

"That's perfect. Okay, go ahead and make seven copies about half scale of this one. You four detectives have two days to get all of your other projects and loose ends wrapped up. This bull pen is going to be running light once you take to the streets. I'll probably have Horbeck and Jamison put in overtime too. Let's go."

Chapter 41

The screams from the basement bounced against the walls and echoed up the stairs. "Somebody get down here, please. We need help."

"What's with the racket down there?" Jeremy asked. He cocked his head toward the door leading to the basement. He and Matt were about to sit down and enjoy a quiet early dinner.

Matt looked over his shoulder and shrugged. He stood at the stove, ready to load up his plate with a Tuesday evening feast.

Scents from the fried chicken wafted throughout the house, and the brothers were hungry. Matt scooped up a large serving of mashed potatoes and poured gravy over the top, and with a slotted spoon, he heaped canned corn from the saucepan onto his plate.

"Dig in, bro. A meal this good shouldn't be left to go cold."

Matt did the cooking in the house. Jeremy was interested only in the amount of money flowing into their joint bank account. He enjoyed the food and appreciated his brother's expertise, but he could live on peanut butter and jelly sandwiches if he had to.

Tomorrow was the day they would be meeting with the buyer's rep for Carley. After dinner, Jeremy intended to go online to see if that final email had come in. The rep would give him further instructions of a time and meeting place in the Milwaukee area to make the transfer.

"Help us." The voice wailed again, irritating Jeremy.

"Who the hell is screaming down there?"

"It sounds like Jenna."

Jeremy pushed back his chair, wiped his hands on the napkin, and threw it on the table. "This better be good."

The basement door slammed against the wall so hard it bounced back, almost hitting Jeremy in the face. That only fueled his anger more as he stormed down the stairs. Matt cursed under his breath and followed.

"What the hell is going on? I swear to God, you're all going to get zapped. I was trying to enjoy a little peace and quiet over a nice, relaxing dinner." Jeremy swatted at the light switch on the wall and flicked it on.

Jenna shook the cage wires, her fingers bloodied from trying to get out. "It's Carley. There's something wrong with her. She's puking and having seizures."

Jeremy spun from the sound behind him. Carley was kicking the sides of her cage, almost in a rage. Five strides and he was in front of her pen. His right knee popped when he squatted next to it. Jeremy winced then stared at Carley as her muscles contracted violently. Her eyes had rolled back, and only the whites were visible. Blood ran out of her mouth and smeared on her chin. He moved in closer to get a better look.

"What the hell? Matt, come over here. Have you ever seen anything like this?"

"Hmm... can't say that I have. She looks possessed. She bit her tongue pretty good too."

"She's epileptic," Jenna yelled, snarling at both men.

Jeremy pushed off the floor, wincing again as he rubbed his knee. He grabbed the chair and sat in front of Jenna's cage. "And how would you know that?"

"I work at a doctor's office. I know what epilepsy looks like, and she mentioned being worried about not having her meds. She's having a grand mal seizure. It could kill her, especially without her anti-seizure medicine. Her blood sugar is probably so low it's off the charts. I'm sure she's feverish too."

"Well, what would you suggest, Dr. Jenna?" Jeremy cocked his head and mocked her.

"She needs medication."

"That isn't going to happen. She needs to snap out of it, that's what she needs."

Jeremy got up and pulled an empty cage forward. "Give me a hand, bro. Unlock her pen. We'll put her in a clean cage for now. She can wait to shower until tomorrow before she leaves."

"Do you think it's safe? I don't want to get kicked in the head." Matt leaned down and took a closer look at Carley.

Jeremy waited. "What do you think?"

"It looks like she passed out." Matt unlocked Carley's pen. He dragged her out, pushed her into the clean cage, and locked the padlock behind her.

"What's happening over there?" Liz's voice echoed from around the corner.

"Don't you worry your little head off, Liz. It's nothing you need to be concerned with. Are we done? I'd like to get back to our dinner," Matt said.

"Yeah, looks good to me." Jeremy headed for the stairs.

Jenna sobbed and kicked her cage. "She's going to die if you don't help her."

"Shhh… don't make them mad," Megan said. "Maybe she'll be okay in the morning."

Chapter 42

"No…no…no!"

The wailing startled Jeremy awake. He sat upright in bed and rubbed his eyes. He wondered if he had dreamed the sounds. He thought the clock on his nightstand showed it was six thirty, but he could barely see through the slits of his burning eyes. His room facing west was still dark, and the blinds were tightly closed.

"You stupid jerks, can you hear me? I knew she'd die. I hate you, I hate you. I hope you both rot in hell!"

The shrill screams sounded through the decorative old iron heat registers piped up from the basement. The noise echoed into every upstairs room.

Jeremy's door flew open, and Matt stood there in his boxer shorts.

"What the hell is going on down there?"

"I don't know, but we're about to find out." Jeremy flung the sheet and blanket to the side and climbed out of bed. He slipped on his jeans still lying on the floor from last night. He exited the room and looked back at Matt. "Put something on."

Jeremy ran down the stairs to the main level of the house and flipped on the light in the living room. An ugly seventies-style chandelier hung from the center of the room and came to life. Cage woke, stretched, and jumped off the couch. Adjacent to the living room, just beyond the arched doorway, was the kitchen. Jeremy continued on, not acknowledging the dog who was at his heels. His hand hit the wall switch next to the stove, and the light above the table lit up. Jeremy turned the dimmer dial to brighten the room. He headed for the basement door, which was just to the right of the pantry.

"Cage, stay," Jeremy ordered. He squeezed through the opening and closed the door behind him before the dog had a chance to follow. He took the twelve steps to the lowest level of the house. He was halfway down the stairs when the cool, musty air hit him.

"What the hell is going on?" He sneered at the women as he turned on the light. The window across the room brought in barely enough light to dim their dungeon at best. Jeremy grabbed the cattle prod out of sheer anger as he walked toward the cages.

Jenna screamed and rattled her cage. Megan joined her, and Liz in the darkened corner did too.

"Carley's dead, you son of a bitch. I told you she'd die without her medication. She had already gone too long without it. That's why she had a seizure, you idiot. I wish you were dead. I wish I could kill you! I wish I could kill both of you."

Matt came downstairs and looked at Jeremy. "What happened?"

Jeremy stood next to Carley's cage and stared at her stiffened body. Her eyes were unblinking and her mouth hung open. "She's dead. I guess the seizure did her in. What the hell are we going to do now? She was supposed to be delivered today."

"Let's go upstairs and talk privately." Matt cocked his head toward the stairs.

Jeremy looked at the two remaining girls staring at him with hatred written across their faces. Liz was still making a racket around the corner.

"Shut the hell up, Liz, or you're going to join Carley," Matt yelled.

The room fell quiet, and the brothers went upstairs.

Matt made coffee while Jeremy sat at the table. His hands were folded under his chin; he was deep in thought.

"I have to get in touch with the buyer's agent." He glanced at the clock. "Shit, I have no idea where he's at. He's probably somewhere over the Atlantic right now. The email I got from him last night said he was at the airport in Delhi and was going to leave shortly. He was supposed to arrive in New York around noon." Jeremy ground his fingertips into his head. "All I know from his calculations was that he wants to meet near Mitchell Field at four o'clock. He said he'd call and give me a location when they stopped in New York for fuel."

Matt poured two cups of coffee and carried them over to the table. He pulled the cream out of the refrigerator and a spoon out of the top left drawer. He placed them on the table then plopped down on a chair across from Jeremy with a loud groan.

"Do you think you can reach him, and what would you say?"

"I don't know. He's come a long way, and the last thing I want to do is piss him off. No matter what, we've just lost nine thousand bucks that's already been paid. Either we fix this somehow or we'll have to give them their money back and likely cover expenses too." The cup bounced, and the coffee splashed out when Jeremy pounded his fist on the table.

"How about replacing Carley with Jenna? She has dark hair, and they were close to the same size and age."

"Yeah, but they didn't look alike."

"So what? Jenna would have sold for more than Carley did. That's like giving the guy in India a bonus. They'll get a better-looking babe, they won't be mad, and we'll skate by."

"True, but we'll still be short the value of one girl."

"Bro, there's plenty more where that came from. Once we get to Vegas, we can cherry-pick from the best of the best."

"Yeah, you might have a point." Jeremy grabbed a banana out of the bowl on the counter then sat back down. He peeled it as he thought about Matt's idea. "It's probably the only thing we can do. I'll be honest with the guy and tell him what happened. Full disclosure, you know. It will keep us honest."

"Where are you going?" Matt stood.

"Downstairs to send an email to the rep—hopefully he'll read it before he arrives in Milwaukee. Surprising him will only make us look sketchy. After that, we have another hole to dig. Beth is going to get herself a roommate. Go ahead and get the shovels ready. Bring the wheelbarrow up to the cellar doors too."

Chapter 43

I thanked Mom for dropping me off before work and took a seat in the doctor's office. Soothing music played on a loop, and a home improvement show was on the TV in the corner near the ceiling. I would like to have heard what the twin brothers suggested to a family that wanted to update their house, but the volume was muted, and the closed captions moved across the screen so quickly I didn't have time to read what was said.

My name was called, and I hobbled with my crutches across the waiting room. I promised Jack I'd call when my appointment was over so he could pick me up.

"Right this way, Jade," the nurse said as I followed her to an exam room. "Have a seat."

I sat and waited for her to begin the preliminary exam. Lisa, the nurse, took my blood pressure, pulse, and temperature. She patted the paper-covered exam table and told me to take a seat. She helped me up. With the cold stethoscope against my back, she said to take a few deep breaths. It still hurt to do that. She did mention that she didn't hear any gurgling—a good thing, I guessed. Lisa gingerly removed the bandages from my foot and gave the stitches a long look, turned my foot slightly to the right and left, and commented on the bruising. She took a seat on the short, backless roller chair and scooted it up to the computer screen and began typing. On the screen, she entered my name, birthdate, and medications I used in my personal medical file, even though that information had been taken several days ago at the hospital. The doctor and hospital all had the same records since it was one gigantic network. I went along with it since I understood protocol.

She clicked off the screen and pushed the chair back. Lisa stood, smiled, and said the doctor would be in shortly. I hated sitting there with nothing to do so I pulled out my cell phone and texted Amber. I apologized again for not being able to join her at the gun range last night. I mentioned seeing the paper target she'd left on the kitchen table and commented on how well she did. I was proud of her.

Footsteps sounded in the hallway, and the doorknob turned. I put my phone away as the doctor walked into the exam room.

"Good morning, Jade."

"Morning, Dr. Dumont."

He sat on the same roller chair Lisa had used and scooted it up to my foot.

"Let's take a look."

He turned my foot left and right and flexed it up and down. "You're lucky, you know."

"Really, how's that?" I hadn't imagined getting my foot half chewed off as being something lucky.

"That dog missed your Achilles tendon. That particular tendon connects your calf muscle to your heel bone and is used when you walk, jump, and run. The stitches look dry and clean, which is good, but the swelling and bruising may take another week to go away. I still want you on light duty for a while, but I think the boot can replace the crutches if you're ready to try putting weight on that foot."

"Yeah, let's give it a shot. I'm not a fan of crutches at all."

The doctor put a clean gauze bandage on my foot and wrapped it so it looked like a club again.

"The wrapping is just to protect your foot from being bumped or getting dirty. The boot will feel more comfortable with the extra padding too."

I nodded.

He slipped the boot onto my foot then pulled the Velcro straps snug.

"Okay, stand up and put normal pressure on that foot. Tell me how it feels."

The doctor helped me off the exam table, and I stood without the help of the crutches. I looked at him and grinned.

"It isn't bad. I think I can do this—anything to get rid of the crutches."

"Okay, but I'm trusting you to take it easy, understand?"

"Yes, Dr. Dumont. I'll behave."

"Fine." He smiled and shook my hand. "I'll send Lisa

back in to set up your appointment in ten days to have the stitches removed."

"Thank you."

I watched him exit as Lisa entered. We set the next appointment, and she told me to keep the crutches. They would come in handy whenever I wanted to give my foot a rest.

In the waiting room, I texted Jack to come and pick me up, then I went back to watching home improvement shows on TV.

Ten minutes later, the front door opened, and Jack walked in.

"Ready, partner?"

"You bet."

I handed Jack the crutches, and I pushed off the chair. It took a second to steady myself on both feet with equal pressure. Jack stood with his hand out, ready to catch me if I fell.

I grinned. "I got this."

"Okay." He opened the door, and I carefully walked out to the car on my own accord.

Jack closed my door and put the crutches in the trunk. He climbed in and glanced my way.

"Don't think this means you're going to run a marathon anytime soon. No driving yet either."

"Who are you, the assistant doctor?"

"Yeah, that's exactly who I am. Today and tomorrow are office days for all of us anyway unless something urgent comes up. I'll keep my fingers crossed that nothing does."

Chapter 44

"Okay, the email is sent, so I'll have to check for a response from Mr. Patel every now and then. Hopefully, his boss will be okay with the switch. I wouldn't be surprised if he wants a photo of Jenna to see what she looks like first. Let's get that out of the way just in case."

Matt set down his glass of juice and rose from the table. "There's no time like the present. Let's just do it now."

Jeremy grabbed his cell phone and followed Matt to the basement.

"Jenna, front and center, you're having a few pictures taken. What do you think, just a head shot for now?"

Matt stared at Jenna with his head cocked to the right and his fists jammed deep in his front pockets. "Yeah. If they ask for more, we'll clean her up later. We have to get rid of Carley first before she starts stinking."

"Good enough. Open the cage."

As Jeremy stepped into the bathroom, Matt knelt and unlocked Jenna's cage. They didn't allow her out, but when Jeremy returned, he had the hairbrush with him.

"Here, fix your hair so you don't look like a mess." He handed the brush to Jenna, and she ran it through her hair. Jeremy snapped five pictures of her, three from the front and two from the side. "Good enough for now. Toss a bottle of water in there for her so we don't have to open the cage again."

Matt nodded and gave her water, then he locked the gate.

Jeremy emailed the photos of Jenna to Mr. Patel then dropped his phone into his pocket. He raked his fingers through his hair as if he were deep in thought.

"What's up?" Matt asked.

"I'm just trying to think of the best way to do this. The wheelbarrow and shovels are outside by the cellar doors?"

"Yeah, they're ready to go."

Jeremy shook his head in disgust. "Fine, let's just get it over with. Go open the outer doors and come back down. I'll pull her out of the cage, then we'll carry her out."

Matt returned to the basement a few minutes later. Jeremy had already pulled her out of the cage, and she lay on the floor, stiff, blue, and with her lifeless eyes wide open. Lividity had marked her backside with imprints of the cage.

"I swear I'm going to puke." Gagging sounds involuntarily erupted from Matt's mouth as he grabbed her legs. Jeremy hooked his forearms in her armpits and lifted her.

"Come on. Let's go."

The heavy thud of her body hitting the metal wheelbarrow was a welcome relief. The worst part was over.

"Beth needs some company," Jeremy said as he picked up the shovels.

Matt pushed the wheelbarrow around the barn and behind the stone fence. He hit a few bumps and downed branches as he struggled to get her back through the woods to the area of Beth's grave.

"This looks about right." Jeremy noticed the somewhat visible mound that he had tried to flatten out with the shovel. "I'm not digging for long. It's too damn hot outside. Three feet is deep enough, and we can't get too close to Beth, either. If we do, we'll stir up her rotting, stinking body. Start digging at least ten feet away." With the back of his hand, he wiped his forehead, then he punched the shovel's pointed scoop through the dirt.

"Okay, dump her in," Jeremy said.

By nine thirty, the hole had been dug deep enough for their liking, and Carley was going in the ground. Matt lifted the wooden handles of the wheelbarrow, tipping the front downward. They watched as she slid and fell into the hole.

"Damn it." Matt groaned and climbed into the hole. Carley's position was off. She needed to be turned on her side or her stiff arm would be sticking out. "Can you give me a hand?" He looked at Jeremy standing above him, his arms tightly crossed.

"Stupid bitch." Jeremy held the end of the shovel for support and jumped into the hole. His bad knee was acting up.

They turned her body so she was completely sideways, then they climbed out and filled the hole with dirt. Jeremy sank down in the shade of a tree and checked his cell phone to see if there was a message from Mr. Patel.

"Here we go. This had better be good." He pressed a few buttons until the email message opened. He read it silently then breathed a sigh of relief. "Thank God, they're going ahead with Jenna. The new owner likes the way she looks. All is well, bro, and the transfer is going forward. We're meeting him at four o'clock, get this, at the Woodfield Cemetery. That's different, but quiet and secluded. I doubt if the dead people will mind. He says he'll be in a blue Explorer."

That afternoon, the brothers pulled Jenna out of her cage and gave her instructions. A freshly washed outfit on a plastic hanger was handed to her as she entered the bathroom.

"I want you to wash your hair and scrub that body good. Use the makeup on the back of the toilet tank. You need to pretty yourself up a bit. You can even take a toothbrush along. It's a long flight to India." Jeremy wiped the tear running down her cheek and flicked it. "You'll be fine, Jenna. Consider this a great adventure. Who knows, you could have gone to somebody in a boring Midwest farm community. Oh, that's right, you already live in one." He grinned and smacked her butt. "Now get busy—you have fifteen minutes." Jeremy locked the bathroom door behind her.

Shade from the large oak tree next to the house cooled the yard and brought welcome relief. The brothers sat outside, each guzzling a frosty can of beer. White ribbed wife-beaters and baggy cargo shorts were the attire for the day. They'd clean up and change clothes before the trip to Milwaukee. Cage lay panting on the grass next to them. A stainless steel bowl filled with water from the hose sat at his side. The well water at the farm was tasty and icy cold.

"Not a bad few months, brother. Liz will be in Tennessee soon, then all we'll have left is Megan. Getting her sold should be easy."

With careful precision, he lined up the blade of grass just right between his thumbs and blew on his knuckles. Whistling sounds made them both laugh. "I wasn't sure I could still do that." Jeremy chuckled with memories.

"Yeah, we had some fun as kids, fishing at the pond and swinging on that rope. Remember when I brought that frog home and forgot to take it out of my pocket?"

They laughed for a brief moment.

"Yeah, until Mom told Dad about it and he beat the shit out of you and—"

Matt interrupted the dark place where Jeremy's mind was heading. "Let's not go there, bro. I just hope that bastard dies in prison." Matt went momentarily silent while he busied himself pulling clover out of the grass. "Did you buy gas for the lawn mower?"

"It's in the barn." Jeremy looked over his shoulder at the black outline on the lawn from where they'd spray-painted the van. "Yeah, we need to get rid of that outline. We'll take care of it tomorrow." He scanned the yard. "Humph… the grass does need cutting. I guess we've had other things on our minds."

Chapter 45

"I'm ready to get started, and I'm not talking about cleaning the bull pen either. I think by tomorrow I can ride along for our door-to-door interviews. It isn't that much work to walk from the cruiser to somebody's front door, and I'd probably be walking that much anyway right here at work."

Clark gave me a frown and rubbed the side of his nose.

"Come on, boss. Look around. We've cleaned our desks already. Yours doesn't look bad either. Why wait an extra day to get started if we don't have to?"

"What did the doctor tell you? And don't lie to me." Clark sat down opposite me and stared in my face. I grinned.

"She's ready to tell a lie. I can see it. Every time she hands someone a line of bs, she smiles. Her face is turning red too."

"Really, Jack? Can you put a lid on it and mind your own business? Come on, Lieutenant. I promise I won't overdo it. We can extend the interviews over three or four days and be really thorough. You're going to hate me if I have to sit at my desk for two more days. It'll drive you nuts."

Clark jerked his head toward me. "Let me see you walk around the room."

"You mean right now?"

"Uh-huh, right now."

I pushed back my chair and stood. Everyone was staring at me. "Wow... you really know how to put me on the spot."

"Jade, you aren't going in the field unless you're capable."

I walked slowly around the bull pen and gradually put a little weight on my right foot. It hurt, but I wasn't about to admit it.

"See, I can do it. I promise, it will only be from the car to the houses and back to the car."

"Fine, but Jack's in charge. Jack, if she misbehaves, bring her back. She'll be sitting it out right here at her desk."

I felt like giving Clark a hug, but I didn't want to press my luck. A simple thank-you would suffice.

"All right, you guys, let's divide up the county and get started," I said.

"You can get everything ready today. The interviews won't begin until tomorrow. Got it?"

"Yes, sir, I got it."

That afternoon, Jack, Billings, Clayton, and I laid out on the lunchroom table the map that Todd had put together for us.

"Jack and I can take the top quarter of the county north

of Highway 60 and Wayfair Road for the first day or so. You guys can mirror that same layout south of Highway 60. On Friday we'll do the same at Division Road. If we cover a little over three miles each day, we'll have our radius taken care of by Saturday afternoon." I looked at each detective, waiting for a nod as an acknowledgment.

Jack spoke up first. "Are you sure you're ready, Jade?"

"I'm more than ready. I'll take along some ibuprofen and a bottle of water if I have to. No big deal."

Clayton nodded. "Let's do it, then. We'll finalize our plans and head out after the morning powwow with Clark."

The lieutenant rounded the corner and entered the lunchroom. "Did I just hear my name mentioned?"

"Yes, sir, Lieutenant. We've put together our interview grid and plan to start up after our morning meeting."

"Show me your search strategy." Clark leaned over the map on the table.

Jack took over and pointed out the search and interview grid we were going to cover each day. "If we narrow down a particular area that seems promising, we'll base our focus there."

"Okay." Clark checked the time above the door. "Why don't you guys call it a day? The bull pen is clean, you have a strategy for tomorrow, and I've already called Jamison and Horbeck. They know for the next few days they're going to be pulling overtime. So are a few of the deputies."

The four of us left and headed to the parking lot. I limped, but I was getting faster at it. I climbed into the passenger seat of Jack's Charger and closed the door, then I waved to Clayton and Billings through the window.

"Can I have my car keys back now?" I stared at Jack, waiting for a response.

"How are you going to drive with that boot on your foot? Look how big it is."

"If there's a will, there's a way. I'll practice when we get to my house. You can even ride along and see for yourself if it seems safe."

"Do you have any beer?"

"Yes, I have beer."

Chapter 46

Matt looked at the GPS on Jeremy's phone. "We should see the cemetery coming up on the right in a few blocks." He turned in his seat and looked over his left shoulder. Jenna sat quietly in the locked cage at the back of the van.

She had been given the same choices Melanie had a week back. She would either sit quietly, get zapped every time she made a fuss, or get the needle. Jenna chose to sit quietly.

"I'm impressed," Matt said as he rearranged himself in his seat and faced forward again.

"About what?"

"She's accepting her fate pretty well. Hell, I wouldn't want to end up in India. No thanks, too many rats."

Jeremy spoke quietly, "Until she's out of our possession, we have to watch her closely, especially when the transfer takes place. We may want to zap her before that."

Matt pointed to the right. "This is it."

Jeremy clicked his blinker and turned in. The cemetery sign was flanked by stone pillars, each holding a coach lamp at the top. Woodfield Cemetery didn't appear large, but it was heavily wooded and had a long gravel driveway. They passed the maintenance building, which sat along a path that veered off to the left. Mr. Patel had mentioned he would be at the farthest end of the cemetery near the back fence. Beyond that, according to Google satellite images, were a nature preserve and a marshy pond.

"That's got to be him," Jeremy said. He jerked his chin toward a vehicle parked farther down the driveway.

"Yep, it looks like a blue Explorer." Matt reached for the cattle prod under the seat. He'd have it ready when they opened the back of the van.

Jeremy slowed at the end of the driveway and pulled up alongside the Explorer. A man looking to be of Indian ethnicity sat behind the steering wheel. He glanced over and nodded. All three men exited their vehicles and introduced themselves. They walked to the back doors of the van, where Jeremy reached for the handles and pulled them open. Jenna sat quietly, wide eyed and trembling.

"She's very beautiful." Mr. Patel leaned in closely and looked her over. "Yes, Mr. Kumar will be pleased, even more than with the other girl. Sorry to hear of her untimely death."

Jeremy nodded. "Yeah, sometimes bad things happen. Anyway, here she is. How do you want to do this? Do you have restraints?"

"You mentioned a drug in your email."

Matt pulled the syringe out of his pocket. "Here it is. Xylazine—are you familiar with it?"

"Aah… yes, we've used that before when it became

necessary. I think it would be in everyone's best interest if you went ahead with that. I don't have any type of containment for her until we're on the jet."

"No problem. Jenna, do you want the prod first or just the needle? You're going to get the needle anyway," Matt said.

Jeremy zapped her as she sobbed into her shaking hands. "Better to just get that over with when she isn't looking." He opened the cage and sank the needle into her neck. There, she's good to go. We'll help you load her up."

The three men lifted Jenna and placed her unconscious body into the back of the Explorer.

"Nice doing business with you," Jeremy said. He handed Mr. Patel the syringe with the remaining Xylazine. He and Matt climbed into the van and watched as the Explorer drove away, creating a wake of dust particles from the driveway.

Chapter 47

I woke up, excited to get to work. We would finally begin our door-to-door interviews.

Over the last few days, I'd given myself an extra half hour to get showered and dressed. The doctor had instructed me to keep my foot dry, so I had to wrap it in plastic bags every time I showered. With my car keys back in my possession, I definitely felt as though I was making progress. Jack involuntarily returned my keys after listening to more pleading than he wanted to. I had to prove to him that I was capable of driving my own vehicle. Pressing the gas and brake pedals didn't hurt. It was just that the large boot was clumsy to drive with. Nonetheless, I was thankful to be back behind the wheel, and I'd make it work. No complaints would come from me.

Wearing my cozy fleece bathrobe, I walked down the hallway, intending to grab a cup of coffee then get dressed. An unusual sound caught my ear as I came around the corner.

"You startled me, Sis. Why are you up so early?"

Amber sat in the kitchen, wearing her flannel pj's and tapping her fingertips on the wooden tabletop.

I did a little shudder and cinched the belt of my robe tighter. The early morning air felt cool with the patio doors open. I reached in the upper cabinet for a coffee mug.

"Morning, Sis. Joey asked me if I wanted to go full-time for the rest of the summer. Would you mind? I really need to save as much money as possible before school starts in the fall. I'm sure I'll be cutting back on my hours then."

I pulled out a chair and sat at the table next to her. The steam wafted off my mug when I blew on my coffee and took a sip. "I understand, hon, and no, I don't mind. School is important, and earning money is too. Hell, look how much I'm gone at the job, and you haven't complained once. I appreciate it, Amber. Things will get easier once you're settled in with your classes in the fall and when people stop getting murdered and kidnapped around here." I smiled at her. "I'm so proud of you." I got up and filled both of our cups. "Let's call Dad tonight and talk to him. He's due to come and visit, especially since we have a new house."

Amber perked up. "Yeah, that sounds good. I'll pick up Chicken Almond Ding and pot stickers for dinner."

"Yum, I can't wait." I carried my coffee down the hall, hoping I wouldn't spill any.

Amber called out after me. "Gimpy."

I heard her giggle as I walked away.

An hour later as I passed the bank next door to the courthouse, I checked the time. I looked at that clock every day out of habit. I always made sure the time on the clock on the bank matched the one in my car. I turned left onto Schmidt Road at eight a.m. and pulled into the parking lot. Other than Clark, I was the first person to arrive from our team, as usual. There was no need to sit at my desk earlier than eight o'clock since the guys rarely did. Our desks were cleaned yesterday, and I was pretty proud at how organized the bull pen actually looked.

One by one they entered, with Clayton last. We went over a few minor details, grabbed our maps, and promised Clark we'd check in if anything important popped.

The lieutenant yelled out to me not to overdo it as we exited the bull pen through the gray steel door. Jack and Clayton each grabbed a set of cruiser keys.

"Geez, he sounds like my dad."

"Clark cares about you, partner, just like the rest of us do."

"Aww…shucks." I held the handrail as I gingerly took the steps down to the parking lot.

"You're a brat, Jade—just saying."

"And I love you too."

Since we had no idea of what we would find or who we would be speaking with, all of us wore exposed service weapons, and our badges were visible on chains around our necks. It was also protocol to keep vests in the trunk. We never knew when a circumstance would arise where they'd be needed.

The four of us climbed into two unmarked black cruisers that were parked in assigned spaces next to each other. Jack got in behind the wheel, and I climbed into the passenger seat and buckled up. He led the way out of town. At the farthest end of the city limits, a gas station with an attached submarine sandwich shop sat on the right side of the road.

"What do you think of that place for lunch?" I asked as Jack sped by. "It shouldn't be more than a ten-minute drive back this way from our locations. We can compare notes with Clayton and Billings then."

"Yeah, sounds good. Give them a call to meet us there at noon if they aren't in the middle of interviews."

I called Billings and told him the plan.

At Wayfair and Highway 60, we turned left and drove the three miles to where Reanne was found. At that spot, we split off from Billings and Clayton. We'd head north, and they would go south.

Following a planned grid of the roads north to south and east to west made the most sense. We'd end the day just east of Division, a north-to-south road. We'd pick up the same pattern tomorrow, starting from the point where we left off. I'd check off every house we went to, make a note of whether anyone was home and whether we actually interviewed someone or not. We didn't want to miss speaking to anybody. If we had to go back a second time, we would.

I pulled out the map and led the way. Deputies had already conducted face-to-face interviews at several houses on Wayfair on the day we found Reanne. Because we were following a precise grid, we'd interview everyone again, even if it was the second time around.

"You know, Jack, this is the best idea. Remember Brad said his grandpa bought their farm in the '60s? Anyone who has lived in this area for a long time is going to be well aware of strangers moving in. There would likely be word among the coffee klatches that a once empty house is now rented out or sold. Checking with Realtors wouldn't be a bad idea either."

Jack nodded. "I agree. That would be a smart thing to do."

I looked at the number of houses in the ten-mile radius marked out on our map. "There really aren't a ton of houses since most of these places are farms. There's more land than buildings."

"Hopefully that will speed our interviews up." Jack pulled into the first driveway on the left and parked.

Even though the families on this road had been interviewed, something might have sparked a recent memory with them because of the news reports. Our questions could ring a bell, especially now that we knew a white van was involved. I pulled myself out of the cruiser and walked alongside Jack to the front door.

An older woman wearing an apron tied around her waist answered the door on our second knock. The look on her face showed how surprised she was at seeing two armed officers standing on her porch. Her suspicion was evident as she peeked out from the barely open screen door. She looked us over carefully before she spoke.

"Can I help you?" she asked as she wiped her hands on the apron and looked down at my foot.

I smiled at her, hoping to ease her concerns. "Hello, ma'am, we're detectives from the Washburn County Sheriff's Department. How are you today?"

"Good." She remained steadfast and didn't open the door any farther.

Jack spoke up, "Ma'am, we're wondering if we can have a minute of your time. We have a few questions about the body that was recently found south of here."

"We already answered questions that day. My husband isn't home, and we don't know any more about it now than we did then. We just make sure to keep our doors locked."

"Ma'am—"

She interrupted me before I got another word out. "The name is Gladys—Gladys and Ralph Knepprath."

I nodded. "Is there any chance that you saw a white van passing by recently, specifically on that day?"

"Can't say that I did, as I'm usually cooking—the kitchen faces the back."

"Mrs. Knepprath, when your husband returns home, would you mind asking him about the white van? If something rings a bell with that, we'd really appreciate a phone call." I handed her our cards, and we said goodbye.

The leather seat squeaked as I slid back into the car and carefully placed my booted foot inside. I wrote down the Knepplaths' names next to the house number on the map. I included a note saying Gladys didn't have anything new to tell us. We moved on to the next residence.

I compared the property we were approaching with the one on the map and made a check mark next to it. "Okay, pull into the driveway on the right," I said. "After this place we'll be turning left and going down the next road."

Jack turned right into the short driveway and pulled up to the garage. The residence was just a country house, not a farm. There wasn't much land to speak of or a barn on the property. We parked and exited the car. A young girl sat cross-legged on the sidewalk that led to the front door. She drew pictures on the cement with pastel chalk.

"Hi, sweetheart, is your mommy or daddy home?"

"Uh-huh." She got up and raced to the screen door. "Mommy, there's two people here."

I smiled at her. "Thank you."

A woman approached and opened the screen door. A towel was draped over her shoulder.

"Hi there, may I help you?"

She looked to be around thirty years old and had white-blond hair, just like the little girl.

"Hello, ma'am, my name is Sergeant Jade Monroe with the Washburn County Sheriff's Department. This is my partner, Detective Jack Steele."

She zeroed in on the badges that hung from our necks then extended her hand.

"If you don't mind, ma'am, we have a few questions for you. We're canvassing the area to gather information about the neighborhood and the residents."

"Is there a problem out here? It seems pretty normal to me, other than that poor—"

I interrupted. "May we?" I didn't want to bring up the dead woman in the ditch in front of her daughter. I motioned toward the picnic table beneath a tree in the side yard.

"Of course, please. I'm sorry, I haven't even introduced myself. My name is Linda Johnson. My little girl is Lucy."

"Are you married, Linda?"

"Sure am." She laughed and looked out in the distance. "My husband, Mike, is a long-haul truck driver. He should actually be back before long. He called about an hour ago and said I should pick him up at the station in town after lunch."

"We won't keep you long, ma'am."

"Oh, no problem, what can I help you with?"

Jack spoke up, and I pulled out my notepad. "I realize the homes are few and far between out here, considering it's mostly farmland, but how well do you know your neighbors?"

"Not that well. The ladies around here are mostly farm wives, late forties or older. We've only lived here for three years. This is our first home."

I could see the pride on her face as she smiled.

"We like the open space and hope to build a pole shed soon where Mike can park his semi. That way he doesn't have to leave it at the station whenever he comes home. We've got two acres here."

"I understand," Jack said. "Do you know of any new people in the area, say in the last few months? Or anyone that drives a white van?"

"No, can't say that I do. The most communication we have with our neighbors is a wave when we drive by if they're outside, and vice versa. As far as vehicles—most are tractors out this way."

We handed her our cards, thanked her, and stood.

"If anything ever seems out of place or unusual for the area, please give us a call."

"Sergeant?"

I turned. "Yes, ma'am?"

"Should I be worried about anything? I mean, Lucy and I are home alone much of the time."

"No, Mrs. Johnson, I don't think so. I'd suggest you be watchful of your surroundings, though, and keep your doors locked at night."

"Maybe we should go inside, honey." With her hand above her eyebrow to shield the sun, Linda scanned the neighboring fields and the road with a concerned look on her face. She took Lucy by the hand and went inside, closing the door behind her. I listened for it and heard the dead bolt turn.

I groaned. "Great, now she's afraid to let her daughter play outside. I don't want to scare people, but we can't get too specific either." We climbed back into the cruiser. "People do have TVs, and I'm sure they can put two and two together." I glanced at Jack then back down at the map, where I crossed off the Johnson residence. The clock on the dashboard showed it was nearing twelve o'clock. "How about two more homes, then we'll break for lunch?" I said.

"Yeah, fine by me. Just lead the way. You have the map."

Nobody at the next two farmhouses answered the doors when we knocked. Tractors in the distance throwing up dust clouds told us the owners of these farms were likely at work—plowing the fields. Others could have been in the barns doing whatever they did in there, but I wasn't going to walk into every building, looking for someone. We'd stick to people that answered their front doors.

We broke for lunch and met up with Billings and Clayton at the submarine sandwich shop. I was surprised at the number of people inside as we entered the restaurant. With an industrial park across the street, I imagined we'd found the lunch spot for most of those people. Clayton snagged the last available booth, and I scooted in to the side against the wall while Jack, Billings, and Clayton went up to the counter to place our orders.

I tore off bits of my sandwich and sipped my iced tea while Billings told us about their progress so far.

"We've gone to six houses but have only talked to four people. It seems like most of them are housewives that don't really spend much time outdoors, unless they're doing something in the garden. Nobody has mentioned seeing or hearing about new people in the area, white vans, or anything unusual beyond Reanne's case."

I leaned in across the booth with my hands folded under my chin as Billings gave us the rundown of their morning. Up to this point, our day wasn't any different.

Jack stretched against the back of the booth and groaned. "I have a feeling these door-to-door interviews are going to be a waste of time."

"It's still something. We can't just sit around and expect the bad guys to come to us. Come on. Let's finish our lunch and get back out there." I ate my sandwich and took my iced tea with me as we headed back to our cruisers. I popped three ibuprofen into my mouth and swallowed them with my tea.

"What's bothering you, your foot or your ribs?" Jack's eyebrows furrowed as he gave me a look of concern. "I can take you back to the station if you want."

"My foot hurts a little, but it's nothing I can't handle. I'll be fine." I looked down at the map and gave Jack directions to the next road on our grid.

The farther out we got from where Reanne was found, the less that people knew anything had taken place.

We reached an intersection with a four-way stop sign. To our right was a train track with a trestle bridge above the river. Six old storefronts stood side by side, dangerously close to the tracks. Across the street, nearly hidden from view, was a fieldstone church. The steeple pierced through the treetops, and a long-forgotten cemetery stood next to it. Many of the limestone grave markers had seen better days. Broken edges and bottoms that were sinking into the ground gave the cemetery a sad, forgotten appearance. Thick grape ivy climbed the wrought-iron gate above the entrance, nearly covering the name—Peaceful Home Cemetery.

"Humph—I'll be darned."

"What?"

"This is Hamilton. I've never been here, but I've read about this little burg. This place is beautiful."

"There's nothing really here, Jade. A couple of rundown, ancient buildings, a bridge over the river, and the railroad tracks. What's so beautiful about it?"

I smirked at Jack's ignorance. "It's historic."

"So, suddenly you're a history buff?"

"I've always been, but I guess we never had a reason to talk about it." I pointed at a building next to the river. "See that place? It looks like an old grist mill." I checked our map again and found Hamilton. "Jack, we're smack in the middle of our grid. See that old timers' bar just beyond the tracks? Looks pretty crowded for one o'clock on a Thursday, doesn't it?"

He looked at the seven cars and two tractors parked out front and shrugged. "I guess so. Why?"

"I bet there are old farmers and longtime residents sitting in there, enjoying a beer and exchanging the latest gossip. Let's go strike up a conversation with them. Somebody has to know something. This *is* their neck of the woods."

"Yeah, okay." Jack pulled into the gravel parking lot that almost reached the front door. That made life easier on me and my throbbing foot.

We got out of the cruiser and stepped over the threshold of the more than one-hundred-year-old establishment. I would have loved to hear stories of the place, but that would have to wait for another time. An old oak bar spanned the length of the room. It looked to be original to the building. Ten barstools, eight of them occupied by patrons, lined the front of the bar. A popcorn machine sat on the back bar, along with dozens of bottles of assorted liquor. Four empty wooden tables on the wide pine-plank floor took up the rest of the room. Several pinball machines that looked to be from the eighties lined the outer walls. Country music played in the background, and every head turned toward us when we crossed the threshold.

I nodded when we walked in. A few farmers nodded back, and others elbowed each other and chuckled.

"Now what did you do, Elton? The law is here." A middle-aged man wearing bib overalls and a baseball cap grinned then laughed out loud.

"I didn't do shit, Bob, but I just might."

They both laughed again.

"Afternoon, officers," the bartender said.

"Do you mind?" I asked as Jack and I took seats on the two empty stools next to the man they called Elton.

"Not one bit," he said, grinning. "I haven't have a pretty girl sitting this close to me since 1998."

I noticed he had a gold front tooth. I grinned back.

"What can I get you?" the bartender asked.

"Two root beers," Jack said.

The bartender nodded. "Coming right up." He wiped the bar top with a wet rag and placed two cardboard coasters in front of us. "What brings you two out this way?"

"Looking for information," I said.

That statement perked up ears, and everyone at the bar looked over their neighbor's shoulder toward us.

"What do you need to know?" Elton asked. "We know everything, so it looks like you came to the right place."

The group chuckled again.

I laughed with them. "Good—that's what I'm counting on."

Over the course of the next hour, we learned more than we cared to about farming, plowing, and milking cows. After gleaning all of that useless information, we did find out a farm had recently sold on Highview Drive, another on Fairfield Lane, and a farm on Division Road had been rented out a few months ago. I gave Jack a look that we both knew well. We were interested in hearing more about the rental.

"Do any of you gentlemen have details about the farm that was rented?" I asked.

"Yep, a bit." The third man down the bar spoke up.

Jack peered around the shoulders of Elton and the man sitting next to him.

"Your name, sir?"

"I'm Leroy Headly. Live just down the road from here." He pointed at the back bar, meaning outside and west of Hamilton.

I wrote that down.

"Could you give us a bit more information?" Jack asked.

I flipped the page in my notepad, ready and waiting for something to pop that would help us.

"Sure can. The farm belongs to old man Miller—John Miller, to be exact. He moved into an assisted living apartment last year in Grafton, after Sarah, his wife, passed on. His farm has been empty for at least a year. Isn't that right, boys?"

They all mumbled and nodded.

"Please, go on," I said then continued writing.

"Joe Laufton owns about seventy acres but wanted more land to plant in corn. He recently inquired about leasing the empty fields, but John's son-in-law told them they had just rented the property out. The tenants wanted the land rights included in the rent."

"That's very interesting. Do any of you know the tenants?"

Leroy glanced down the length of the bar. Everyone shook their heads. "Guess not."

"Okay, then. That information is very helpful, and the farm is on Division?"

Leroy nodded. "Yep, just after the second pond on the east side of the road. Long driveway and empty fields—you can't miss it."

We got directions and descriptions of the sold properties as well. We left our contact information, and by the time Jack and I walked out, we were fast friends with the farmers and bartender at Hamilton Inn Bar and Grill.

We climbed back into the cruiser. I pulled out the map from the door pocket and looked for the roads I had written down in my notepad. I circled each one, and even though we were going off course, I wanted to check them out next. The properties were still within our grid, and the farm on Division definitely piqued our curiosity.

Chapter 48

"The guy from Tennessee should be here in a half hour. After Liz is gone, it's only Megan left, and she's going to get lonely in the basement with nobody to talk to." Jeremy smirked and turned the crank on the handheld can opener. Chicken noodle soup would suffice for now. He carefully pulled off the sharp metal lid and poured the soup into a bowl. After placing it on the glass carousel in the microwave, he set the timer for two minutes and pressed the start button.

Matt chuckled. "Maybe Cage can hang out downstairs and keep her company until she leaves. I'm sure she'll be gone within a week's time. After that, we can start packing. Why are you eating now?"

"Because I'm hungry. As soon as Mr. Adamson leaves, we'll go to town and buy groceries." Jeremy tipped his left arm and looked at his watch. "Liz should be done in the bathroom by now. Want to check on her?"

"Yeah, sure." Matt went downstairs and banged on the bathroom door. "Are you done?"

A meek-sounding yes came from inside the room. He unlocked the door, turned the knob, and pulled it toward him. Liz wore a clean dress, and her hair was shiny and secured with a rubber band at the nape of her neck. Matt gave her back the original pair of shoes she had worn when they kidnapped her months ago.

"Did you brush your teeth?"

"Yes."

"Okay, get back in your box for now. The buyer will be here soon." He pushed Liz forward with the prod touching her back.

She complied and crawled into the cage.

Matt found Jeremy filling out the notebook when he returned to the kitchen. "Last-minute entries?"

"Yeah, just making sure I'm up to date with everything. I have each name, description, the amount they sold for, and where each girl went." He closed the book, crumbled a handful of crackers, and dropped them into his soup. When the temperature was tolerable, he ate it.

The sound of gravel crunching under tires alerted them. Matt ran to the living room window and turned the wand on the blinds. He peered out at the driveway, waiting for the vehicle to get closer. "What kind of car does he have?"

"A green SUV with Tennessee plates."

"Yep, it's him."

Jeremy put his notebook in the drawer and the empty soup bowl in the sink. "Bring her up through the cellar doors. I'll show him where to back up his vehicle. Don't forget the Xylazine." Jeremy went out through the front porch, and the screen door slammed at his back. He directed Mr. Adamson in and had him back up to the cellar doors. With the key in hand, Jeremy unlocked the outer doors and swung them open. They bounced against the dirt.

Jeremy gave Mr. Adamson the once-over when he exited the SUV. He looked to be sixty years old, thin, almost frail, but snarly nonetheless. The few wisps of hair left on his head were tinted a light shade of gray. His clothes looked disheveled. Jeremy chalked that up to a full day of driving and sleeping in his vehicle. The end of the cigarette pinched between his lips glowed orange in the light breeze. He shook Jeremy's hand, made small talk, and waited for Matt to bring Liz up the cellar steps.

"Well, aren't you the pretty one," he said. A wide grin spread across his face when he saw Liz. He looked her up and down slowly. "Oh yeah, I'm going to have a damn good time with you."

Liz spat at him. He slapped her across the face, almost knocking her over.

"Apparently somebody has to teach this bitch who's the boss." He wiped his cheek and grinned. "Feisty little tramp, aren't you?"

Liz glared at Matt and Jeremy. Her face welted bright red. "I hate you. I wish both of you were dead." She turned her head and looked away.

"Okay, then, that's it. Enjoy Tennessee. It's been a riot, Liz," Jeremy said.

Mr. Adamson opened the back doors and shoved her into the cage, then he padlocked it.

"Do you want the Xylazine for the road?" Matt asked.

"Nope, I'm good. I know how to handle these girls. This isn't my first rodeo, young man. I've got a prod inside, and I like to keep them awake. They're a lot more fun when they're conscious." He laughed out loud and slammed the back doors. "Nice meeting you boys." He climbed into the SUV and drove away. His tires kicked up small gravel stones as he exited the driveway and turned left.

"That guy was definitely a freak," Jeremy said.

Matt nodded and cracked his knuckles. "Come on. Let's put a grocery list together and go to the store."

Twenty minutes later, Jeremy and Matt climbed into the van and headed to town. The afternoon sun was right at eye level, causing both of the brothers to squint. Jeremy dropped his visor, rearranged himself in the seat, and put on his sunglasses.

Matt spun in his seat and craned his neck, trying to look out Jeremy's side mirror.

"What the hell are you doing? What did you see?" Jeremy adjusted the mirror and looked back.

"I swear it looked like an unmarked black police car. It had a spotlight next to the outside mirror, and extra antennas. There were two people inside. I wonder what they're doing way out here."

"Don't know, but keep your eyes peeled to make sure they don't turn around."

"I don't think they noticed us behind this milk truck, but I'll keep a close watch. Good thing we painted the van."

Chapter 49

Jack drove up Division Road as I called out the directions. "I think it's the next house on the right. There are empty fields on either side of the driveway, just like Leroy said. This has to be the place. I saw something that looked like a dried-up pond back there."

Jack ducked down and craned his neck, looking through the passenger window as he slowed the cruiser.

"What do you think?" I asked.

Wind gusts blew and kicked up small dust devils in the vacant fields ahead. I watched them spin. Their power mesmerized me. Dust devils, fire devils, and water funnels—the spinning entities were an unusual force of nature, and I considered myself lucky when I saw them.

"Yeah… it's probably the right place."

Jack turned in and drove down the long gravel driveway that took us to a farmhouse in need of a fresh coat of paint. The barn wore a similar appearance. Jack pulled up to the driveway's end, twenty feet from the sidewalk that led to the screened porch. We exited the car and walked across the dusty driveway. I knocked several times when we reached the porch, but nobody answered.

I looked around. "No vehicles. No farm equipment either." I pressed my face against the screen. "There's a pair of dusty work boots next to the front door."

Jack kicked the dirt in the driveway. "At least whoever lives here takes their shoes off before going inside. I see tire-track patterns, and they look fresh. Somebody was here earlier."

I carefully stepped down from the porch to the sidewalk and walked over to the burning barrel. I stuck my nose in and took a deep breath. "This was recently lit. It still smells like smoke." I picked up a foot-long stick and poked at the rubble inside, looking for something, even though I didn't know what.

"Maybe this isn't the right place. It seems more like the kind of homestead that belongs to an elderly farmer and his wife. You know the type—settled in and not wanting for much. The old couple could be in town at a church bingo game or something like that."

"It does belong to an elderly couple—or did, according to Leroy. Old man Miller, remember? And what do you mean, I know the type?" I cocked my head and gave Jack a questioning stare. "I've never talked to a farmer in my life until Brad found Reanne."

"Really? I didn't know you were that sheltered."

I continued to walk the property and turned left at the end of the porch.

"Hey, take a look at this."

Jack rounded the corner just beyond the cellar doors. He stopped, stared, and rubbed his chin.

"Hmm... looks like an outline."

I knelt down and pulled out a few blades of grass. I studied them and rubbed them between my fingers. "Black paint." I backed up and stared at the outline again. "Looks like something about the size of a vehicle. Let's check the barn."

Jack checked the distance then looked at me, his eyebrows furrowed. "You still doing okay with that foot?"

I dismissed his question with a hand wave. "I've been eating ibuprofen all day." I jerked my head toward the barn. "Come on."

Jack yanked hard on the double doors when we reached the building. They creaked and resisted but opened grudgingly.

"Do you see a light switch?" I asked.

"No. I can barely see my own hand, but there isn't a vehicle in here, if that's what we're looking for."

"Should we come back with a warrant or just come back and hope to catch someone at home?"

"No judge is ever going to give us a warrant without probable cause."

"I guess not. This is going to be the first place we come back to tomorrow."

"People do have jobs, Jade. They could be at work."

"Whatever—try the screen door again."

Jack shouldered the barn doors closed, and we walked to the sidewalk for the second time. He gave the screen door a pull—it was unlocked. We entered the porch and gave it a methodical side-to-side once-over—nothing unusual stood out. With his knuckles pressed against the inner door, Jack rapped on the glass. No answer. He slowly turned the knob, but the door was locked.

"Darn it. Where the heck are they?" I asked the rhetorical question not really expecting an answer. "Isn't it too early to go out for dinner?"

Jack spoke up with his typical sarcastic wit, "Not unless they're still at church, enjoying the after-bingo buffet."

I huffed and climbed back into the cruiser. North Bend was fifteen minutes up the highway. I checked my watch—four o'clock.

Billings and Clayton's car was already sitting in the parking lot when we pulled in at the sheriff's department. Either they struck out too or they had something important to report. We went inside. Clayton stood at the coffee station, scooping grounds into the paper filter. He filled the carafe to the top with water. Billings was leaning against the doorway of the lieutenant's office.

Clark lifted his head and set his pen down when we walked in. "Here they are. Let's gather in the bull pen, guys. Hopefully you four have something to report. How's the foot, Monroe?"

"I'm good, boss. Ibuprofen helps." I turned toward Billings as I plopped down at my desk. "You guys just get back?"

"Yeah, five minutes ago."

Everyone sat at their respective desks. The lieutenant

pulled the roller chair out of his office and got comfortable next to me.

"Coffee ready?" Jack asked as he began to stand.

I glanced at the carafe. It was nearly full. "Give it a few more minutes. It will beep."

Clark spoke up, "Okay, you two first." He nodded at Clayton and Billings. "Learn anything, and how many houses did you have time to hit?" He drummed the side of my desk with his knuckles.

Billings answered, "We stopped at six homes and spoke to four residents. Nobody was home at the other two places."

"Okay, not bad. Did anything pop?" Clark leaned back in his chair—it creaked in protest.

Billings absentmindedly rubbed his forehead. "Two families didn't know of anything unusual going on. They said they were longtime residents and were acquainted with everyone in the general area. Nothing out of the ordinary has given them reason to be concerned. One family complained of teenagers' toilet papering their maple trees. The last family had information that sounded interesting. It's on your side of the grid, Jade, so you and Jack are welcome to it."

"Really?" My interest level increased. I leaned forward with my elbows on my desk and my chin resting on my fists. "What did they say?"

"Only that a couple of farms have sold in recent months. It might be something you want to check out."

I exhaled slowly, almost feeling defeated. I was hoping

for something I wasn't already aware of. "Yeah, we heard about them. We're checking them out tomorrow." I opened my notepad that I had tossed on my desk. "Um... on Highview and Fairfield?"

Billings flipped the pages of his notepad until he got to that bit of information. "Yeah, looks like those are the places."

I got up and filled five coffee cups. I jerked my head toward Jack to help. Since Billings and Clayton took their coffee black, I handed Jack those two cups to carry over while I doctored up the rest.

I talked while I prepared the coffee. "We started on Division Road after lunch. Kind of detoured off the normal route of the grid, I guess, but we were told about a rental in the area. A retired farmer named John Miller owns the place, and it's been sitting empty for nearly a year, until recently. He's in a retirement home in Grafton, and we intend to contact him for more information. Nobody was home at the farm we think is the rental. We were only given a description of the place, not an actual address. We did see an odd paint outline in the grass at the property, though. That piqued my curiosity."

Clark sat up straight. "Really? That's definitely something to follow up on."

I nodded. "For sure, boss. That's the first place we're hitting in the morning. I want somebody to explain that paint to us."

Jack took a sip of his coffee and told the lieutenant what we found out from the residents we did have a chance to speak with. It didn't amount to much.

"So far, we haven't learned anything new. One person we spoke with is a married woman whose husband is a long-haul truck driver. She didn't seem to know much about the neighborhood activity. Unfortunately, we probably made her more worried than anything else. Another woman was the typical farm wife that said she talked to the cops on the day Reanne was found. She didn't have any more to offer. There was also an executive guy we spoke with. He lives in a fancy-schmancy gentleman's farm and had to buzz us through the gate to enter. He didn't seem like the type that paid attention to the goings-on around him. He said he's out of town a lot. We saw farmers working the fields at a couple of other places. The only thing that could be a possible lead is the farm on Division."

"Okay, that's something." Clark rubbed his red eyes and squinted. "Damn allergies. I want to be updated as soon as you talk to the people at that farm. I don't care if it's an actual lead or not, just let me know either way."

"Roger that, boss," I said.

"All right, let's call it a day. Go home and relax. Rest that foot, Jade, and we'll start fresh tomorrow. Hopefully something will pop, and we'll apprehend these sickos before the weekend is over. Jade and Jack, you're on that farm before anything else. If nobody is home, track down the owner. What's his name again?" Clark asked.

"Mr. Miller, boss, and he lives at Meadowbrook Manor in Grafton."

"Good enough. Okay, good night, guys."

"Night, boss,"

We packed it up and left the bull pen. Jack and I were the last ones out. We passed Jamison and Horbeck coming in as we were leaving and updated them about our door-to-door interviews.

"So, are you going straight home?" I held the handrail for support as I walked down the outer steps. We headed to our parked cars in the lot.

"I guess so. Maybe I'll hit a drive-through for some chicken wings or something. How about you?"

I looked at my watch. "It's early. I think I'll go to Joey's and hang out with Amber for an hour or so. She was supposed to have tonight off, but somebody called in sick. I was looking forward to Chinese, but now I don't have any dinner plans. Come with me. Joey's food is better than drive-through anyway."

"Yeah, that sounds good. What's with Amber's extra hours?"

"Joey asked her if she'd work full time. She agreed but only until school starts in the fall. She's taking all the hours she can for now."

Jack nodded. "Okay, I'll meet you there. Drive carefully."

"Yes, Mom." I pulled out of the parking lot and headed west at the lights. Every time I turned into the parking lot at Joey's, the flashbacks of Doug abducting Amber returned. I shook the images out of my head and knew that, in time, they would diminish. I caught Jack's flashing blinker right behind me as I glanced up at my rearview mirror. We both turned in and parked close to the door. At this time of day, the beer crowd hadn't arrived yet. I was thankful that I didn't have to walk very far. Jack and I entered and sat at the closest of three empty tables. Amber stood behind the bar, filling a pitcher of beer, and waved hello. I was looking forward to a couple of Scottish ales and a delicious, greasy hamburger with a side of home fries, garnished with the usual dill pickle spear that I would give to Jack. I loved spicy brown mustard, and my burger would be slathered in it.

"You know you're predictable, don't you?" Jack said as he arranged himself on the chair.

"What the heck does that mean?"

"You don't even pick up the menu. I already know your meal is going to be the same as always."

"Yeah, so? Why mess with perfection? I'm not a foodie anyway, and the burgers and fries here are the best in the county. Scottish ale? That's like mother's milk to me."

Jack laughed out loud. "You're a crazy one, Jade Monroe."

I grinned. "Blame it on my folks."

Amber made a quick stop at our table. "Hey, guys. I didn't know you were coming in. Your timing is perfect—not too busy yet." She kissed each of us on the cheek. "Sorry about dinner, Sis. Are you guys eating here?"

"Sure am. I'm hungry, and Jack is always starving."

Amber laughed. "I'll send Pete over to take your order. I've got to get back to the bar. Talk to you guys later."

"She seems to be doing well," Jack said after Amber was out of earshot.

"Yeah, she's one tough girl."

"I wonder where she gets that." Jack picked up the menu. "Now, what am I hungry for?"

Chapter 50

Jack turned the wand on the blinds on the south-facing windows to reduce the glare coming into the bull pen. We were all seated at our desks by eight o'clock. The aroma of a fresh pot of coffee brewing filled my nostrils. I poured out the tepid coffee leftover in my travel mug and washed it out. A handful of Styrofoam cups sat on the counter, waiting to be filled. Chances were, we would be knocking on doors all day, and I made extra coffee to take along.

The lieutenant received a courtesy update from Colgate before we headed out that morning. He was told that the police from the Riverwest area had expanded their search. They were still hopeful they'd get some leads in Carley and Gina's disappearances. According to Colgate, after the press conference and the news report, a hotline had been set up by the families. They even had their own search parties going, but so far, nothing had panned out. I wasn't surprised and didn't think either girl was in the Milwaukee area anymore. Colgate wasn't sure, but they were still actively looking.

We finished our morning powwow with Clark, filled our cups, and left. Jack and I started back at Division Road, and Billings and Clayton picked up where they left off yesterday.

"I hope somebody is home at the rental, if that's even the right farm. That paint outline has been weighing heavily on my mind."

Jack nodded and lifted his travel mug. He took a gulp of coffee. "We'll be there soon."

Within ten minutes, Jack slowed at the rusty mailbox at the end of the driveway.

"Hang on a second."

He shifted the cruiser into park. "What?"

"Humor me. Will you just look in the mailbox quickly? By some off chance there could be something inside."

Jack checked his surroundings and made sure no front-facing windows from the house were visible. He got out, ran to the box, and pulled the door open. With his six-foot frame bent over, he peered inside, then he slammed it shut.

"Nothing."

"Damn it. Okay, let's see if anyone is home."

Jack drove in slowly and parked in the same spot he had yesterday.

"Hmm… no cars again." I opened the passenger door and got out.

Jack pushed off the steering wheel and grabbed the top of his open door. He pulled himself out and elbowed the door closed. We walked up the sidewalk, just like yesterday, except this time a nice-looking man came outside and met us halfway.

"Hi, there, what can I do for you?" He stuck his hand out to shake ours. "I thought I heard a vehicle pull in. I'm Luke."

His surprisingly friendly demeanor caught me off guard. I shook his hand. "I'm Sergeant Jade Monroe"—I pointed at Jack—"and this is my partner, Jack Steele. We're from the Washburn County Sheriff's Department."

He nodded. "Nice to meet you."

He stared at us and waited as if he didn't have a care in the world. I couldn't get a good read on him yet.

"We're canvassing the area, Luke, and talking to residents."

"Okay. What can I help you with?"

"Have you noticed anything unusual out here? Any strange people, newcomers, weird carrying on, that sort of thing?"

"No, can't say that I have. What's this in reference to?"

"Nothing really in this area, but a deceased young woman was found recently about ten miles from here. Heard any gossip out this way?" I asked.

"Wow, that's terrible, but no, not at all."

"So, how long have you lived here?" I reached in my breast pocket, pulled out my sunglasses, then slipped them on.

"Well, let me think about that for a second. I'm pretty sure my folks bought this place when I was a toddler. I guess I'd say twenty-five years or so."

I gave him a long stare. "Really? This isn't a rental home?"

Luke chuckled. "Nope, not at all."

"Where are your folks now?" Jack asked.

"They've been out on the road for the last two weeks. They travel the Midwest to different art fairs four times a year. Mom and Dad are pretty talented artists. My mom paints still life on canvas, and my pop is a woodworker. He makes furniture and decor." He pointed back at the woods behind the barn. "See the woods back there?"

We looked in the direction he pointed at and nodded.

"A lot of the furniture my dad has made came from that forest."

"Uh-huh." I walked to the end of the porch and glanced at the ground. The outline was gone. "Looks like you've been busy this morning."

"Sorry, I don't follow."

"Nothing, just early, that's all. It looks like the grass has just been cut."

He laughed. "My bad. I guess I like a freshly mowed lawn. Actually, I cut the grass yesterday evening."

"So, what do your parents drive when they go from show to show?" Jack asked.

"They have an RV. It's seen better days, but Dad keeps it in pretty good shape."

"When do you expect them back?"

"In a week or so. Anything else?" Luke's eyes darted from Jack to me, then back to Jack.

"Yes, your last name, please, and your folks' first names."

"Yeah, sure, it's Parker. My mom and dad are Bethany and Gerald."

Jack wrote that down and handed Luke our cards.

"Okay, thanks for your time. If you notice anything out of the ordinary, please give us a call." I nodded at him and we left.

"Will do. Thanks, officers. Have a nice day."

Jack and I walked back to the cruiser and got in. Jack backed up and started down the driveway. I gave Luke a long stare as he stood on the porch and watched us leave.

"What do you make of him and his story?" I asked.

"Hard to say. He seemed friendly enough and not at all nervous talking to us. I didn't notice anything actually suspicious about him. Are you getting a different vibe?"

"Not sure. I guess the jury is still out." Then I told Jack that I'd brought a couple of Granny Smith apples along. "Want one?" I reached into the plastic bag on the floor well and pulled out two apples. I handed one to Jack.

"Thanks."

I took a bite of my apple. "Yeah, he seemed unusually friendly. I'll admit, he's a good-looking guy, that's for sure."

"What? Now you want to rob the cradle?" Jack raised his eyebrows at me.

"Don't be ridiculous, I'm just stating the facts. I don't think it's considered robbing the cradle if the person is three or four years younger than me."

"Oh, so you've already calculated your age difference?" Jack laughed.

"Whatever, I was just making an observation. Anyway, he's either lying or that was the wrong house. That still leaves the paint outline. Damn it, why didn't I take a picture of it?"

Jack shrugged. "If the parents are actually artists, they must work with a lot of paint and stain."

"True enough, but I've never heard of an artist that paints still life with spray paint, or a woodworker that does, either."

"If it makes you feel better, we can look up the property owner's name in the county records," Jack said.

"Great, so what's the address? Was it on the mailbox?"

"Nope. Out here it's going to be one of those with the north and south or east and west coordinates. That's probably why it isn't on the mailbox. It's too long. As a matter of fact, I didn't see anyone's addresses on the mailboxes out here."

"Well, somebody has to know. Still, something about Luke Parker isn't sitting right with me."

Chapter 51

Jeremy picked up his ringing phone that sat on the passenger seat. He looked at the screen—Matt was calling.

"What's up?" He slowed the van and clicked on his left blinker.

"Where are you?"

"Just turning off Highway 60, why?"

"Find a different way home. The damn cops were here. They just left."

"What the hell?" Jeremy checked his side mirror, then he pulled back out into traffic. He needed a minute to think. "What did they want?"

"They were snooping around and checking door to door. They mentioned Reanne."

"Shit. They couldn't have been city cops. It's out of their jurisdiction."

"Son of a bitch, that's why she looked familiar to me. It was that sergeant we saw on TV. It was probably her damn medical boot that distracted me."

"Medical boot?"

"Yeah—whatever, I know it was the same woman."

"Crap—they're getting too close. We're going to have to pack it up and move on. Open the barn doors and make sure nothing is in the way. I'm going to park in there. We have a lot of thinking to do, and I want to hear everything they said to you. I'm taking the back way around. Go upstairs and watch out the windows in both directions. I need to know the coast is clear before I turn in. I'll call you back in five minutes."

Jeremy hung up and pounded his fist on the dash. He'd wanted to get rid of Megan before they left the area. Now everything had changed. They'd have to either take her along or put her in the ground with Beth and Carley.

He made four turns before he ended up on Division Road. The farm was a half mile farther south. Jeremy hit the name Luke on his contact list, and Matt's phone began to ring.

"Yeah, the coast is clear in both directions as far as I can see."

"Okay, good. Are the barn doors open?"

"Yep, pull in—you're good to go."

Jeremy sped up and headed for the farm. Gravel kicked up on both sides of the driveway when he turned in. He pulled the van into the barn and got out, then he closed the heavy wooden doors at his back. He ran up the driveway to the sidewalk and into the house, then he locked all of the doors and drew the blinds on every first-floor window.

"Okay, sit down and tell me everything." He grabbed two beers from the refrigerator and sat at the kitchen table.

He twisted the cap off the bottle and threw it across the room. It hit the stove and bounced to the floor, where it spun before falling over.

Matt sat and began from when the cruiser pulled into the driveway. "I know it was the same unmarked black cruiser I saw yesterday after the Tennessee guy took Liz. They've obviously been snooping around since then. They said they were canvassing the neighborhood and talking to everyone."

"I wonder if they stopped at the house yesterday. If they did, they might have seen the paint outline. Maybe that's why they came back."

"Don't know, but it's gone now. What proof would they have?"

"Yeah, you're right. A paint outline isn't proof of anything. It would only be their suspicion, and that's if they actually were here." Jeremy ground his fingertips into his temples and yelled out. Cage tucked his tail and left the room.

"I gave them my fake name and didn't even mention that a brother existed. I said my mom and dad were artists and they were gone doing the art-fair shows."

"How did you hold up?"

"Fine. I'm not about to let those pigs rattle me."

"Okay, good. There's no time to sell Megan now unless I list her right away at a bargain-basement price. I really don't want to take her with us."

"Let's do it now, then. I'll get her ready."

Jeremy nodded and finished his beer. "I'll put her on a two-hour auction. If she isn't sold by then, she's dead."

Chapter 52

We had already left the last farm on Division Road. We turned right on Elmwood. I looked at the map and checked off the houses we had been to. Other than Luke Parker, nobody answered their doors.

"Don't you think it's weird that a mom and dad would leave a grown son alone without a vehicle to use for weeks on end? And why would he be there anyway? Shouldn't he have a job?"

"Yeah, definitely, but how would he get to a job without a vehicle? It isn't like he can go far on a bicycle."

"Precisely my point. I'll admit, something about him sticks in my craw." I checked the map again when we reached the next intersection. "Okay, Highview Drive must be the left turn just ahead. Let's see who these new owners are."

The farmhouse was vacant, but a small trailer sat on the edge of the driveway. The man that greeted us said he was the handyman hired by the new owners to restore the house. He was living alone at the site but had a crew that came in to help every day. By the looks of it, there were at least five guys on the roof.

"Sir, why do you stay overnight in the trailer and the rest of your crew comes in during the day to work?" I asked.

"The new owner wanted it that way. I guess there are some unsavory characters around here."

I cocked my head. "Really? What have you heard?"

"I haven't heard anything. The owners said they were told some kids have been toilet papering properties, knocking down mailboxes and the like. They wanted me to stay out here as a deterrent so expensive building supplies don't go missing, if you know what I mean. I don't want my tools to disappear either."

"Have you seen or heard anything since you've been staying here?" Jack asked.

"Nope, it's been real quiet except when my crew shows up. We've just started on the roof, but I guess you can see that."

I nodded. "Okay, thank you, sir." I handed him our cards, and we left.

"You know, we still didn't locate the house that's supposed to be a rental. It doesn't look like any of them on Division are."

"We only talked to Luke Parker. Nobody else was home. Maybe we should have asked him if he knew which house was a rental. It could have been a lease-to-own property. Maybe Leroy got the details wrong."

The radio in our cruiser squawked. Peggy from dispatch was calling.

"Hey, Peggy. What's going on?"

"Jade, Lieutenant Clark wants everyone to report back. Somebody just called in a 10-57 out at the intersection of Rustic and Linden Roads. Apparently a car just ran into a house. Don't know the circumstances yet, but there are two fatalities and several injured people. An ambulance is on the way. Clark has already informed Jason, Lena, and the forensic team."

"Roger that, Peggy. We're on our way." Then I said, "Hit the lights, Jack. It sounds like a bad one."

The drive took us twenty minutes. That location was on the far west side of the county. We arrived at a chaotic scene. People familiar with that intersection knew it to be a dangerous one. To anyone else that had never been to that area, they'd understand the danger once they'd see it. A hill hid the stop sign that was just below it at the intersection and a house stood dead center across the road. Anyone driving too fast that didn't realize a stop sign was just beyond their field of vision could easily be involved in an accident.

The front of the brick bungalow, right at the picture window, had been pushed in by the car. Skid marks told us the driver had had no idea a stop sign was there. The lawn was furrowed by tire tracks that continued on until they stopped where the car hit the house. The EMTs were assisting several people inside the residence. Jason's head was buried behind the steering wheel, and Lena was on the other side of the car, looking in. Both the driver and the passenger were deceased. Neither of them had on a seat belt, according to Jason.

"Holy crap, this is bad."

"Jade, Jack. We've got two deceased in the front seat. The backseat passenger is already in the ambulance. The EMTs said it doesn't look good for her. They're getting ready to take off for St. Joe's."

"Does anyone know what happened?"

Lena spoke up, "I can tell you this, there are plenty of empty beer cans on the floor of the car."

"It's only eleven a.m."

Jason nodded. "And these are kids. Their driver's licenses show they aren't even legal drinking age. The car is registered to the driver's parents."

Jack shook his head. "What a waste. Let's go inside and find someone to talk to."

The door-to-door interviews were temporarily put on hold. We had people in the house to interview and parents to contact. Nothing about this scene would have a good outcome.

We drove to the hospital and let Billings and Clayton finish up the interviews with the homeowners. Luckily the husband and wife were sitting at the kitchen table instead of watching TV in the living room. That alone probably saved their lives. Cuts and scrapes from flying debris seemed to be their only injuries.

We were told at the hospital that the third person in the vehicle, a seventeen-year-old girl named Stephanie Cane, had also passed away. Now it was our job to track down the families and break the bad news to them. Not only had their children died, but also there could be an insurance suit filed against the driver's family. Thankfully, that was something we didn't have to address. Jack and I sat with each family at their home and told them what had happened. We gave them Jason and Lena's contact information as well as our condolences, then we left.

I looked at my watch when we finally walked out of the last home. It was nearly five o'clock.

"Let's head back to the station. We'll update Clark and call it a day."

I agreed with Jack and climbed into the cruiser. We turned onto Schmidt Road at five fifteen and parked. Inside, I made coffee, and we sat with the lieutenant, going over the day's events.

"That accident was not only tragic, boss, it was so senseless. They were just kids."

"And likely drunk ones, I might add," Jack said, shaking his head. "What I want to know is who bought the beer for them. That in itself is a criminal act which resulted in three deaths."

Clark agreed. "That is something we'll probably never find out. Might be better left for North Bend PD to check into. All of the kids lived in town. What about the door-to-door interviews earlier?"

"I'm on the fence with someone we talked to. It was at that house with the paint outline."

"Something suspicious going on?" he asked.

"Not really, just off. I've got to think about it some more. For now, I'm going home."

"Yeah, sounds good. Get out of here. I'll see what

Billings and Clayton found out when they check in."

"Okay. Night, boss. Night, Jack."

"Night, Jade."

The late afternoon sun felt warm against my skin as I walked to my car. I pictured lying on the chaise on my deck, the sun on my face and a cold beer in my hand. Living close to work was something I was thankful for. I drove the short distance home with a lot on my mind. Amber worked until closing so I had the house to myself—and plenty of time to think. I pulled into the garage and hit the button on the passenger side visor. The door lowered. Inside the kitchen, I opened the pantry door and pulled out the cat food. Spaz purred at my feet and rubbed his side against the Velcro tabs on my blue boot. I was sure he didn't care about me, he just wanted to be fed, but I petted him anyway. In my bedroom, I changed out of my work clothes and put on a pair of jeans and a T-shirt. I poured fresh birdseed into the plastic feeder for Porky and Polly, then I dumped their water and filled the cup from my bathroom faucet. Polly sat on my shoulder while I changed the newspaper at the bottom of their cage.

With all of the animals taken care of, I opened the refrigerator and pulled out a Scottish ale. With two hours of daylight left, I sat on the deck with my beer and a notepad in hand.

I thought back to yesterday when Jack and I were at the Parker residence. I remembered Jack commenting on the fresh tire tracks in the driveway. I tried to rationalize them. The UPS man could have pulled in, or Luke might have had a friend that came and left—anything was possible. And without a car, was he home yesterday when we were there? Did he see us snoop around and enter the barn while he peeked out from behind a closed curtain? Did he know we saw the paint outline? Was he on to us? Maybe he wasn't even home when we did our snooping. I had too many questions and not enough answers floating around in my head.

I'm overthinking this. He's probably exactly who he said he is and hasn't done anything wrong. But what about the rental Leroy mentioned? It has to be that house. No matter what, there's still something about Luke that bothers me. Call it police intuition or whatever, but I need to find out more.

There was still an hour of daylight left, and Luke didn't know my personal car. I could sit a good distance away and watch the property with my binoculars. I needed to know if there was another vehicle somewhere and who might be coming and going. I knew Jack would be furious if I told him I was going back to Division Road, but it was only for surveillance—what was the harm?

I made myself a quick sandwich, chowed it down, and left. From my house, the drive was only twenty minutes. I tried to recall the layout of the property as I drove east, a direction from which I was less likely to be noticed. In reality, I didn't want to be noticed at all. I knew in my gut that the outline we saw in the grass came from a vehicle being recently painted. There was no other logical explanation. If the paint came from his parents' artwork, the black would be at the outer tips of the grass as the lawn grew. Luke said they had been gone for several weeks, yet the grass where the paint was couldn't have been more than a few inches tall. His story didn't jibe with the facts. For some reason Luke Parker had lied to us, and I needed to know why.

I turned off Highway 60 a few miles before I needed to. The back farm roads would be better for me, less obvious than the most direct route. I'd come in from the north and sit about a quarter mile from the house. I had known that at some point in my life, the high-powered binoculars I owned would come in handy, and lately they had.

My heart raced when I saw the green street sign that said Division Road. I wanted to turn back and go home to the safety of my pets and a glass of wine, but the detective in me said to continue on. I turned and slowly drove south. The farm was on my left about a half mile down the road. As soon as I saw the rooftop of the barn, I'd slow down and creep closer to a safe place to park. Out in farm country, there weren't too many hiding places. Wide, open fields took up most of the real estate as far as I could see.

I pulled over and wished the crunching gravel on the shoulder of the road didn't sound so noisy. I parked and waited. I patted the gun on my side for reassurance, picked up the binoculars from the passenger seat, and placed them against my eyes.

Chapter 53

Jeremy sat at the computer, nervously tapping his foot against the cracked cement basement floor. Matt had just put Megan back in her cage. The photos and one-minute video of her were uploaded, and now it was just a waiting game.

Jeremy was pissed. Megan could have easily gone for twelve thousand dollars, but now? He'd be lucky to get half that price since the auction was so short, and she would have to go to somebody nearby. The luxury of time was a thing of the past. The brothers needed to leave the area as soon as they could.

"How's it going?" Matt asked as he pulled up a chair and handed Jeremy a beer. He sat and looked at the screen. "You wrote a really good description of her. I like the 'feisty Irish' part. That should attract more people."

"True, but we only have an hour left. This auction is short. There hasn't been much time to get a lot of eyeballs on it."

"So what are you thinking, somebody from the Chicago area?"

"Yeah, probably, and hopefully they have deep pockets. We'll have to take her tonight once the money wire has cleared. If those cops are still trolling the neighborhood tomorrow, I don't want them to see us. At this point, they're probably suspicious of any van."

"Yeah, you're right." Matt leaned back and took an extra-long swig of his beer. "What did you set her reserve at?"

"Five grand."

"Man that sucks. What can I do to help?"

Jeremy looked at the time on the bottom right corner of the computer screen. "Let's see, it's almost seven o'clock. Why don't you pull the van up to the cellar doors and load an empty cage in the back. You can get a syringe ready and give her something to eat. I want to leave as soon as the payment goes through. We may be driving farther than Chicago, just so you know. You can pack some food up for us and Cage too."

"Yep, I'm on it."

Jeremy breathed a sigh of relief when he saw the reserve icon go from red to green.

"Yes! At least the reserve hit." He checked the time again—seven fifteen. In forty-five minutes the auction would be over, and Megan would be gone. He hoped they wouldn't have to drive too far.

Jeremy went up the steps when he heard the cellar doors bang against the ground. He saw Matt outside.

"The reserve hit—we're almost there, only a half hour to go."

"Good to know. I'll get the van ready."

Darkness hadn't set in yet, but the sun hung lower in the sky. The cellar doors stood in the shadows of the house. Matt flipped on the yard lights before he walked to the barn.

Chapter 54

"Damn it." I craned my neck out the passenger side window and looked west at the setting sun, trying to calculate how much time I had left. Daylight was quickly slipping below the horizon, and a deep pink-and-purple glow took over the sky. It would be dark in a matter of minutes. So far I hadn't seen anything that would warrant suspicion.

I continued to peer through the binoculars, hoping to see movement, but with each passing second the shadow of night was filling the sky. I gave up and turned the key in the ignition, with plans of spending the rest of my evening in front of the TV. Lights suddenly illuminated the backyard from the house to the barn, breaking the darkness. I quickly shut off my car.

"Shit. I hope he didn't see my headlights."

I saw Luke open the barn doors, then a vehicle backed out. It drove in reverse to the house.

So Luke did lie to us earlier. I wonder what he's up to.

I had to decide if I would check it out on my own or call Jack for help, and I had to make my choice quickly. By the

319

time Jack would arrive, Luke could be gone. It looked as though he was getting ready to leave and needed the cover of darkness to make his move. I couldn't walk to the house on this bum foot, but I could get a little closer as long as I didn't turn on my headlights.

I turned the key, and the car's engine came to life. On the blacktop with the headlights off, and the quiet of my barely moving vehicle, I inched closer to the farm. I was only a few hundred feet away, and I was sure I could walk that distance. My adrenaline would help me get there. I needed to see what was going on.

Before I exited the car, my conscience told me to call Jack. I knew I would get a tongue lashing, but as an officer of the law, I had a duty to check out a suspicious situation, or at least convince myself that there was nothing to be suspicious of. Jack's phone rang.

"Hey, Jade. What's up?"

"I know you're going to be really pissed at me, but as a responsible adult, I have to tell you."

"Now, what did you do—or is it something you're in the process of doing?"

"I'm parked down the street from Luke Parker's house and—" I held my phone away from my ear as Jack yelled at me.

"Are you out of your mind? What part of that do you call responsible? Don't do anything. As a matter of fact, get out of there right now!"

"I can't leave. He's up to no good, I just know it. He backed a vehicle out of the barn and up to the house like he's going to load something. I have to check it out."

"Jade, don't! At least wait for me to get there."

"He'll be gone by then. I'll be careful."

"Jade—Jade—son of a bitch."

I hung up and got out of my car, then I closed the door as quietly as I could at my back. I dropped my keys and my gun's extra magazine into my back pocket then double-checked my sidearm. The ditch was the best place to walk, not only to hide myself as much as possible but also to avoid the crunching sound of the gravel under my feet.

At about a hundred feet out and lying low behind a row of trees, I saw a black van and what looked like open cellar doors. A lone window at ground level on the side of the house told me the basement lights were on. I was certain I could reach that window undetected. From there, I would be able to see what Luke was doing downstairs.

Crouched low, I moved through the shadows. I had to be careful and deliberate with each step. The slightest sound of a twig cracking could give me away.

Finally, when the window was only ten feet from me, I belly-crawled the rest of the way. The basement window was surrounded by a metal window well. I had to drop my upper body into the well to see through the dirty glass. Thanks to the windows having years of exposure to the outdoor elements, cobwebs and dried leaves filled the space and clouded my view. I didn't want to give what normally disgusted me too much thought. I had to see what was going on downstairs. Holding my body in that awkward position and scooting in as close as possible, I was able to see inside, and what I saw made me want to shoot Luke right then.

Chapter 55

Matt circled around and entered the house from the porch. He took off his shoes, then he tiptoed downstairs from the kitchen. He entered the computer room with his announcement. "We have company."

Megan's auction was over, and she'd sold for ten thousand dollars to somebody from Barrington, Illinois. Jeremy was ecstatic—until Matt said those three words.

"Son of a bitch, what does that mean?" He pounded his fist on the desk so hard, the computer mouse bounced off and hit the floor.

"I saw headlights a few minutes ago. They came on then went off immediately. I circled the house on the driveway side and crept down the road. I found an empty Mustang parked a few hundred feet north of here. I saw a set of binoculars on the passenger seat. That's telling me there's only one person, and they're definitely watching the house. That person is outside somewhere, it's just too dark to see them."

Jeremy pushed back the chair and grabbed the stun gun

and cattle prod out of the jelly cupboard. "Did you load a syringe?"

"Hell yeah, I have it right here." Matt handed it to Jeremy.

"Okay, go upstairs and put your damn shoes back on. Make plenty of noise in the kitchen. That should be all it takes to lure them through the cellar doors and into the basement. I'll be ready and waiting for them down here."

"Got it." Matt ran upstairs and into the kitchen.

Jeremy prepared himself for whatever was about to happen. He remained out of sight with the syringe in his pocket and the stun gun and prod in his hands. There were plenty of empty cages for his next guest.

Chapter 56

I felt for my phone then remembered I had left it in the car. I had only so many pockets, and I definitely didn't want it to ring when I was trying to be quiet and surveil the situation. Jack knew where I was, and that was what mattered right now.

My focus was on the girl being held captive. I couldn't see who she was; the room was dimly lit at best. She lay curled in a fetal position at the back of her cage, her knees almost touching her chin. The cage was secured with a large padlock. I didn't see anyone downstairs other than the girl. Eight empty cages were lined up against the far wall. That room looked to be the main area, yet there were corners and doors going off in different directions.

The noise continued from inside the house. Luke was preoccupied, likely packing up. I had to think of a way to rescue the girl in the cage—and any others that might have been down there. As far as law enforcement knew, four young women were missing, and one was definitely dead.

I stood up slowly and pulled out my weapon while

hugging the side of the house. I crept forward. I knew the van was around the corner just ahead of me. I neared the edge of the house and peeked around the corner. Nobody was there. I inched forward and looked in the back of the van. The interior was white, just as I suspected. My heart pounded triple-time in my chest.

A large cage and some supplies lay in the back of the van. Luke was preparing to make a run for it. I didn't have much time. I crouched and looked down the basement steps—I didn't see any movements. From the window well, the girl was to my right. That meant once I reached the basement floor, she would be directly across the room from me. With my head on a swivel, I took in my surroundings outside and saw nothing. I saw a light flicker on the second floor. Luke must have been upstairs. I needed to make my move. The cellar steps would be a challenge with this boot, but there was a handrail. I descended with my gun drawn.

At the bottom of the stairs, I peeked around the corner. Everything was still. I looked at the cage. The girl must have been sleeping; she hadn't moved. I heard footsteps walking from room to room upstairs. I still had a little bit of time and headed to her cage.

Chapter 57

He watched her from the darkened corner where Liz's empty cage still sat. He was sure she thought she was alone and could rescue Megan. Jeremy almost laughed.

He watched her fumble with the lock, looking for something to open it with. She sat her gun down for a second, and that was all he needed.

Bad move on your part, Jade. He crept out of the darkness until he was only a few feet behind her. "The keys are on the hook around the corner, Sergeant."

She reached for the gun, but he kicked it across the room. It slid to a far corner and disappeared from sight. Jade stood and spun, almost stumbling on her bad foot, but he got her in the throat with the cattle prod. She went down like a ton of bricks.

"Matt, get down here and help me with her," Jeremy yelled.

Matt ran downstairs. He laughed when he saw Jade lying on the floor, writhing in pain. He kicked her bad foot just because he wanted to. She groaned.

The commotion woke Megan. She scooted back in her cage, trying to look small, and cupped her knees against her chest. She quietly whimpered.

"Grab a lock," Jeremy said as he stood above Jade. He watched her squint as she tried to focus on his face.

"You?"

He chuckled. "Yeah, go figure. I guess you decided to come to my house party after all, right, Jade?" He looked at Matt. "Got everything?"

"Yep, the cage and lock are ready to go."

She tried to get up. Jeremy nailed her again with the prod. She screamed, then she went quiet.

"Grab her arms. Let's get her into the cage. She might have called for backup, so we've got to hurry. They could be on their way. Grab everything you want from here. The plan has changed—we aren't coming back."

They locked the cage door. Jeremy found Jade's gun and handed it to Matt. He slipped it into his waistband. "Run upstairs and grab everything you can think of. We're leaving in five minutes. Get some clothes and food. I'm going to load Megan in the van."

Jeremy ran up the cellar steps and opened the cage door at the back of the van. He tossed the cattle prod and stun gun in through the side door then ran back downstairs.

"Get over here," he yelled to Megan. "Lean against the side of this cage, and I'm only saying it once. Do it now or I swear, I'll kill you."

She sobbed and crawled over to him. He sank the needle into her neck and waited. She was unconscious in less than a minute. He spun at the sound behind him. Jade shook the cage, yelling at him.

"Shut up, bitch. Consider yourself lucky to be alive. I'm feeling a little merciful right now or I would have killed you earlier."

Jeremy pulled Megan out and threw her over his shoulder. At the back of the van, he tossed her into the cage. A whistle sounded to his right. He turned and was hit with the cattle prod.

Chapter 58

I heard a familiar voice calling my name and footsteps running down the cellar steps.

"Jack, thank God—I'm over here. Get me out of this damn cage. The keys are hanging on the wall around the corner to your left."

"Damn you, Jade. One of these days, you aren't going to be so lucky." Jack found the keys, unlocked the cage, and helped me out.

"Where's Luke? Where's Jeremy?"

"I only found one person, and it wasn't Luke. I nailed the guy with the cattle prod. He's handcuffed to the van."

"That means Luke is still in the house. Jack, I think one of them has my gun."

"Shit—I need to find him. Jamison and Horbeck are on their way, but they were both fifteen minutes behind me."

"Jack! Look out."

A shot fired from the cellar steps, catching Jack in the left shoulder before he had time to take cover. He turned and fired back. Luke went down. I ran to Jack's side and saw that he was bleeding badly.

"Don't move. Give me your gun." I took Jack's service weapon and hugged the basement wall, not knowing if Luke was dead or alive. I did a quick look around the corner—he lay motionless on the steps. I approached cautiously with Jack's gun pointing at Luke's chest. I kicked his foot—he didn't move. A pool of blood was spreading across the steps beneath him, then I noticed the entry wound. Jack got him center mass. I knelt down and checked for a pulse—there wasn't one. "He's dead." I retrieved my gun and went back to help Jack. "Do you have your phone?"

"Yeah," he groaned, "it's in my shirt pocket."

I pulled it out and called Horbeck. "Brian, it's Jade. We need an ambulance. Jack's been hit, and we have a drugged girl here too. Don't ask me the address because I don't know it, but we're on Division, a couple of miles north of Highway 60. You'll see my car parked on the road. Hurry."

"We're only a couple of minutes out, Jade. I'll radio for an ambulance right away."

I hung up and sat Jack's phone down. "I have to see what's going on with the girl."

"The guy upstairs put her in the cage but didn't get a chance to lock it. She was unconscious when I was up there." Jack winced when he moved his arm.

"Yeah, he nailed her with the Xylazine. Don't move, Jack. Horbeck and Jamison should be here any second, and the ambulance is on its way." I looked around and found a towel in the bathroom. "Here, use this. Put pressure on your shoulder. I'll be right back."

I went outside through the cellar doors and found Jeremy handcuffed to the van. The girl was still passed out in the cage. I saw the cattle prod lying on the ground out of his reach and picked it up.

"Just so you know, Jeremy, Luke is dead."

He spewed the words at me. "His name isn't Luke, it's Matt, and he was my brother."

"Is your name really Jeremy?"

"What's it to you, bitch?"

I knelt down so I could be eye to eye with him. "You know, Jeremy, pretty soon you're going to live in a cage. I'll even come to visit you so you can tell me how you like your new digs."

I looked around to make sure we were alone. I didn't hear the sound of cars coming up the road or the ambulance's siren piercing the night's quiet, just yet. The stillness seemed peaceful for a second until he screamed. I pressed the prod against Jeremy's side and gave him a solid three seconds with it. I cocked my head. "How was it? Nice?" Then I nailed him again.

Horbeck and Jamison arrived within minutes. I explained to them that a body was blocking the cellar steps. We needed to call forensics and the ME and get them out here.

"Jack is downstairs. There has to be a basement entrance through the house somewhere. Let's get him outside. I can hear the ambulance getting closer."

We found the stairs leading to the basement and helped Jack outside. Jamison shoved Jeremy into the back of the cruiser and slammed the door. I heard him yelling profanities at me through the glass. I smiled.

Jack and the girl, who after closer examination I assumed was Megan, were taken away in the ambulance. I explained to the EMTs before they left that the girl had been injected with Xylazine. The shock on their faces spoke for them.

Chapter 59

"I'm fine. Stop fussing over me." Jack sat in his hospital bed, swatting away my intentions to help him with his lunch.

"Shut up and let me do this." I leaned in from the olive-green guest chair next to Jack's bed and cut the unidentified chunk of meat on his plate into bite-sized pieces.

"I still have one good arm, you know."

I shushed him with a hand wave and continued what I was doing.

"So tell me about the interrogation with Jeremy."

"Neither of the brothers had prints in the system, and Jeremy won't tell us his last name. So there's no way of knowing if anything he's said is true or not. The only thing I got out of him is that he's twenty-nine years old. His brother, Matt, was twenty-seven. They both had fake names to use when necessary and a made-up family story, which you and I heard yesterday. It sounded as though they lived a pretty shitty life growing up in Idaho. The mom was abused, and so were they. He said his dad hit them in the knees with baseball bats, or whatever he could find at the moment, when they misbehaved. Jeremy also said he and Matt spent a lot of time in dog cages."

Jack rubbed his forehead. "That explains a few things, I guess, if it's actually true. The cages were something they were familiar with and understood."

"Yeah… according to Jeremy, the dad went to prison years ago for nearly killing their mom. She eventually abandoned the boys in their early teens, and they've been doing who knows what since then. I guess this human-trafficking thing started a few years back."

I looked out the hospital room window at everyday life going on around us. If people only knew the type of sick characters that really lived among them, they'd be horrified. I sighed.

"I can see that gerbil on the wheel. What's going on in that head of yours?"

"Do you think I'm going to be reprimanded for going rogue?"

"Nah—don't worry about it. Who knows if we would have caught them otherwise? Plus, I'm not going to press charges against you."

I saw the twinkle in Jack's eye when he laughed.

"You're lucky I don't disable your good arm. Anyway, the girl at the house was definitely Megan. She was the only one left at the farm. She said Jenna was sold to someone in India and left a few days back. Carley was supposed to go, but she died at the farm from an epileptic seizure." I wiped my eyes with the back of my hand. "I'm going to visit Megan again after I'm done with you. She's actually right down the hall. Her folks are in there now." I saw the concern on Jack's face. "She gave us quite a statement this morning. I don't know the process on trying to find the other girls. Megan didn't know all of them. She did say some of them were dead and buried in the woods behind the barn. There's a team out there looking right now with cadaver dogs. The house has been gone through by forensics, and Lena and Jason have Matt in the morgue."

Jack sighed. "I'll never understand the sick ways of a criminal. All we can do is try to stay ahead of them or at least apprehend them as soon as possible. This one was a little daunting."

"Yeah, I agree. Forensics found a journal of sorts in the house. Evidently, Jeremy kept very detailed records going back several years when this abducting-and-selling-women thing began. It's going to take a while to sort through it. I have no idea how to explain to families that they may never see their loved ones again, and it isn't because they're dead. They're somewhere in another state or country. I really don't know which is worse."

Jack squeezed my hand. "I'm sure the FBI will get started on that right away."

I nodded. "Yeah, I know. Okay, I'll be back later. Amber wants to come with me tonight. Take advantage of some downtime, partner. You'll be out of here in a couple of days." I got up and headed for the door.

"Hey, Jade."

I turned back toward him. "Yeah?"

"Can you hand me the remote?"

I shook my head then handed him the TV remote. "You're something, you know that? Get some rest. We'll be back later. Your family should be here soon."

Chapter 60

Two weeks had passed since that night on Division Road. Life in North Bend fell back into what we called our normal routine—for now. Jack came back to work last week on light duty. I told him to take advantage of the quiet, he'd be working his butt off again soon enough. I knew Jack well enough to know desk duty wouldn't last long. He was too stubborn that way. I guess we were a good fit.

The medical boot was off, but with my still-swollen foot, I had to wear sneakers every day. I knew I looked ridiculous and had to plan my outfits to coordinate with my shoes. My coworkers ribbed me constantly.

We finally had a weekend off, and the Saturday barbecue at my condo, on the deck, was in full swing as promised. The weather cooperated, and the bright sun filtered by the woods shined through just enough to give us the perfect balance of sun and shade. Friends and family gathered for brats, burgers, chips, potato salad, baked beans, and all the trimmings that went along with the barbecue theme. A wine table was set up for the red, and the beer and white wine sat beneath the table in the cooler filled with ice.

Living up to his word, Jack manned the grill, wearing his left arm in a colorful sling his mom had made for him. Amber stood at his side and helped with the cooking.

Jack called out, "Okay, let's dig in. The grill master has completed his duties."

Amber held the platter while he loaded it with brats and burgers.

The table was set, and we all took our places around it. My mom and Bruce, Jack's folks and brothers, and Amber and I all said a word of thanks and appreciation for good food and wonderful friendships. Spaz circled the table at our feet, crying out for scraps. Amber dropped a few baked beans on the floor for him.

Jack slapped away my attempt to help him prepare his hamburger.

I ignored him and continued on. "I got this, partner. Let me give you a hand."

He gave me a nod and a grin, and we all dug in.

THE END

Thank you for reading *Captive*, Book 2 in the Detective Jade Monroe Crime Thriller Series. I hope you enjoyed it!

Stay abreast of my new releases by signing up for my VIP email list at: http://cmsutter.com/newsletter/

You'll be one of the first to get a glimpse of the cover reveals and release dates, and you'll have a chance at exciting raffles and freebies offered throughout the series.

Posting a review will help other readers find my books. I appreciate every review, whether positive or negative, and if you have a second to spare, a review is truly appreciated.

Again, thank you for reading!

Visit my author website at: http://cmsutter.com/

See all of my available titles at:
http://cmsutter.com/available-books/